GIFT OF
Continence

TABITHA ORMISTON-SMITH

Paradox
Publishing
Covers & Formatting
http://paradoxbooktrailerproductions.blogspot.com.au

❧DEDICATION☙

For Samson, Fionn, Magnus, Ogre, RooRoo and
Beau.
Wait for me by the bridge.

ACKNOWLEDGMENTS

Thank you:

To Bruce Pippett, solicitor, for information about solicitors and their jargon.

To the late Dr Marion Colville for refrigerator measurements.

To Owen Davies for advice on physical presentation.

To Patti Roberts for endless help with producing the print edition and for wonderful cover art.

And to the late Fionn The Magnificent and the late Magnus Maximus II, without whom I could not have survived to write this book.

ɞPROLOGUEʗ

I never really wanted to get married. Tim had been pestering me for years, on and off, I generally tried to avoid the subject.

But then, one day, I saw this incredibly perfect dress. Of course I had to try it on.

The dress was magic. I still think so. It had some supernatural quality that defied analysis, as Tim would have said. He often said things like that, which I suppose should have been a warning. Anyway, when I looked in the glass I almost didn't recognise myself. Except for my red hair, I could have been Scarlett O'Hara.

I didn't just get married on the strength of that, though. After all, I'm not stupid. I checked it out most carefully.

It was pure silk, and all hand-finished. How

could I go wrong?

CHAPTER ONE

First the Banns of all that are to be married together must be published in the Church three several Sundays, during the time of Morning Service, or of Evening Service (if there be no Morning Service), immediately after the second Lesson...

Book of Common Prayer

'Fiona! Get out of there this instant, do you hear me? It's after ten, the hairdresser's here.'

'Go away, I'm busy.'

'Fiona!' The doorknob rattled violently. For all I knew, my mother had a passkey. I wished I'd thought of putting a chair under the knob. Although why that would stop anyone coming in, I've never been able to figure out. Ah well, life is full of mysteries. I turned on the hot tap to drown out my mother and a cloud of steam filled the bathroom. Moses, crouched on the basin, watched me balefully through the swirling mist, rather like the Hound of the Baskervilles.

It was a great comfort to me to have Moses with me on my wedding day. My mother had wanted to put him in a kennel, but I had really had to put my foot down about that. I was already going to be separated from him for the whole honeymoon. Men are so funny about things like that. I lay back in the hot water and imagined that I was the captain of a vast schooner, carrying a precious cargo of peacocks and ivory to the Spanish Main, whatever that is.

'Fiona! Open this damn door or I'll break it down.'

Thank God, Gloria had arrived. Now it was safe to come out. I had been locked in the bathroom for the last two and a half hours because I couldn't face my mother unadulterated. Having dodged out on her parental responsibilities for twenty-two years, she had been hounding me for the past week, trying to give me a talk about the birds and the bees. I could hear her scuffling with Gloria in the hall.

'But I have to talk to her.'

'Don't worry, Mrs M, Fiona knows all about

sex. She got it off the lavatory wall, same as the rest of us.'

Evidently my mother retreated in some confusion, because when I came out there was only Gloria, looking evil and dangerous in a black mask. She took it off when she saw me, revealing a stupendous black eye.

'I didn't want your old bag of a mother to see this. Got it at karate last night. Bloody moron, I told him I was being your bridesmaid today, you'd think people could show a little consideration.'

'D'you want to see the cake? It's amazing, six layers.'

'Christ. Did she make it herself?'

'Of course. She's been at it nonstop for weeks, in between trying to give me The Talk.'

'Still trying, I noticed.'

We sneaked furtively down the stairs to the sitting room. My mother had insisted on having the reception at home, just the way she'd insisted on everything else. I sometimes wondered if everyone realised who was getting married here.

The cake rose majestically from a sea of white tulle with little pink rosebuds scattered through it.

Six layers of white frosting, lace, and God knew what else. I had to admit it looked lovely. Gloria tiptoed over to the cake and bent to examine it.

'Holy Jesus, there's a hole in it!'

'What d'you mean, a hole? There couldn't be. What sort of hole?'

But when I looked, it was all too obvious what sort of a hole it was. You could even see the tongue marks around the edge if you looked closely.

'Oh God, Moses. It's the marzipan icing, he loves it. Someone must've left the door open.'

'Well Jesus, Fi, we've got to do something. Cover it up or something. Did she have any icing left over?'

'God, I don't know. I've been staying out of her way so she wouldn't start telling me about sex.'

'Go and have a look in the kitchen. I'll stand here in front of it, just sort of casually.'

I left Gloria standing casually in front of the cake and dashed for the kitchen, clutching my towel. My little brother, Patrick, was there, eating something out of a large mixing bowl. I skidded to a halt.

'Patrick, thank God! Moses ate a hole in the cake, is there any of that marzipan icing left we can cover it with?'

Patrick looked innocent, which I knew meant trouble.

'Well, not actually left, not as such, no.'

I grabbed the bowl. Sure enough there were a few tiny scraps of marzipan icing clinging to the edges.

'You greedy little shit!' I howled. 'Now what am I going to do?'

Attracted by the noise, my father wandered into the kitchen.

'Ah, Fiona. I think your mother was looking for you. Is something wrong?'

It's not easy to break the habit of fifteen years.

'Oh no. Everything's fine. I just wanted to spend some time with Patrick, things won't be the same after...'

My father went predictably misty.

'Well do put something on, you'll catch cold wandering about like that. Although in some areas of Central Australia...'

He wandered off, mumbling to himself. I quickly filled Patrick in on the situation.

'Oh, don't worry. They always freeze the bottom layer for your anniversary. So no-one'll be looking at it down there.' He sniggered; presumably the words 'down there' had sparked off some association in his incessant preoccupation with sex. I looked at him doubtfully. Wedding protocol wasn't something I'd really expected Patrick to know much about.

'Are you sure?'

'Yeah, the bottom layer, or else it's the top one, Mum was on about it the other day.'

'Oh, great. What if it's the top layer, you dork? Quick, we've got to hide it before Mum sees it.'

'What about Tippex?'

'Have you got any?'

'No.'

I looked about for something to hit him with. Speed was definitely of the essence.

'What about flour and water? That's white. Quick, give me that bowl.'

We mixed some flour and water and dashed

back to the sitting room with it. Gloria was there, standing casually in front of the cake and listening to our father, who seemed to be describing the burial customs of Samoa. She didn't miss a beat.

'Good heavens, Mr M, Mrs M'll have a fit if she catches you in here with your pipe. I'd better open a window. And I think Fiona was looking for you, she's upstairs.'

Patrick and I dodged behind the hat stand as our father wandered past. It wasn't difficult to avoid notice; he's never really quite there.

We filled in the hole with the paste we'd made.

'That's no good, I can see the finger marks.'

'We'll have to sort of scrape it over. Get a piece of cardboard or something.'

'What about this?'

Using the bottom edge of the china shepherdess, Gloria masterfully scraped over the patch. We all stepped back to admire her work.

'Jesus, it's not the same shade of white.'

'Don't be silly, white's white. You can't have shades in it.'

'No, look. You can see it.'

It wasn't the same shade of white.

Gloria rose to the occasion, as I knew she would.

'Well, we'll just have to cover it up with something. Look, we'll pull a bit of this material up in front of it.'

'Why don't we just turn the whole thing around so it's at the back?'

'God, you're a dork, Patrick. It's on a semicircular thing, look. No, this is the best way. Look, all we've got to do is pull it up a bit, see?'

She let go and the tulle fell back down.

'We'll have to stick it with something. A pin or something.'

We looked around the immaculate room. Of course there were no pins. Superfluous objects are not allowed to hang around in my mother's rooms.

'Fiona, go and get a pin. We'll stand in front of it.'

'No way, I'm not going back upstairs without you. Mum's up there.'

I wiped the china shepherdess on my towel, to give myself time to think. I didn't think of anything.

'Shit, I've got one!' Gloria was unbuttoning her shirt.

'Look the other way, Patrick.' He was getting a glazed look to his eyes which was positively obscene. Gloria pulled a safety pin out of her bra strap.

'You'll have to lend me a bra, okay?'

'Mine won't fit you.'

'Oh, never mind, I don't really need one. What's the point of all that martial arts and stuff, if your tits don't stay up?' She jabbed the safety pin into the cake.

'That's no good, you can see it.' I didn't want to be negative, but it stuck out a mile. Patrick didn't say anything, he was angling around trying to look into Gloria's shirt.

Gloria looped a bit of the tulle around the exposed part of the safety pin. It sort of worked.

'Well, that's going to have to do.'

***

My mother was practically foaming at the mouth by the time we got upstairs. She followed me and Gloria into my room; the hairdresser was curled up

17

in my armchair reading a magazine.

'Here they are, Kerry. At last. And mind you keep Moses out of the room if he comes back inside, Fiona. Kerry's allergic.' She shot me a filthy look. Moses was on top of the wardrobe, luckily she hadn't noticed him. I wondered what she was so upset about, after all the wedding wasn't until four o'clock.

Gloria threw herself onto my bed and lit one of her black cigarettes. She hadn't done her shirt back up. The bra was red satin. I hastily got into position in front of my dressing table to distract my mother, she didn't like Gloria anyway. I'm not sure why. I looked at Kerry in the glass. I wasn't sure I wanted my hair done by someone with green spikes, but it was too late to get another hairdresser. I closed my eyes and imagined that I was the captain of an interstellar spaceship, on a mission to save the galaxy.

***

I felt really weird when I woke up. I couldn't remember who I was, or anything about my life. I grasped futilely at shreds of my dream, which might have had something to do with the Navy. No good, I couldn't remember that either. Panicking, I opened my eyes and saw two strange-looking women and a huge black cat; I seemed to recognise the cat, but had no idea about either of the women.

Fortunately this state only lasted a few seconds, actually until I moved and one of the strange women moved with me, and I realised I was looking in a mirror. Then everything came flooding back, and I really started to panic.

I looked like Elizabeth the First. My hair rose vertically up from my head into what appeared to be a solid mass about eight inches high. My fringe had totally disappeared, and the whole thing was the wrong colour, sort of a pale washed-out ginger. I had gone to sleep with nice, thick red hair, and woken up a freak. I turned and looked at the hairdresser in total disbelief. She didn't look so good herself, her nose and eyes were bright red, which clashed unpleasantly with her green spiked hair. I'd cry too, I thought bitterly, with remorse, if I'd done this to a fellow human being. If she even was human.

The hairdresser sneezed all over me. It was the last straw, and I'm afraid I rather lost it. After the hairdresser had departed, weeping pitifully between sneezes, I ripped into Gloria for not watching what she'd been up to. By this time my mother, attracted by the noise, was outside tapping at the door in a ladylike manner.

'Go away,' I shouted, in a frenzy of grief and terror.

Gloria, who had been reading some trashy paperback while I was being mutilated, was quick enough to save her own neck. Quick as a flash she did up all her shirt buttons and resumed her mask just as my mother opened the door.

'Darling, whatever is the matter?'

'Look at my hair, just look at it!' I shouted.

'It looks lovely. Darling, I came up to tell you Tim's on the phone.' She bustled off to ruin someone else's life.

'I can't talk to him,' I wailed. 'Oh God, this is the worst day of my life.'

'For Christ's sake, Fiona, settle down. You're getting married in four hours.'

'No way! I am not getting married looking like this.'

'Well, it's too late to get out of it now.'

'I don't care. I am not leaving this house. Tim wouldn't want me looking like this anyway. What did she do to my fringe, for God's sake? She must have plucked it, the bitch.'

'Look, go and talk to Tim. We'll fix your hair, don't worry.'

'Fix it! How can you fix it, it's the wrong colour! Oh God, I wish I was dead.' I got into bed and pulled the covers up over my head. I wasn't exaggerating, I really felt suicidal. My hair had always been my best feature.

I heard Gloria going away. Good, I thought. If everyone would just leave me alone perhaps I could go to sleep and wake up and it would all have been a bad dream. Moses thudded onto the bed and raked at the doona. I pulled him under it and buried my nose in his lovely rich smell. Nothing smells quite like a tomcat.

Presently Gloria came back and ripped off the covers. I wondered how I had come to have a best friend so devoid of sensitivity.

'Come on, get up, you can't lie there all day feeling sorry for yourself. Tim's ringing back in half an hour, I told him you were in the loo throwing up.'

Perhaps it wasn't so bad after all. Gloria certainly didn't seem to think it was the end of the world. I got up cautiously and sat on the edge of the bed.

'Okay. Now we'll just take it all out and start again.' Gloria sat down beside me and poked at my hair experimentally. A worried frown appeared on her face and she poked around a bit more.

'Jesus, Fiona, it's got no ends.'

***

Ten minutes of poking later, we were both seriously worried. Gloria's temper was showing signs of fraying.

'Jesus Christ on a bicycle. It can't be a perpetual fucking Mobius strip. What the hell has she done?'

'It must be the hairspray.'

'That or the fucking snot she kept spraying all over you. Fuck, I thought we were all going to drown.'

I felt sick, both at the thought of the Hairdresser from Hell sneezing all over me while I was asleep and also what my mother would say if she overheard Gloria's language.

***

We were in the bathroom washing out the industrial strength spray when a shriek of outrage ripped through the house. I had been dreading the moment when Patrick discovered he was to wear the kilt. I had realised some weeks ago that, as he had failed to show any interest whatever in my wedding plans, this detail had escaped him. It didn't really seem kind to warn him, so I hadn't. Truth, the enemy of kindness, as my grandmother always says. It had been my mother's idea for Dad and Patrick to be in Highland dress, but who argues with my mother?

We found Patrick standing in the middle of his room, arms folded, looking bootfaced. Our mother was facing him, they were squared off like two tomcats disputing a garbage can.

'I don't care. I'm not looking like a poofter in front of everyone.'

'Patrick Aloysius MacDougall, how dare you use that language. Your father isn't ashamed to wear the kilt, and you shouldn't be either. Now I don't want to hear another word...'

And so on, and so forth. I had to admit Patrick had a point. Our father might not have been ashamed to appear in Highland dress, but then he didn't have weedy little skinny legs like Patrick. Really an ankle length job would have been better.

As there was clearly nothing to be done, Gloria and I started to ease gently backwards out of the room. With my mother in full cry, I was uncomfortably aware of my hair dripping on the carpet, and Gloria's mask.

Just as we were about to accomplish a silent escape, with verve, elan etc, another cry of outrage rang through the house. This one sounded more like a wounded bull. It was my father, who presently erupted from my parents' room clutching his kilt and roaring incoherently.

'Jesus, what's his problem?' screeched Gloria.

A general confusion ensued, with my mother trying simultaneously to look reproving at Gloria's language and to be a ministering angel to my father. Gloria and I retreated a little way to be out of the centre of it.

'Holy God,' muttered Gloria. 'It's a wonder she doesn't trip over her own back legs.'

The trouble emerged. Moses, at some stage since it was laid out on the bed, had slept on my father's kilt (when had he found the time?). The kilt was now covered in black fur.

Cat fur, as my readers will no doubt be aware, is extremely difficult to remove from any woollen material. Added to this injury was the insult that, my father seemed to feel, had been sustained by Clan MacDougall. I couldn't really see the problem myself, Moses leaves fur on all my stuff and I don't feel insulted. Still, my father is, as I may have mentioned, a bit eccentric. I think something happens to people's brains when they turn forty. As for the actual fur itself, you could hardly see it. The

MacDougall tartan is one of those ghastly boring old ones with just black and red, in a sort of nasty blocky design. I was glad I didn't have to wear it, it would murder my hair.

'God, my hair!' In the excitement I'd forgotten about it.

'And what the devil, may I ask, are you doing, dripping all over the carpet with the hairdresser already gone?'

Oh, shit.

'She fell in the bath, Mr M. Don't you worry, we'll have it good as new in two shakes. Come on, Fiona.'

I was left wondering why nobody but me had noticed the mask.

❧CHAPTER TWO☙

Whose adorning, let it not be that
outward adorning of plaiting the hair,
and of wearing of gold, or of putting on
of apparel...

1 Peter, 3:3

By lunchtime I was starving and ate four chicken salad sandwiches. I had gone right off the whole marriage thing, and couldn't even remember why I'd agreed to it in the first place. I tried to stiffen my resolve by considering the even more ghastly alternative of having to send back all the presents.

My mother, as always, was critical.

'Dear, do you really think you ought to eat quite so much?'

Gloria was less tactful.

'Christ, Fiona, gutsing yourself like that, how

are you going to get into your dress? It'll probably burst open when you're saying your vows.'

I felt a small moment of uneasiness at these words. It was true that I hadn't quite stayed on my diet lately. But the dress had fit perfectly when I picked it up three weeks ago; I knew I had nothing to worry about really. Anyway, the diet didn't allow for giving Moses half my meat under the table, so I knew I had some leeway.

Actually, I didn't feel worried at all. My hair, washed and left to dry naturally, had gone back to its normal colour, and my fringe had come back from wherever it had gone. I breathed a silent prayer of thanks that she hadn't plucked it after all.

***

Presently my mother started jumping up and down insisting that it was time for everybody to get dressed. I didn't see what the hurry was, after all the wedding wasn't till four o'clock, and it was hardly two, but I was pretty keen to get Gloria away from the table before a) my mother noticed her mask, b) she said anything else outrageous, or c) she lit one of her black cigarettes, so I didn't argue.

The hassle started as soon as we got upstairs. I'd thought I was getting away from nagging for a while, but Gloria was almost worse than my mother. First she wanted me to have a bath. I didn't see any point in that as I'd already spent two and a half hours in the bath that morning while I was waiting for her to arrive, and I didn't want to risk getting my hair wet again just when I'd got it looking decent. I ignored her and got out my dress from its wrapping.

'Let's see yours, I haven't seen it yet.'

Gloria had picked her dress up from the dressmaker herself and taken it jealously home, refusing to let anyone look at it. My mother, with her mania for supervising everything, had been pretty annoyed about it, actually.

'Okay, get ready to die.' Gloria ripped off the plastic cover and held the dress up against herself. It was beautiful, scarlet as sin. Gloria always looks her best in red.

'It's gorgeous. Put it on and show me.'

Then a thought struck me.

'Wait on, wasn't it supposed to be pale blue?'

Gloria looked a bit shifty.

'Fiona, a pale blue dress is the ultimate in dorksville. Grace Kingsley wears pale blue dresses, for Christ's sake. I want to be able to wear this again.'

I couldn't really say anything, she had a definite point. Grace Kingsley was an old acquaintance of ours from school, she was a sort of Deb of the Year type, enormously fat with a complexion like purple porridge. Since getting married two months ago in a blur of artificially generated publicity, she and her husband, judging from the occasional postcard she sent me, heaven knows why, had been eating their way around Europe like Pac-man. My mother had always thought Grace was a lovely girl, probably because she was a compulsive writer of thank-you letters, which she sent on the least excuse, even if someone had given her a cup of tea. Anyway, Gloria and I had always regarded Grace as a sort of ultimate guide to anti-chic, and if she wore something you just knew it was gross, even if you hadn't seen it.

'Well, it looks great. What are you going to do when Mum sees it?'

Gloria shrugged. 'What can she do about it?'

There was a gentle tapping at the door. Gloria whipped the plastic back over the dress.

'Darling, how are we going? Have you had your bath?'

Dear God, not her too. Had I suddenly developed BO?

'Mum, I just got out of the bath a couple of hours ago.'

But this cut no ice with my mother, whose major interest in life is hygiene.

'Fiona, you simply cannot be married without even having a bath. Gracious, I don't know what's got into you lately, you never used to be so difficult. Now I'll just run you a nice warm bath, and perhaps Gloria would like a shower.'

'What about Patrick, don't you think he should have a shower?' I knew I could rely on Patrick to waste all the hot water. Although perhaps that wasn't so smart, I wouldn't put it past my mother to make me have a cold one. How nice to be an orphan, I thought longingly. Then I wouldn't have to go through any of this, since there'd be no-one to pay for a wedding at all.

'After you, darling, then we can all have one while you're getting dressed.' My mother bustled off to run me a nice warm bath. Gloria collapsed across my bed.

'Don't worry Fi, once you're married you can spend all day in your dressing gown watching soap operas.'

Sometimes I really think life is unfair. On your

wedding day, everyone is supposed to be nice to you, and here I was being monstered from all directions. At least in the bathroom I'd be able to have peace for a little while and they wouldn't be able to get at me.

***

I had the foresight to take my mobile into the bathroom with me in case Tim rang again. Then I sank blissfully into my second bath. It was nice and warm, my mother has no idea about these things. I ran in lots more hot water and some lilac bubble bath, and settled back for a relaxing game of toe fishing with Moses.

***

Of course it wasn't really all that peaceful; various relatives kept banging on the door to remind me of the time, like some kind of airport announcement service.

'Fiona, darling, it's nearly half past two.'

'For Christ's sake Fiona, have you fucking drowned in there? Get a bloody move on, will you?'

'Just in case you'd forgotten, Fiona, the rest of us would like to use the bathroom too.'

That was my father, who usually stays out of these disputes. Serve him right for not putting in a second bathroom, I thought. On the other hand, I didn't actually want Patrick being my page boy without a shower. Perhaps I'd better get out soon. On the other hand, my mother was lurking around waiting to give me a talk on Married Life.

I was saved from my dilemma by my mobile playing Eternal Flame. It was Tim, of course, no doubt ringing to check up on me. Men are so possessive. I ran in a bit more hot water to tide me over while he rabbited on. His conversation was so frightfully soppy that I can't bring myself to repeat it, even now. I tuned him out as much as I could and tried to concentrate on how handsome he was and how envious all my friends would be when they saw me in The Dress.

The hot water didn't seem to be as hot as it had been. I stretched my leg out to turn it off with my toes, an accomplishment of which I have always been very proud. It was unfortunate that Moses chose that precise moment to leap onto my exposed stomach.

Well, naturally I submerged, didn't I? After all, people do bend in the middle. I suppose it would have been better if Moses hadn't grabbed my mobile as he went under, but you could hardly expect him not to try to save himself. I wrapped it up in a towel as soon as I got myself and Moses out of the bath, but it seemed to have stopped working already, or else Tim had hung up, which didn't seem likely. I tried calling him back, but the phone didn't have any sound at all, not even a dial tone. I propped it up on the heated towel rack to dry out. The real problem was that my hair was saturated.

I was just wrapping it gently in the last dry towel (always squeeze gently, never rub) when an appalling screech reverberated through the house. Moses arched his back and jumped onto the lavatory cistern, trying unsuccessfully to bristle his dripping fur. I wrapped him in the towel instead and cautiously unlocked the door. Voices came to me from the direction of Patrick's room.

'I am not wearing it, and that's final. No way!'

'But, dear –'

'NO!'

For once I decided to abandon my non-interventionist policy and get involved. After all, blessed are the peacemakers. I think that's in the Bible. Perhaps a good deed on my wedding day might bring me luck.

'What's the matter?'

'What's the matter? You can actually stand there and ask me what's the matter? Just look at this thing.'

He waved the jacket. It was rather cute, I thought, and there really isn't anything more flattering to blond hair than black velvet.

'What's wrong with it?'

'It's got a tail!'

'A tail?'

He spread the jacket out under my nose. It did, indeed, seem to have a thing that was rather like a little tail. I thought fast.

'Well, um. That's the way the highland jackets always are made. It's like that because, well, you know...'

'No, I don't bloody know. Easy access for sodomy, I suppose?'

'Patrick!'

We dropped the jacket and eased my mother into a chair. She looked very pale and was clutching her heart, as usual when things don't go her way. Gloria, however, with her more robust ethnic tradition, was horrified.

'Jesus, Mary and Joseph. Is she having a heart attack?'

'No, don't worry. Just nick down to her room and grab the smelling salts off the dressing table.'

'Smelling salts? I thought they were only in old books.'

'No, they're real, it's a little green bottle.'

While Gloria was getting the smelling salts, I had a little heart to heart with Patrick.

'Listen, shitface, I don't want Mum popping off on my wedding day and wrecking my wedding, so will you please keep your opinions to yourself and just wear the damn kilt, okay?'

'Jesus, Fi, it's totally faggoty.'

'Look, I was about to tell you, those slit things are for wearing a sword. It's the Highland tradition to always bear arms in the defence of your clan. That's why you have the little knife tucked into your socks.'

'Oh, what bullshit.'

I was cut to the heart. I had almost broken out in a sweat making that up on the spur of the moment, and the little creep didn't even have the grace to swallow it. I decided to appeal to his better nature.

'Look, when I'm married and living in my own place, you can come and stay with us.'

'Oh great, watch you and Tim suck face all day, terrific.'

'Well, it's up to you, but I would have thought you'd like to be away from the house when Father Simpson and Father Morelli come to dinner.'

There was a pregnant silence. Then Patrick put on the kilt.

I nicked off just as Gloria got back, leaving her to revive my mother with the smelling salts. Patrick knew how to work them anyway, he'd had enough practice.

I was really pissed off about my hair, though.

***

My hair wasn't as shiny as it had been before I got it wet for the third time. It was okay, though, because along with all the subversive literature, packets of black cigarettes, condoms and God knows what else, Gloria had in her bag a can of stuff that you spray on and it goes instantly glossy. I tried it on Moses first and it looked excellent; Moses was pretty cross, but he was in a bad mood anyway, from falling in the bath and injuring his dignity.

Despite all the hassles of the morning, and everyone constantly shouting at me to hurry, my make-up went on perfectly. By the time I was ready for The Dress, I was feeling quite relaxed and ready for anything.

Gloria had been ready for ages and looked stunning. The red dress was sensational, and she had somehow managed completely to cover her black eye. I couldn't help feeling, though, that somehow she didn't look quite like a bridesmaid. It wasn't the mask, she'd taken that off, but there was something, all the same. Now I came to think of it, the design of her dress didn't really look familiar at all.

I took a deep breath and unwrapped my own dress. Hundreds of yards of beautiful cream silk glowed softly at me, making all the dramas of the past weeks seem worthwhile. I held my breath and stepped into it, ready to turn into a fairy princess.

Once again the dress worked its magic and I stood in front of the glass, lost in admiration. I was six inches taller and ten pounds lighter.

'Do it up for me, would you, Gloria?'

'Sure thing.'

She moved around behind me. Better her than me, I thought to myself, visualising the thirty-six tiny pearl buttons. I could hear her swearing and muttering to herself.

'Christ, Fiona. Couldn't you have got into the

fucking dress before I did my nails? Jesus.'

I pointed out, in tones of sweet reason, that I would then have been in the dress since early that morning.

'Fuck! So what? You haven't been doing anything all day except lie around in the bath and stuff your face anyway. Right, that's ten down, bloody four hundred to go. Jesus, why couldn't you get a zipper put in?'

I wasn't going to listen to a word against The Dress. 'I think the buttons look sweet.'

'Yeah, well you could still have them on the outside of the zipper, just not doing anything. Jesus, didn't it occur to you when you tried it on what a bloody pain it'd be to get into?'

It had, but of course I knew I wouldn't be the one doing up the little buttons. It didn't seem like the time to say so, though, with Gloria's scarlet talons hovering near my spinal column.

My mother tapped at the door yet again.

'Darling, are you nearly ready?'

'Nearly, Mum. Just doing up the buttons.'

'Well, don't be too long, dear. We want to get a

picture of all of us before we leave for the church.'

'Sure Mum, we won't be a minute.'

Gloria had stopped doing up buttons and was lighting another of her black cigarettes. I wondered uneasily if she was about to spring a blackmail demand, and then remembered that Patrick or even, in an emergency, my mother, could just as easily do them.

'Come on Gloria, get on with it.'

'Yeah, well. About those buttons.' She was looking at me in a funny way, I didn't like it.

'Why are you looking at me like that? What about the buttons?'

'Fiona, weren't you supposed to be on a diet?'

'Yes, so?'

'You didn't stick to it, did you?'

'Of course I did. Well, sort of. Nearly, anyway. What's that got to do with anything?'

'Well, I wonder. What could not sticking to your diet possibly have to do with getting the buttons done up on your wedding dress? I just can't think of a connection. Help me out here, Fiona, I'm really at a loss.'

'What are you talking about?'

'I can't get the fucking thing done up, you idiot. You're too fat, it won't meet in the middle.'

Through a grey haze, I wondered where the smelling salts were.

&CHAPTER THREE&

It's funny, how you can go through your whole life using something on a regular basis and never really knowing all that much about it. My mother was always being overcome by faintness, whenever anyone said a rude word or she saw anything that wasn't germ-proof; pretty much every day, really, or at least four times a week, and whoever was handy always dashed off for the smelling salts and waved the bottle under her nose. It used to bring her round pretty smartly, and I'd always assumed it was some delicate scent that would make you think beautiful thoughts and waft you gently back to consciousness on a wave of perfumed air; something along the lines of Devon Violets.

So when Gloria rushed in with the familiar little green bottle, I grabbed it with total confidence and had a good big sniff.

Night fell. My whole perception of the universe was reduced to pain, and the sensation of the top of my head coming off. I was blind, deaf, mute. Novas burst behind my eyes, and an express train ran up the inside of my nose on red hot wheels.

When I eventually regained some vision, the first thing I saw was Gloria hovering in front of me, looking horrified.

'Holy Infant Jesus, they must have gone off.'

I could only gasp weakly at her, I seemed to have lost my voice. She handed me a glass of water.

'Christ, we're going to have to do your whole make-up again.'

She was right. Great black streaks ran down my face, and I had broken out in a sweat, too. The whole lot was going to have to come off. I looked at my watch; it was just after three. Then there was the dress. It was all too much to contemplate, so I invoked my all-purpose remedy by bursting into tears. Somebody always does something.

It's not always the best way with Gloria, though.

'Jesus Christ on a bicycle, will you stop your howling? I can't hear myself think with the racket.' She fished around in her bag and handed me a kleenex which seemed to have seen better days.

'Look, start getting your face clean while I think. I'll be back in a sec.'

She opened the door and I panicked.

'Don't leave me!'

'Look, I'm just going down the hall to confer with my colleague, okay? Two heads are better than one, you know.'

'What about my head?'

'Two functioning heads, Fiona. I'll be right back.'

She disappeared, leaving me to wonder a) who in my house she considered her colleague, if not me, b) what would happen when my mother saw the red dress, and c) why I couldn't teleport myself to Uluru. I thought about life in an Aboriginal community. The peace, the timelessness, the days ordered by ancient custom. I saw myself, tired but happy, coming home after a three day hunt, proudly bearing a gigantic kangaroo which I had single-handedly tracked through a waterless waste, relying on the stars for my bearings and my bushman's skills for my survival. I would be greeted by my tribe with cheers and acclaim. Then I remembered about witchetty grubs. I sighed and started to take off my makeup, wishing I hadn't put it on quite so thickly.

Time passed. I got my foundation on properly on the third attempt. Moses jumped heavily onto my lap and settled down, purring. Thank goodness cat hairs don't stick to silk, I thought, imagining myself going down the aisle with a great black patch on my front. On the other hand, the other problem with the dress still hadn't been resolved. I wished the whole business was over, it had been nothing but dramas ever since we'd decided to get married. No, actually that wasn't fair, the hassles started when we told my mother. I imagined her hovering around the bed on our wedding night, trying to disinfect the pillow. The image of Tim's face cheered me up a bit. I thought about living in my own place and never, ever buying another bottle of White King or having to get up for work in the morning.

It seemed it was all worthwhile, in the balance. I remembered my horrible job at Marsh and Spacknall, working for a homicidal maniac, where I had been treated like a slave, forced to get up at the crack of dawn, and, finally, sacked for accidentally shutting down the computer with the Emergency Stop button. I'd never have to work again now. Work really isn't my thing.

My reverie was rudely shattered.

'Christ, Fiona, haven't you even done your eyes yet? Get a move on, for God's sake. And get out of that dress.'

'I can't take it off, I can't undo the buttons.'

She had brought Patrick in with her. I had to admit he looked sweet in Highland dress. You'd never have guessed what evil lurked beneath the angelic surface. He was holding something behind his back in a furtive way.

'Listen, Patrick, if you've got that water pistol there, it's not funny.'

'Would I do that? What I have here, my dear sister, is your salvation.' He produced something that looked like an old rag.

'What is it?'

'I found it in one of those old boxes of Gran's in the hall closet. Go on, put it on.'

I examined the item cautiously. Looked at close up, it was an old-fashioned corset, the kind with bones in it and lacing up the back. It had a strong smell of moth balls. Moses jumped off my lap and retreated huffily to the bed. He hates moth balls.

'I'm not wearing that, it stinks.'

Gloria was briskly undoing the bottom buttons. 'Come on Fiona, don't be a wuss. You can drench yourself in perfume.'

I sighed and stepped out of the dress, resigning myself to fate. At least I could be certain that anything found in our house would have been thoroughly washed.

'Now you hang onto the bedpost and we lace it up. Come on, get moving, we've still got to do up all those buttons once we get this on.'

'The bed doesn't have posts.'

'Well look, just grab onto something, okay? The back of the chair, or something.'

I stood behind the chair and held onto its back. Patrick sniggered.

'What's your problem, you dirty little boy?'

'You look just like one of those French tarts in those old postcards of Grandad's.' He evidently found this highly amusing, going into one of those giggling fits that are so annoying when other people do them. I was pretty narked that Gloria started laughing too.

'Come on, do the bloody thing up, will you?'

'Well, breathe in.' Gloria started pulling on the laces. It wasn't very comfortable.

Patrick had to put in his two cents' worth.

'In Gone With the Wind she puts her foot up on her bum.'

'Don't you dare get shoe polish on my knickers.'

'Keep still, will you? Patrick, come here and hold this bit.'

'Ow, that's too tight, I can't breathe.'

'Yes you can. Close your eyes and think of England.'

Patrick started sniggering again. If I had to get married again, I'd really try to do it without the assistance of a fourteen-year-old boy.

'What are you laughing about now, you little creep?'

'I was just thinking how funny it'd be if the string breaks when you're at the altar.'

I wanted to hit him with something, but Gloria had me in a grip like a boa constrictor.

'Okay, just put your finger here.'

'Where?'

'On the knot, fuckwit.'

'Oh. Right.'

Gloria started sniggering again.

'What is it now?' I asked crossly.

'Something old, something borrowed... Oh, God!'

'What, what is it, what's the matter? Gloria, what, dammit?'

'What's he doing?'

'Who?'

'Moses, look at him. I don't like the look of it.'

'Jesus Christ! Moses, stop it, get away from that!'

But he'd already finished, and was sitting down to lick his backside, staring at me with his yellow cat expression.

He had sprayed on my wedding dress.

***

After I got my breath back, I remembered that I had a bottle of magic elixir that I'd discovered in the pet shop, that you spray on and all the smell goes away and there's no stain. Well, it had always worked on the carpet, sofa etcetera, so I assumed it would also work on The Dress. I dispatched Patrick to the bathroom to bring back a damp cloth, and offered Gloria the smelling salts. She wasn't grateful.

'Jesus shit, woman, are you trying to kill me? Get me a martini if you want to be medicinal.'

Patrick came back with a dripping face washer.

'Look, that's much too wet. Go and wring it out.'

Gloria revived.

'No, give it here, I'll do it. Patrick, you nick downstairs and see if you can pinch a bottle of gin and some orange juice or something. No, better make it vodka, it doesn't smell on your breath.' She wrung out the cloth in my wastebasket and applied it vigorously to the sprayed patch.

Everything seemed to be under control, and I was about to resume my interrupted makeup when I noticed something tickling my leg.

'Oh God! Help! There's a spider on me!'

'Where?'

'I don't know, it was crawling up my leg, get it off for God's sake.'

'Look, there's no spider. You probably felt the suspender dangling.'

'Suspender?'

'Yeah, look, those little things hanging off the corset are for holding your stockings up.'

'I'm wearing pantyhose.'

'God, Fiona, it doesn't know that. Just get your eyes done, will you?'

Patrick sneaked furtively back into the room with a large bottle of vodka and one of orange juice.

'Great. Now just spray that stuff on the dress, and I'll make us all a stiffie to get us through the rest of the day. Holy mother!'

Patrick squatted down and squirted the damp patch.

'Patrick?'

'What?'

'Where's the glasses?'

'Oh, well she's got them all laid out on a table,

and she was in there, so I couldn't get at them. Give us it here, I'll drink some and we can stick the vodka in the bottle.'

In the glass I saw Patrick scull half a pint of orange juice. It was probably the first vitamins he'd had all week, I hoped he wouldn't go into shock. I also hoped he wouldn't spill the orange juice down his shirt front. Actually, I decided, I couldn't bear to watch. I went back to doing my eyes. Then a thought struck me.

'Gloria.'

'Yeah?'

'These little suspender things, I can't have them jumping around under my dress. Let's cut them off.'

'Okay, just a sec.' She screwed the top back on the fortified orange juice and shook it vigorously. 'Here, Patrick, try this.'

Patrick took a long drink. 'Great stuff. Here you go.'

We passed the bottle around a few times and all felt better. Then I finished my eyes while Gloria crawled around on the floor cutting the suspenders off my grandmother's corset with my nail scissors. It was unfortunate that my mother chose that moment to walk in.

The smelling salts couldn't have gone off, because they worked just fine on her.

Everything works out in the end if you stay calm, as my grandmother always says. The dress fit perfectly.

&CHAPTER FOUR&

At the day and time appointed for solemnisation of Matrimony, the persons to be married shall come into the body of the Church with their friends and neighbours...

Book of Common Prayer

We were only slightly delayed leaving for the church. This was not my fault, as my mother suddenly dug in her heels and refused to promise to put on Moses' ribbon after the ceremony. I couldn't see what the problem was, after all she had to be the first back at the house anyway, to let all the guests in, so she could just as easily put on his ribbon, but she wouldn't promise to do it. I think she might have been a bit shocked with Patrick for drinking the vodka.

So I had to put it on him myself before leaving,

which meant coaxing him down off the top of my wardrobe where he'd gone to sulk when my mother made a noise like a fire engine, and then persuading Gloria to tie the bow while I held him still, and watching him for a minute to make sure he didn't rip it straight off, and then getting him a bowl of milk to distract him from trying to rip it off, and getting Gloria a band-aid... anyway, it wasn't more than fifteen minutes, twenty at the outside, I couldn't see what all the fuss was about.

I wanted Gloria and Patrick to go in the car with me (actually what I really wanted was to curl up in the sun and go to sleep for a week, but since I couldn't have that I'd have settled for moral support) but my mother wouldn't let us. Perhaps she thought we'd drink more vodka or something. Instead, I had to go with my father in one car, and Gloria and Patrick in the next one, and then my mother in the last one, accompanied by my grandmother who turned up at the last minute with her dog, Euthanasia. I really think the argument Gran had with the hired car driver about Euthanasia took longer than decking Moses out in white satin, especially as, having browbeaten the poor man into letting Euthanasia ride in the car, Gran delayed us further by spotting Moses in the window and insisting on Euthanasia having a white satin bow too. I had a bit of the ribbon left over, but the problem was Euthanasia is quite a large dog, and takes a sixty centimetre collar, and I only had eighteen inches of the ribbon left. We eventually compromised by making it into a bow and attaching it to his collar.

Anyway, we finally got underway. Things were pretty sedate in my car, with my father brooding darkly on past injuries to Clan MacDougall and throwing out the odd bit of information on Highland betrothal customs and sheep stealing. This was extra galling, as every time I turned around I could see Patrick and Gloria having a right merry jape in the car behind, swigging out of the orange juice bottle, which Gloria had shoved in her handbag.

***

I felt pretty relaxed by the time we arrived at St Arnulf the Lesser. The damp patch on my dress had dried out pretty well, and I was getting used to the corset. Getting married was really a piece of cake, I thought to myself, although I could have done with a bit more orange juice.

Father Simpson was waiting for us at the church door. I hardly recognised him in his best robes. He was looking a bit strained, but then he generally does. There was an awkward moment when he saw Euthanasia; there nearly always is when people meet him for the first time. I'm not sure why, he's just a big fuzzy black and yellow dog. Of course he is quite big; he weighed a hundred and eighty pounds the last time Gran was able to get him on the scales, and that was before he finished growing. He can't be weighed any more, because he doesn't like it.

Anyway, they all nicked off into the church, and I was left standing pitifully exposed on the steps, with only my father, Gloria and Patrick. That was when I had the sense of deadly foreboding. If marrying Tim was a sensible enterprise, why didn't I have more sensible people helping me do it?

There was no time to worry about it just then, the organ started playing our entrance music and we had to get into formation and process down the aisle. I could see Tim standing at the other end, he looked very tiny and far away. I couldn't remember anything about the wedding service, and wished I hadn't been too busy to go to the rehearsal.

We made it to the front of the church without incident, although as we passed the front pew I could hear Gran restraining Euthanasia, with some effort, from rushing out to greet us. The church looked great with all the white flowers and everything polished. Tim looked more handsome than ever. Perhaps everything would be all right after all.

Father Simpson can really be quite impressive in priest mode. He led off in the usual way:

'Dearly beloved brethren...'

For a horrible moment I thought he'd got the wrong service and was going to give us Evensong.

'...we are gathered together here...'

A faint whisper floated to me from Tim. 'Tautology...'

'...of God, and in the face of this congregation, to join together this Man and this Woman...'

Thank God, he'd got the right service after all. I relaxed slightly. Actually, I thought, now that we'd got past all the hassles and dramas and actually got here, it was rather fun. And soon I'd be living in my own flat and whipping up little gourmet creations every night. It was true that I didn't actually know how to cook anything except roast beef and a rather unreliable omelette, but I wasn't worried about that. After all, I thought, if the people who host cooking shows on the television can master it, there can't be all that much to it. I imagined my dinner guests fainting with astonishment and demanding third helpings.

Father Simpson thundered on majestically. Was that a snigger from behind me? He seemed to be saying something about carnal lust, surely that wasn't in the service? Not that I was necessarily against it, but it didn't seem really to fit the St Arnulf's ambience, and I didn't want Patrick getting a giggling fit and dropping the rings off their little cushion. I tuned in to make sure Simpson was really on track.

'...for which Matrimony was ordained. First, it was ordained for the procreation of children...'

That was an idea I hadn't thought of. A sweet little baby all our own. I would get some of those Laura Ashley smocks, in soft shades of blue, with perhaps a hint of broderie anglaise. And I might change my perfume to something a bit more demure. Pregnancy is supposed to do wonders for your complexion. Perhaps the freckles on my nose would go away.

'...to avoid fornication...'

That was a definite snigger. I wondered if I could kick Patrick without anybody seeing, and decided I didn't dare risk it.

'...that such persons as have not the gift of continence might marry...'

What on earth was the gift of continence? I supposed it must have something to do with those advertisements on the television, where the old dears are enabled to play bowls despite the fact they wet their pants all the time. I couldn't quite see what it had to do with getting married though. Your wedding night couldn't be much of an event if you had to wear a nappy. I sniggered myself. Serve them right for not doing their pelvic floor exercises.

Father Simpson was frowning at me. I made a big effort and pulled myself together.

'...Therefore if any man can show any just cause, why they may not lawfully be joined together, let him now speak, or else hereafter for ever hold his peace.'

A ghastly silence fell over the whole church. I could feel the eyes of the congregation boring into my spine. I realised that I had no idea who was there from Tim's list. Could there be one of his old girlfriends, who would now leap up and bring the whole thing crashing to a halt?

The seconds dragged on towards eternity. I reminded myself firmly that Tim and I had been going out for three years, so he didn't have any old girlfriends. But what if he'd been secretly leading a double life and was already married? I could feel a cold sweat breaking out under my powder.

And then my worst fears were realised.

When I got my breath again I realised that Euthanasia had only barked once. It just seemed like a whole pack of hounds because of the way sounds echo in a church. Of course, Euthanasia has a very loud bark.

Father Simpson was definitely glaring at us now. He resumed thundering, sounding even more deadly and terrible than before.

'I require and charge you both, as ye will answer at the dreadful day of judgement when the secrets of all hearts shall be disclosed, that if either of you know any impediment why ye may not be lawfully joined together in Matrimony, ye do now confess it. For be ye well assured, that so many as are coupled together otherwise than God's word doth allow are not joined together by God; neither is their Matrimony Lawful.'

I could feel the blood draining out of my face. A yawning chasm seemed to open up before my feet, with hellfire, demons etcetera. I felt sure there was some awful thing that had to be confessed, but couldn't really think of what. The only impediments to marriage I could think of was the list of people in the prayer book, where it says you can't marry your grandmother. What if Tim had been switched in the hospital, and was really my brother? We'd both go to hell, and also it would mean that Patrick wasn't even my brother, which after everything I'd done for him over the years would be a total rip-off.

Fortunately Father Simpson didn't pause for so long this time. In fact, he hardly paused at all, and while he did he kept looking nervously over my left shoulder, presumably towards Euthanasia.

'Timothy Charles Cedric Alfred, wilt thou have this woman to thy wedded wife...'

I couldn't believe my ears. Cedric! He'd always claimed not to have a middle name at all. I should have known it was suspicious, I thought furiously. Nobody doesn't have a middle name. I wondered if it was sufficient grounds to call off the wedding. But it would be so embarrassing, and I'd have to send back all the presents. I bit my tongue and shot Tim a filthy look out of the sides of my eyes.

'...and forsaking all other, keep thee only unto her, so long as ye both shall live?'

'I will,' said Tim, looking unbelievably soppy. He didn't seem to have the slightest consciousness of guilt for having such a disgusting middle name. I wondered if it was possible that Patrick might have missed hearing it. He didn't like Tim much anyway.

'Fiona Bridget Mary, wilt thou have this man...'

I just wasn't sure if I would or not. Cedric is a bit much to swallow, when it's thrust on you all at once like that. I took my time replying, both to be really sure and to make him squirm. I was also pretty annoyed that he had more names than I did. Actually Father Simpson squirmed pretty well, but my father had less patience and poked me in the ribs.

'I will,' I said crossly. I hate it when people rush me.

Then we had to hold hands and there was all the better or worse bit. I couldn't help sniggering a bit when I said, 'I, Fiona Bridget Mary, take thee, Timothy Charles Cedric Alfred...'

'...to love, cherish, and to obey...'

WHAT! Tim had just said to love and to cherish. I wasn't going to say obey if he didn't, I never heard anything so outrageous. There was a longish pause while I thought rapidly.

'To love and to cherish,' I said firmly, looking Father Simpson right in the eye. As I'd thought, he didn't argue about it. What a nerve, slipping in something like that. Probably Timothy Cedric had put him up to it.

After that bit it was Patrick's big moment, handing the rings to Father Simpson. He had them on a cute little black velvet cushion. Patrick is a bit unreliable at times, but I didn't think he could screw up anything as simple as holding out a cushion.

I was wrong.

When Father Simpson went to pick up the rings, they stuck. He was pulling and tugging away, and they were stuck fast to the cushion. The horrified look on Father Simpson's face was quite something; he looked even more upset than the time Moses had jumped on the dinner table with a rubber spider in his mouth. I was tempted to laugh, but it was my wedding, and it really wasn't funny. I had no idea whether our marriage would be valid without rings, and didn't want to find out.

For once in his poisonous little life, Patrick had the grace to look worried. I pinched him, hard, under cover of my bouquet.

'What have you done?' I hissed.

'Sorry, Fi. I was afraid they might fall off going up the aisle, so I stuck them on with Superglue. I've got the solvent in my sporran.'

'Well get it out, you little creep.'

The congregation was then treated to the entertaining sight of Patrick fiddling with his sporran. Eventually we got the rings unstuck and Father Simpson, hands visibly shaking, continued with his routine. Tim looked really upset too. I wasn't too pleased myself. I was sure Aquadhere would have been enough, or some Blue Tack.

✃CHAPTER FIVE✃

...reverently,   discreetly,   advisedly,
soberly, and in the fear of God...
                                    Book of Common Prayer

We got to sit in the choir pews while everybody received communion. It got a bit boring after a while, and I wondered if it had been a good idea to go for the full nuptial mass. Gloria and Patrick, who had both taken an almighty great swig of the altar wine, got restless after a while, and started a running commentary on the guests.

'Oh Christ, there's Miss Peemoller. What's she doing here?'

'Come off it, she couldn't be called that.'

'She is, she was my form mistress at school year before last. The old bag.'

'She's no old bag. What did she get you for? Don't bother with that innocent look, you must have done something evil in a whole year.'

'Will you two shut up?'

'Shut up yourself, Cedric.' They both started giggling. Tim looked furious. His best man didn't look like anything, I've never seen such a colourless person. I'd never met him before and had no idea of his name.

Gloria sat up straight. 'My God, who's that?' Her eyes had lit up like traffic lights.

'Oh shit, don't you start going into heat. We could hardly restrain Fiona. That's Joe Morelli, he's a Dominican priest. Pure as the driven snow, and a total prick as well, so no use getting your hopes up.'

Gloria raised an eyebrow.

'So what did he get you for?'

'Same as Miss P. Don't ask.'

'Christ, he's good looking. What a waste.'

Tim was goaded past endurance. 'Jesus, Gloria, anything in pants. Could you just keep your filthy speculations till the reception?'

'Shut up, Cedric. I hope your penis falls off.'

'Trust you to think of that.'

I thought I'd better intervene before they came to blows. Tim and Gloria had never liked each other all that much.

'Look, guys, will you please not squabble at my wedding?'

Of course they both turned on me.

'Your wedding, Fiona? I suppose I don't count at all.'

'Oh, come on, Tim, I didn't mean it like that.'

'Oh, God! Who on earth's that?'

'Who?'

'Him, there, in the pink velvet.'

'Oh, that's Peter, we used to work together at Marsh and Spacknall.'

'What a freak! How on earth did you convince your mum to send him an invitation?'

'She didn't know who he was.'

'Has she met him?'

'Well, yes, sort of.' I remembered the night I'd brought him and Sean home for dinner, under the impression that my parents were out for the evening. We'd all been pretty drunk and Peter, in particular, had disgraced himself. I wasn't looking forward to introducing him to my mother again on the receiving line. Perhaps I could get him quietly on one side and persuade him to avoid it, but I didn't like my chances.

'Hey Gloria, I'm thirsty. You got any of that orange juice left?'

'No, I left my bag in the car.'

'Shit.'

They went on like this for some time, after a while I got bored and tuned them out. I looked at the church, all polished within an inch of its life and covered in white flowers. I seemed to remember reading somewhere that nuns taking the veil have a wedding service, just as if they were getting married. I imagined myself taking the veil as a Bride of Christ. Presumably the dress and everything would be the same. I supposed you must get changed into the habit at the reception, as if it were your going-away outfit. But then they cut off your hair, didn't they? Or perhaps that had been relaxed after Vatican II. Maybe now they just plaited it or something. Not that plaits are a great idea if you have a natural wave, of course. I imagined myself the next morning, embarking on a boat for some remote Third World country, to minister to the heathens. Perhaps Father Morelli would be on the boat, I thought hopefully. We would spend our lives in the service of the poor, gathering our precious harvest of souls and storing up treasure in Heaven.

I found this picture so moving that I shed a few discreet tears.

'For Christ's sake, Fiona, pull yourself together. Whatever are people going to think at all, with you howling and snivelling at your own wedding?'

***

I think we were all relieved when everybody finally finished receiving communion. It took an extra long time because Patrick and Gloria had both drunk so much of the wine that it ran out, and everybody had to stay on their knees while Father Simpson rushed off to bless another lot. Then a whole lot of people at the back of the church didn't go up for communion, so there was heaps left; we could tell by the time it took Simpson to quaff it. He looked quite pale. Patrick started sniggering again:

'God, Fiona, I hope he's not too squiffy to sign your certificate. They won't let you book into the hotel without it.'

'Don't be stupid. People book into hotels all the time, they don't ask to see your marriage certificate.

That's what you have a ring for.'

'For Christ's sake, Fiona, will you shut up?'

'No, why should I?'

'You just promised to obey me.'

'Oh, no I didn't.' There, I knew I'd been right to insist.

***

As it turned out, I had been more right than I realised. Who would have dreamed that Tim would expect me to change my name? And to Pinkpank, for heavens' sake? I said I'd think about it, by which I meant no, but I didn't want to have an argument right then. I mean, everybody was waiting for us to sign the register so they could get off to the reception. It just wasn't the time, I felt, to have major lifestyle discussions. Well, I mean, is it ever?

***

It's pretty tiring getting married. By the time we got home my feet hurt, and I was just about ready to kill for a gin and tonic. What I really wanted was to get out of Granny's corset, but I knew there was no hope of that until we left on our honeymoon. I cheered myself with the thought that I was now a married lady with my own residence, and would never have to worry again in case my mother found out about Moses spraying.

***

Receiving lines are the ultimate in torture. The worst of it is that while you're accepting the banal compliments of normally intelligent people who seem to have been specially lobotomised for the occasion, you have to watch everybody else at the party drinking and having a good time. I had hoped Gloria or Patrick might notice how stuck I was and bring me a drink, but no such luck – they were both too busy getting stuck back into the vodka and orange. The worst of it was that my mother had nailed me into place the minute we arrived at the house, and I hadn't even had a chance to find Moses.

At least you don't have to concentrate on this sort of thing. I allowed my mind to drift, imagining that I was a Secret Service agent on a mission to discover a new top secret military device being developed by the Axis of Evil. Dressed in close-fitting matt black (so flattering to the complexion) I scaled the wall of the enemy fortress using a Batman rope, and dropped lightly to the ground sixty feet below; special high-technology boots cushioned my landing. I knew the guard would not pass this way on his patrol for another thirty-nine seconds, giving me plenty of time to gain access to the building with my miniature diamond-bladed glass cutter. I moved carefully towards my target window and positioned the rubber suction cap above the catch. Suddenly my concentration was broken by a low growl – an enormous German Shepherd was leaping for my throat. With reflexes specially honed at the Secret Service Academy, I swung the cutting tool up, instantly severing the dog's jugular. Blood fountained over the snow, seeming black in the moonlight. I calculated that fourteen seconds remained before the guard would appear round the corner; speed was now of the essence.

'...Fiona? Are you alright?'

My father was shaking my shoulder. Father Simpson was waiting to say some mundane ritual remark to me. I realised that I had dropped into a fighting crouch, and straightened up.

'Well, I'm feeling a bit...' I allowed my voice to trail off artistically, seeing a chance for early release. Sure enough my father led me to a chair and pressed a glass of lemonade into my hand.

I sat for a minute, for verisimilitude, while my father resumed his duties. Then I nicked upstairs to look for Moses.

***

Moses was curled innocently on my bed and had not destroyed anything or removed his white satin bow. I took this to be a good omen for my marriage. I picked him up carefully and carried him downstairs, noticing as I did so that the party seemed already to be spilling out into the hall.

I went into the sitting room, carrying Moses. I was looking for Patrick, I wanted him to take our picture. I knew he would have the camera with him, as he had told me the day before that he thought wedding pictures were too contrived, and he planned to supplement ours with some candid snaps. People were everywhere, I didn't seem to know half of them. I pretended to recognise everybody though, just in case.

I found Patrick out on the back steps, smoking one of Gloria's black cigarettes and talking to Peter, who let out a hoot like a train whistle when he saw me.

'Dragon Woman! Have you consummated your marriage yet?'

'Don't be disgusting, Peter, we haven't even cut the cake. Listen, Patrick, could you take a picture of me and Moses, while he's got his bow on?'

'Sure. Can you get him to face this way?'

I sat on the step and arranged Moses nicely on my lap, assisted by Peter. He seemed unusually docile.

'Okay, smile.' We all waited anxiously for the picture to appear. It was lovely, except that I had bright red eyes, like a pervert. It was a good likeness of Moses, though.

Peter squinted at Moses, who seemed to have fallen asleep on my lap.

'Jesus, it's a wonder that thing doesn't rip your face off. It was totally hyper last time I was here.'

'Oh, that's because I gave him one of Mum's Valiums.'

I couldn't believe my ears. 'You did what?'

'Well, you didn't want him charging around the place climbing up the curtains and snatching people's food, did you? It's just calmed him down a bit, that's all. It won't hurt him.'

I was horrified.

'You bastard, he'll probably be a drug addict now. We'll have to make him sick it up. How much did you give him, you creep?'

Patrick assumed an expression of wounded

innocence. 'Only one.'

'Only one! You break pills in half for cats! Jesus, when he was on the hormones last year I had to break them in quarters! How long ago did he have it?'

'Oh, about twenty minutes I suppose.'

'Well, you'll just have to stick your finger down his throat.'

'Oh, what? No way, he'd have my hand off.'

'Look, if he dies I'll never forgive you.'

'He won't die, Fiona. Jesus.'

'Stick your finger down his throat right this minute, or you're never ever coming to stay with us when we're married.'

'You're married now.'

'Yes, well. Look, I'll hold him, he won't do anything.'

Patrick assumed the demeanour of a virgin martyr and squatted down in front of Moses. Moses yawned widely at him. I got a good grip on his shoulders, then I had a terrible thought.

'Wait a sec, if he sicks up it'll go all over my dress.'

'Pull your skirt up, there's no-one around.'

'Right. Hang on. Okay, go for it.'

I prised Moses' jaws apart and Patrick nervously inserted his finger. Nothing happened, except that Moses chewed gently on it.

'It mustn't be in far enough.'

'Are you kidding? I've got teeth marks up to my elbow.'

'Don't be a wimp. Here, let me do it.'

I stuck my own finger in with no discernible effect.

'It must be different with cats. Well, we'll have to give him a lot of milk, that's what you do for poisoning. It says so on the fly spray tin.'

'Jesus, Fiona, he's not poisoned. Look, I'll prove it.'

'How?'

'I'll take one myself.'

'Oh, big deal. You only weigh about ten times more than him.'

'Well I'll take ten times as much. I'll take ten,

that'll prove it.' He disappeared back into the house. I looked around for Peter, but he had drifted off, presumably bored with our argument. I went inside to find a drink, carrying Moses with me so as to keep an eye on him in case he started having convulsions.

In the few minutes I'd been outside, our reception seemed to have become a scene of unbridled debauchery. Or perhaps it was only the effect of suddenly coming in from the peaceful dusk. A quick scan of the room revealed the trouble spots to be avoided, to wit:

My mother was near the door talking to Father Simpson.

Miss Peemoller and Father Morelli were in the far corner. They were swigging champagne and laughing. I wondered what they found to laugh about. Probably they were planning how to totally disrupt some innocent person's life. I shuddered at the memory of the interminable counselling sessions that had ensued upon Miss Peemoller's catching Patrick with a pornographic magazine the year before last. We had all suffered.

My grandmother was sitting by the window with a large group of people; fine except that she had Euthanasia with her. It is the one wish of Euthanasia's life to make friends with Moses. Moses, however, loathes Euthanasia, and couldn't be trusted even in his drugged state.

I looked around for my own friends, and located Peter and Gloria over by the fireplace with Tim and some other people. It seemed safe enough, so I headed in that direction.

Tim was touchingly pleased to see me.

'Christ Fiona, do you have to cart that smelly cat everywhere?'

'He's not feeling well.'

'Well fucking put him outside before he vomits everywhere.'

I wasn't worried by Tim's apparent callousness, because I knew he loved Moses really. I arranged Moses, who was now fast asleep, nicely on a chair, poured myself some champagne and surreptitiously took my shoes off. I felt instantly better, except for Granny's corset, which was now digging red hot furrows in my ribs.

Presently Patrick appeared with a bottle of pills.

'Okay, Fi, just keep an eye on the olds while I take these, will you?'

'Right. You're taking ten?'

'How much does he weigh, exactly?'

'Sixteen pounds last time I weighed him.'

'Well I only weigh nine stone, so I reckon eight would be about the same dose, okay?'

I did quick sums in my head, but couldn't remember how many pounds in a stone.

'Okay.'

Patrick swallowed eight of the pills, washing them down with champagne.

'There, you see? Absolutely harmless, no effect at all.' He took another great swig of champagne. I wondered uneasily how much he'd had to drink. Gloria evidently had the same thought.

'Jesus H Christ, what are those things?' She snatched the bottle. 'Valium? Fuck, you'll be on your ear!'

'Bullshit. Look at Moses, he's hardly affected at all.'

Moses had, in fact, woken up and was polishing off the remains of a plate of salmon mousse that someone had unwisely left on the coffee table.

***

Actually, I had a wonderful time. After all, when do you get to invite all your friends to a party that's paid for by someone else, and you're guaranteed to have the most stunning dress there?

I had settled in for a good gossip session with Tim, Peter, Gloria and Patrick, who didn't seem to be showing any effects at all from all the Valium, when Gloria suddenly froze, pointing, like a retriever that's just seen a rabbit.

'Holy shit, who's that?'

I looked. I couldn't see anyone particular.

'Who?'

'That man. God, he's gorgeous. Introduce me at once.'

I still couldn't see who she was talking about. The only men in that direction were Father Simpson, my father, and deplorable Uncle Mike, who seemed to have just arrived. Presumably he'd been held up between the church and our house by the urgent necessity of calling his bookmaker.

'What man?'

'God, Fiona. You're looking right at him. There, talking to your Dad.'

'That's my uncle. You don't want to meet him, he's boring.'

'Jesus, when it looks like that, who cares?'

'Oh, come off it Gloria. You couldn't possibly fancy him, he's frightfully old, he must be fifty.'

'And looks every day of it too, the old whore. You could pack for the weekend in those bags under his eyes.' Peter never could stand anyone else being admired.

'Is he married?'

'No. He's always got some girlfriend, but it's never the same one. He used to come and stay with us, but Dad won't let him now, because he reckoned the last one was only fifteen.'

'Shit. I'm probably too old for him.'

'Oh, I don't think he's fussy. Some of them were quite old, too.'

'Hello, darling. Or I suppose I should say congratulations.'

Uncle Mike had sneaked up on us while we were discussing him. He kissed my cheek and I nearly choked on his aftershave.

'You look scrumptious, darling. Almost enough to make me consider incest.'

You can always rely on Uncle Mike to say

something utterly tasteless. I couldn't for the life of me see what made Gloria fancy him, with his great beer gut and his white pants two sizes too small. Perhaps they'd split up the back, I thought hopefully.

'Uncle Mike, this is my friend Gloria Jackson. Gloria, Mike O'Brien.'

Of course, Uncle Mike made a complete prat of himself bowing over her hand. I really thought his pants actually were going to split, but they didn't, which just goes to show that God isn't always on the side of the righteous. Then he straightened up and stood very close to her, looking down the front of her dress. God, he was so obvious. I edged away and left them to it, only to be seized by my mother who wanted us to cut the cake.

And what a primitive ritual that is, I thought as we all clustered around it, keeping still so that all our ghastly relatives could take their blurry snapshots. At least Tim wasn't in the army, so we didn't have to risk life and limb with him waving a sword about.

'Wait a minute darling, I just want to get some of this material out of the way.'

My mother was fussing with the cloud of tulle around the bottom of the cake. I wasn't really paying attention, I was actually noticing that Uncle Mike, a fast worker if nothing else, had his arm around

Gloria. Or perhaps it was Gloria who was the fast worker. They both looked disgustingly pleased with themselves, so I supposed it didn't really matter.

Then I remembered about the hole.

'Ah, Mum, I think that'll be okay like that...'

But I was too late.

'Merciful Heaven, what is this?'

I thought I'd better come clean, not that it isn't totally against my way of life, but at least it would save us having the Spanish Inquisition in front of everybody.

'Well, Moses just ate a tiny bit, you know how he loves marzipan, I patched it up...'

My mother showed imminent signs of fainting. She didn't get to hog the limelight on this particular occasion, though. It was at that moment that Patrick gave a little sigh and slid slowly under the table.

I can hardly bear to remember the ensuing events. One thing followed another with a sort of horrible inevitability, like dominoes. Of course Euthanasia had been specially trained by our grandmother to rescue people from drowning. So it was quite natural, wasn't it, that he should be concerned when Patrick fell down and lay still. And, I suppose, that he should rush over and slobber on Patrick's face. And he's always loved Moses, even though Moses despises him, so I suppose it was fairly understandable that when he caught sight of Moses he should be distracted from his mission of mercy and bound off after him. And, with his being such a large dog, I suppose it would have been reasonable to expect that, if he stood up under the table, then the table would fall over.

But it was lovely getting the corset off.

৪০CHAPTER SIX೦೪

*For this cause shall a man leave his
father and mother, and shall be joined
unto his wife...*
                    Book of Common Prayer

By the time we came back from our honeymoon I was more relaxed than I've ever been in my life. Not that I'm normally a tense person, but the thing about most holidays is that, however great they are, you always have that little awareness at the back of your mind that you have to go back to work, or uni or whatever, at the end of it. Since Tim didn't believe in working wives, I was happily aware that for me the holiday was going to go on forever. As we drove through the depressing Northern suburbs into Melbourne, I congratulated myself yet again on marrying someone who was both handsome and incredibly old-fashioned.

Of course, life is never a total bed of roses. In between congratulating myself and planning how to redecorate Tim's flat (mine now, of course) I was uncomfortably wondering how to break it to him that I hadn't actually got around to packing yet.

On the other hand, I thought, why did I need to tell him at all? He'd only be upset. I had my make-up, hair dryer and a suitcase full of my favourite clothes which I could throw in the wash, so except for Moses there was really nothing at home that I couldn't live without indefinitely, and I could sneak over there and pick my stuff up when he went back to work. Yes, that would be much the best way. Then I wouldn't have to listen to one of Tim's patronising lectures, that he always trotted out when I'd forgotten something or behaved in a non-Tim way.

Presently I noticed that the car had stopped in front of Tim's flat.

'Hang on, Tim, this is your place.'

'Our place now, darling.'

Yuk. I wished he wouldn't call me darling in that soppy way. It's funny how some people can call you darling and you hardly notice, like my mother, and then others, like Uncle Mike for instance, always sound as if they're calling you that because they've forgotten your name, and then you get someone like

Tim, who only has to say the word and you get visions of Bambi. Perhaps he'd get over it, once we'd been married for a while.

'Yes, but listen Tim, we've got to pick up Moses.'

'Oh, for Christ's sake. Can't we spend our first night at home together without that fucking smelly animal?'

I couldn't believe my ears. I had already been separated from Moses for two weeks, and although I'd rung home most days, it's just not the same, he never says anything back. I knew how to deal with this sort of problem, though. I concentrated on the injustice of it all and allowed my eyes to slowly fill with tears. Crying is something I do really well.

It had the appropriate effect on Tim. He looked all horrified and put his arms around me.

'Oh God, Fiona, please don't cry. Look, we'll go straight there now. Or would you rather get settled in and then go and fetch him? Or you could have a nice hot bath and I'll nick over and get him, how would that be?'

I took care to make my voice small and sorrowful. 'Could we go now?'

'Of course we can go now, whatever you want,

sweetheart.' He started the car again.

***

I found Moses in my room, which was still just as I'd left it, except that someone, presumably my mother, had tidied it up a bit. Well, quite a lot really, and I was sure I could smell disinfectant. Moses was frightfully pleased to see me, and I nearly started genuinely crying with homesickness. I cheered myself up thinking that I'd soon obliterate the techno minimalist flavour of Tim's flat. All it needed was a few lace tablecloths and some nice curtains, really.

My parents were pleased to see me too, of course. My mother asked a lot of silly questions about the hotels we'd stayed in and whether they were hygienic. My father stuffed his pipe morosely and remarked how quiet the house had been since I'd left, and followed up with some entertaining facts about the mating habits of tribal Eskimos.

Patrick fell on my neck and demanded to know when he could come and stay with us. I was still a bit narked with him for drugging my cat, passing out at my reception, and sticking the wedding rings to the cushion with Superglue; it had been days before all the black fluff had come off them, so I told him he'd have to wait until I was settled. Whatever that means, but it always sounds terribly convincing when other people say it.

Tim shook hands with my father in a way that I can only describe as manly, and kissed my mother on the cheek. It was quite nauseating actually, but at least they didn't ask him to call them Mum and Dad, like people's parents do when they're the sort of people who call each other Mum and Dad. All the same, I was glad to get out of there.

Moses kicked up a fearful row in the car, he hates going anywhere by car. Usually if I have to take him to the vet or anything I take him on the tram, which he quite likes, but something about cars really brings out the worst in him.

Tim was in a pretty bad mood by the time we got back to his flat, I think the long drive must have given him a headache. I explained about the magic bottle of stuff that takes the smell of cat pee out of the car upholstery, but it didn't seem to cheer him up at all. Just as well, I suppose, as I remembered afterwards that it was one of the many things I had not packed. In any case, he moped and stamped about the place, and when I explained about the litter tray I thought he was going to hit me.

Well, of course Moses had to have a litter tray, didn't he? After all, if you live in flats there are certain concessions you have to make, and one of them is that you have to have a litter tray for the cat. After I had explained this to Tim there was a long silence. Then, in terms of the utmost forbearance, he asked me why I had not brought it from my parents' house.

'Well, I haven't got one, have I? We've never lived in a flat before.' I thought it was better not to bring up the one disastrous time when I moved into the residential college at Uni. Anyway, we'd both been thrown out with such dispatch that I hadn't remembered to bring the litter tray with me. Perhaps it was still there under the desk, perplexing some undergraduate with intermittent odours.

'Well, please excuse me for being dense, Fiona, but I would have thought you might have bothered to do something about it before now. Where the fuck do you expect me to get a fucking litter tray, for Christ's sake, at seven o'clock at night?'

'Um. Could we borrow one from the neighbours?'

'No, we bloody couldn't. Jesus!'

Fortunately for all of us, I then remembered that it was Friday, and all the shops would be open in the city. I don't know why Tim wasn't more pleased, it would have been dreadful for Moses to go all night without being able to go to the lavatory. He insisted on shutting Moses in the bathroom while we went out, and then he muttered and grumbled all the way into the city. Men are so unfair, after all it wasn't my idea to take the car, it would have been much quicker on the tram, especially as Tim, like most men, felt it was a stain on his honour to pay for parking, so that we had to drive round in circles for three quarters of an hour looking for somewhere free to leave the car. We could have jumped on the tram right outside Tim's flat and got off right outside Pets' Paradise, and the whole thing would have taken about fifteen minutes, but when I mentioned this Tim snarled at me. Evidently it is beneath the dignity of a solicitor to be seen on public transport carrying what he referred to as a shit box.

He was wrong, as it turned out. It was not called a shit box, but a Booda Box. We had another argument.

'I'm not paying fucking ninety bucks for a box for that fucking smelly cat to crap in.'

'But look, it's got a little roof and a charcoal filter. You won't be able to smell a thing.'

'Why would you smell anything? Cats cover up their droppings.'

'What if he's going at the same time as you? Then you'll smell something alright.' It didn't seem to be quite the right time to mention that Moses wasn't really into covering up.

'WHAT! Just where were you planning to put it?'

'Well, in the lavatory, of course, where else?'

'Why can't he have it on the balcony?'

'It's got to be inside, it might rain.'

'Well, the fucking lid can keep him dry, can't it? I'm not having it inside.'

I didn't miss the implied capitulation. Once we got it home, we could discuss where it was going.

'So we can get this one then?'

'I'm not fucking paying ninety bucks for it. You can pay for it, he's your cat.'

'I haven't got any money.'

'Put it on your fucking credit card then.'

He was really cross. I didn't really feel it was the time to tell him that my credit card was already maxed. Well, I had to have some decent clothes for my honeymoon, didn't I? And you can't get married without new underwear. Perhaps I'd better change the subject.

'Oh, look! Kittens.'

They were really sweet too, there was a tortoiseshell one and a little grey one with the narrowest little stripes, like a tiny pinstriped solicitor. When I pointed this out to Tim he was not amused. But at least, by the time I'd stopped crying because the kittens had no home, he had paid for the Booda Box and a big sack of Kittyflakes.

All in all, I guess you could say our first night of married life wasn't a success. Although I don't know why Tim was so cross with me. After all, it wasn't my idea to go out to dinner in the city, and I couldn't very well help it if the waiter sniggered when Tim asked him to put the Booda Box in the cloakroom. As for the parking ticket, if he'd taken my advice and paid ten dollars to park in the parking lot, it wouldn't have happened. And nobody with an ounce of sense could have expected Moses to wait that long. I thought he'd been really clever to go down the plughole like that, and I must say I thought it was a bit excessive to make me scrub the whole bath. But it was when we went to bed that the trouble really started.

I had no idea to expect any problems. After all, Tim and I had been going to bed together every night for two weeks, and I knew honeymoons weren't supposed to be anything like real life, but there had to be some continuity, didn't there? We were both the same people, if nothing else. We had established some habits even during the short time we'd been married, like for instance Tim always had the right side of the bed and I had the left. So we just got into bed, as usual, and of course Moses came in and settled down on my feet. It wasn't cold enough for him to want to get under the covers.

Tim froze.

'You're not going to let that smelly cat sleep on our bed, I hope.'

I couldn't believe my ears.

'What on earth d'you mean? Where else would he sleep?'

'Well he's a cat, Fiona. There are plenty of places he could sleep. The floor, for instance.'

'Why would he want to sleep on the floor?'

'It's not really about what he wants, is it? He's an animal, for Christ's sake. I think the floor would be a lot more appropriate than our bed.'

'Don't be ridiculous. How would you like to sleep on the floor? It's not even a proper floor, it's all concrete under the carpet.'

'Look, I don't want to have an argument about this. Kick him off, he'll soon get used to it.'

'No way. He's always slept with me.'

'Fiona, I do not want a fucking smelly tomcat in my bed, am I making myself clear? In fact I don't really want him in our bedroom, but I can live with it. But not on the bed.'

'He's not smelly, he has a bath every month.'

'Are you kidding, he fucking stinks. You ought to get him fixed.'

'What d'you mean, get him fixed? There's nothing wrong with him.'

'Fixed, spayed, neutered. Cut off his fucking balls, Jesus, Fiona, how can you be so fucking dumb?'

I was horrified.

'How would you like to have your balls cut off just because of somebody else's stupid idea?'

'Jesus, Fiona, he's not a person.'

'He is so a person. And I'm not kicking him out of bed, he's always slept on the bed, it's his bed too.'

'Fuck.'

Tim turned his back on me and refused to say anything else. I put out the bedside light, and then I lay in the dark and wondered. Eventually I must have fallen asleep, because I woke up later on and Moses had crawled under the doona with me, and was nestled up against my shoulder.

***

I couldn't wait to call Gloria as soon as Tim went off to work on Monday morning. Actually, I couldn't wait for Tim to go off to work, I'd had no idea he was like that early in the morning. Determined to be a perfect wife, I'd got up when he did and made him what all the magazines say is the perfect breakfast: a lightly boiled egg, a glass of orange juice and one slice of wholemeal toast. I had it all ready when he came out of the shower, and the coffee dripping through the filter, and I expected him to be really impressed, so it came as a real shock when he just growled at me.

'I never have anything in the morning.'

'Well, you should, it's terrible for you to start the day on an empty stomach. At least have the orange juice and a cup of coffee.'

'Look, I haven't got time, I have to get to work.'

'But it's only seven o'clock.'

'I like to start work early.'

He went into the bedroom and started getting dressed.

'Look, what if I bring you in a cup of coffee and you can have it while you're getting dressed?'

'Fiona, not everyone takes half an hour to get dressed. I'd be finished by the time you poured it. Anyway, I don't want any coffee. I never drink coffee in the morning.'

He was already knotting his tie.

'But I made it all specially.'

'Well, you should have asked me first.' He grabbed his briefcase and his coat and charged off, brushing past me in the doorway. I would have thought he'd at least kiss me before going to work, but all I got was the sound of the front door slamming. I raced out after him and shouted down the stairwell.

'You'll get an ulcer.'

But all I heard, apart from my own echoes, was the sound of the car starting. So I went back inside and ate his breakfast myself.

The day stretched ahead, full of possibilities. I couldn't call Gloria yet, it was still too early. Most people can be called after nine, but with Gloria it's really better to wait till ten. But I had the whole day, to do whatever I liked with. Well, at least until about six o'clock or so, when Tim would get home. And I was completely alone in my own flat, except for Moses, of course. What a luxury. Perhaps I'd do my nails, and then go shopping. But I'd already bought all the new clothes I fancied before I got married, which is why my credit card was full. Remembering that put a bit of a damper on my mood until I also remembered that, now that I was a housewife, Tim would pay it for me. Surely he would be over his bad mood by the time he got home. But just in case, I'd better impress him with my housewifely skills. It was true that I didn't actually have any housewifely skills, but this wasn't a problem, as my mother had given me a copy of Mrs Beeton's *Book of Household Management*.

Tim had brought all the wedding presents to his flat since that was where we'd be living, so all I had to do was find it. I breathed a mental sigh of relief that he was so teutonically organised; it would have been so embarrassing to have to rush over to my parents' house on the first day.

I poured myself a second cup of coffee, and had a nice long bath. I was able to have it by myself as Moses never gets up before nine. Then I realised I had nothing clean to wear. I'd have to stay in my dressing gown and do some washing. Well, that wasn't a problem. Tim, being a born consumer, had every electrical appliance known to man. I loaded up the washing machine and left it to hum quietly to itself while I explored the flat. Of course I'd been there stacks of times, but it was different now, being mine.

I found all the wedding presents in a pile in the spare room, dripping gift wrapping, a depressing reminder of all the thank-you letters I'd have to write. Perhaps I could persuade Tim to do them, or at least some of them, although I knew really that it's the wife's job. But perhaps Tim wouldn't know that. The pile wasn't a bit neat by the time I'd found Mrs Beeton, but I could tidy it up later. In fact, I decided, I'd put each present away as I wrote the thank-you letters, thus eliminating the dreadful possibility of writing the same letter twice. Anyway, my fountain pen was still at my parents' place, and I couldn't go there until I'd done the washing and ironing, so that was alright.

Moses was still asleep, so I poured myself another cup of coffee and settled down to read Mrs Beeton.

'As with the Commander of an Army, or the leader of any enterprise, so it is with the mistress of a house.'

Great stuff, I thought to myself, although I

wasn't sure Tim would see it in quite that light. I rather suspected he saw himself as the commander of the house. Never mind, he'd adjust in time. I read on.

'Early rising is one of the most essential qualities which enter into good Household Management...'

Well, I didn't think that really applied. There hadn't been much point in getting up at the crack of dawn this morning, since Tim wouldn't eat the breakfast I'd cooked for him. I skipped on to the next paragraph.

'Cleanliness is also Indispensable to Health, and must be studied both in regard to the person and the house, and all that it contains.' I was beginning to see why my mother thought it was a good book. I hoped Mrs Beeton didn't expect me to spend all day scrubbing. But I'd had a bath already, and put on a load of washing, so I reckoned I was doing okay so far.

'Frugality and Economy are Home Virtues, without which no household can prosper.' This was really getting a bit boring, perhaps I'd have better results by opening the book at random.

The book fell open to a page of recipes for things I'd never heard of, interspersed with little paragraphs about the water supply in ancient Rome and the fountains of Athens, which reminded me of my father. I tried again.

'Bill of Fare for a Picnic for 40 Persons.' I was starting to feel quite faint, and on the opposite page there was a dissertation about how you shouldn't hire footmen solely on the strength of their having nice legs. I'd give her one more chance.

'The dairy-maid receives the milk from the cowkeeper, each pail being strained through the hair sieve into one of the milk-basins.' On another part of the page I learned that a hair-sieve is used to strain out any of the cow's hairs which may have fallen into the milk. What a disgusting thought, if I found hairs in the milk I'd complain to the factory. I decided Mrs Beeton must have been quite insane. I propped her up in the corner of the kitchen bench and went to see if my washing was finished.

***

The washing machine was still going back and forth. It was still only eight-thirty, so I couldn't call Gloria yet. Moses wouldn't be awake for at least half an hour. I decided I'd wash up the breakfast things and get his breakfast ready for when he woke up, and by that time the washing might be ready to go in the dryer. I felt quite smug about how organised I already was, until I went back to the kitchen and discovered that I'd used the last of the cat food.

I hunted everywhere, but there wasn't even a bag of whiskettes. There was nothing useful in the refrigerator either, I supposed Tim must have thrown everything out before leaving for the wedding; no doubt that explained why he'd insisted on going out for all our meals over the weekend. I'd have to go shopping, but I had nothing clean to wear. Perhaps Moses would be satisfied with an egg flip for breakfast. I could ring Tim at his office and get him to bring me some cat food on the way home. But he'd be sure to ask why I didn't go out and get it myself. It would better to wait until my washing finished and then nick out to the supermarket. I'd have to buy groceries anyway, there was nothing in the house except a few eggs and the bread, milk and orange juice, which we'd had to pick up from the seven eleven on Friday night.

I had just poured myself another cup of coffee and settled down to do my nails, when I noticed the water running along the floor.

❧CHAPTER SEVEN☙

...for the mutual society, help, and comfort, that the one ought to have of the other, both in prosperity and adversity.
Book of Common Prayer

My first thought was that a pipe had burst somewhere. I must stay calm and find out where, and then call the State Emergency Service. I knew they were the right people to call for a flood, because you always see them on the television, rescuing people from the tops of houses.

The trail of water was coming from the bathroom. Inside the bathroom it could more accurately be described as a flood. I noticed that the washing machine, now on rinse cycle, was purring away happily as if nothing were wrong. I'd better turn it off in case it short circuited sitting in that pool of water.

Hitching up the skirts of my robe, I paddled carefully over to the washing machine. As I reached for the switch, a sudden horrible thought assailed my mind: weren't you supposed to get an electric shock, or something, from standing in a pool of water to turn off an appliance? Was I, even now, courting death? Perhaps I should just not touch anything and leave it for the State Emergency Service.

I backed out of the bathroom to think about it. On the one hand, I was quite sure I remembered that you mustn't touch electrical things while standing in a pool of water; it was one of the things one's mother goes on about when one's little, like sticking a pair of scissors into a power point. Of course, no-one but a mother would ever think of sticking a pair of scissors into a power point, but once they'd given you the idea, I remembered, it was a hell of a temptation to resist. I had tried to persuade the neighbour's little boy to do it when I was three, thereby having the best of both worlds, but his mother had apparently been on the same track, and not even taunts of 'Chicken, chicken, chicken' had been sufficient to break his iron conditioning.

I dragged my mind back to the present dilemma. Concentrate, Fiona, as Miss Riddlestone used to say in the fifth grade. On the other hand, I had dropped my mobile in the bath just a couple of weeks ago without any ill effects. Well, the mobile did seem to have some ill effects, but I hadn't felt a thing, and neither, I was fairly sure, had Moses, who had also been in the bath at the time. Perhaps the whole thing was an Urban Myth, like the monster under the bed.

On the other hand, if it wasn't an Urban Myth, I'd probably be dead. And I couldn't face the thought of being found dead without my makeup on.

Of course, I could do my face and then hope for the best, but I remembered dismally that my cleanser was in the bathroom cabinet. You can't put on makeup without cleansing, toning and moisturising, that's one of the first rules of life. Perhaps I could call Gloria and ask her to bring over some cleanser and things? But it was still too early to call, and meanwhile the water level was presumably rising, although it didn't seem to have risen perceptibly while I was standing there.

While I was pondering this apparently insoluble dilemma, a freezing jet of cold water hit me in the knees. When I got my breath back I noticed it was coming out of a big black tube at the bottom of the washing machine.

Oh, shit.

***

I spent the next several hours mopping up water from the floor. As if that weren't enough, I had to wash all the towels. The exercise was not made easier by Moses jumping from furniture to furniture, screaming for his breakfast. I tried to explain to him that I had an emergency on my hands, and that if he could wait for lunch it would really be a big help, but my calmly reasoned arguments didn't make much impression on him; they usually don't on cats. I gave in and mixed him an egg flip.

By about two o'clock I had got the carpet about as dry as it was going to get. I shoved the last lot of towels in the washing machine and flopped onto the sofa. I was all sweaty, the bottom of my dressing gown was soaked, and I had broken a nail. I also had an uneasy sort of feeling that Tim was going to expect me to have known to put the black hose thing into the bath before starting the washing machine. Perhaps I could tell him it had sprung a leak? But solicitors are hard to lie to, they have this depressing sort of way of wanting to see hard evidence. The first thing he'd do would be to look for the leak, and then where would I be? I was sure he'd be frightfully cross.

But wait on, I thought, with mounting

excitement. What if there actually was a leak? If reality doesn't fit one's expectations, as my grandmother says, it's always a good idea to alter reality.

It was quite easy to pierce a little hole in the black hose thing with my nail scissors.

***

Having attended to all the domestic emergencies, I was now free to have a nice leisurely shower, put on my makeup and get dressed. Of course, I still had to iron my clothes first, and for that I had to find where Tim kept the iron, which took some doing. By the time I had everything sorted out and felt human, it was nearly five o'clock; too late to call Gloria as Tim would be home any time. I hoped all my days weren't going to be like this.

Then I remembered there was nothing in the house for dinner.

***

'Hello, Tim?'

'Hello, darling. How's your first day as my wife?'

Yuk. I pressed on bravely.

'Well, actually there's been one or two problems, that's why I'm ringing.'

'Oh, God. You're not hurt, are you?'

'No, I'm okay, but the washing machine sprung a leak and flooded all over the place, and it's taken me all day to get the water cleaned up so I didn't have time to go shopping, and I wondered if you could sort of pick up a few things on the way home?'

'Jesus, what happened to it? Are you sure you're not hurt? You could have been electrocuted.'

'Well, I wasn't. So could you get some cat food, Snappy Tom's his favourite, and a bag of whiskettes? And something for dinner.'

'Of course, no problem. I'll be home around seven-thirty.'

'How come you're going to be so late?'

'I'm not, I always leave about six-thirty or seven, you know that. Listen, I have to go, I'll see you tonight, okay?'

For a person who had to go, he certainly had time to say a lot of mushy things over the phone, which I won't repeat. I wondered why he was working such long hours when we'd just got back from our honeymoon.

***

I had had visions of white linen and crystal, and little gourmet delights like salmon mousse and Beef Wellington (I was sure Mrs Beeton would have the recipe, despite her worrying deficiencies in other areas), but Tim's idea of dinner turned out to be pizza with ham and pineapple. If there's one kind of pizza I absolutely can't stand, it's ham and pineapple. I said so in no uncertain terms.

'Um, Tim?'

'...so I told him to get stuffed. Bloody little nerd. Just because he's got his name on the letterhead, you'd think he was frigging God.'

'Do you think next time you could sort of get, well, something a bit...'

'Then old Pratt shambled in and chucked a whole pile of files on my desk, about four-thirty. I mean, he expects them to be ready by tomorrow lunchtime, the prick. Jesus, who does he think he is?'

I knew the answer to that one, actually. Mr Pratt was the senior partner.

'You know, I don't actually like ham and

pineapple.'

'Then on top of all that, bloody Katherine had to go and get pregnant.'

This got me in spite of myself.

'What, right in the office? How could you tell?'

'Jesus, Fiona, you're so fucking dumb. She announced it, you twit, and she's taking twelve months' bloody maternity leave, the bitch, just when I'm up to my eyeballs.'

'Oh. I suppose you'll miss her.'

'Damn right I'll bloody miss her, she's the only one that's got any bloody sense. The rest of them are hopeless. Gina deleted a whole bloody great will the other day, that took me days to draw up, reckoned I never told her to save it. Christ. And Louise is no bloody better.'

I thought I would inject a positive note. Always look on the bright side, it's prettier, as my grandmother says.

'Well, I suppose it'll be nice for her husband, having her home.'

Tim shot me a filthy look. He didn't like anybody looking on the bright side when he was grumbling.

'She's not married.'

'Oh.'

After that, I didn't really know quite what to say. Perhaps I was old-fashioned. It didn't really matter in any practical sense, as Tim continued to rabbit on about his boring office for the next hour and a half, all through coffee and the washing up. I refrained from telling him to shut up as he'd obviously had a rotten day, nothing he said was positive.

He was just winding down to a dull mutter, and I was getting ready to have another go at explaining about the pizza, when he suddenly jumped up and raced into the bathroom. Moses, who had been idly playing with his shoelaces, was deeply offended.

'Well, come on. Where is it?'

I was completely baffled.

'What?'

'The leak, in the washing machine, where is it?'

Ah. Thank God I'd thought of it first. I went into the bathroom to show him the hole.

Of course I knew where the hole was. I'd put it there, hadn't I? Fifteen minutes passed as I searched the hose, more and more frantically. In the end I had to admit there was only one explanation.

It had healed itself.

Well, after all, rubber is an organic substance.

***

Tim was frightfully cross. I couldn't really work out whether he was more cross about me saying that the machine had healed itself, or about the spurious leak. Somehow he figured out almost instantly that I had made the whole thing up to cover up the fact that I'd forgotten to put the hose thing in the bath, and he was so mad with rage he was almost gibbering. It quite reminded me of the old days at Marsh and Spacknall. He went on and on until he ran out of breath and wound down like a clock.

'...why you have to fucking lie about it.'

Disoriented, as I always am by being shouted at, I wondered myself, for a moment. Why had I lied about it? Then common sense reasserted itself. After all, if this was how he carried on when I took the trouble of thinking up a perfectly good lie, what would he be like if I hadn't even bothered?

After having shouted at me for what seemed

like hours, Tim developed the need to have a Deep and Meaningful conversation about Our Relationship. In the end Moses and I both fell asleep, which I supposed accounted for Tim's mood the next morning.

***

At least I knew better than to get up early and rush around making breakfast. I couldn't help waking up, because the clock radio alarm went off at six o'clock and Tim left it blaring away while he went to have a shower, but I felt the next best thing, judging from the ferocious way Tim was banging around, was to pretend not to have woken up. After all, if you pretend a thing, it nearly is, as my grandmother always says. My grandmother was right as usual, it took a lot of self-control not to turn the radio down at first, but I must have really gone back to sleep, because the next time I woke up it was ten o'clock and someone was breaking the front door down.

Moses opened one eye resentfully as I struggled into my dressing gown. Can't you keep the noise down, he seemed to be saying. I staggered out of the bedroom. There was a little hole pierced in the front door, so you could look through and see who it was before opening it. I looked through it, but couldn't see anything, so I opened the door anyway.

It was Patrick in his school uniform.

'Patrick! What on earth are you doing here?'

'Hello, Fi. I wagged off school. Now that you've got your own place, I thought it'd be a shame to waste it.'

'But what are they going to say? They'll send a truant officer after you. Quick, get inside.'

I put on a pot of coffee, and made some instant to tide us over until it was ready. Patrick, of course, was properly appreciative of my hospitality.

'Jesus, Fi, what's this muck? Can't Cedric afford Moccona?'

'Don't call him that.'

'I'm starving, have you got anything to eat?' He already had his head in the refrigerator, so I didn't bother to reply. There was nothing in there that hadn't been in there yesterday, since Tim's grocery shopping had been confined to three cans of Snappy Tom, a box of whiskettes and the pizza. I sipped my disgusting coffee (Patrick was quite right, Tim had no idea of what to buy) and waited for the reason for his visit to become clear. Not that Patrick and I weren't close, but turning up this early in the day had to mean he wanted something.

Presently Patrick closed the refrigerator door, having let out all the cold air, and sat down opposite me, staring greedily at the coffee machine. Some time passed. Moses wandered into the kitchen and sniffed Patrick's ankles. Patrick leaned down and stroked him reflexively. I began to get bored.

'Okay, what's the trouble you're in?'

Patrick fixed me with a look of saintly innocence, so I knew it was really bad.

'Well, um. You know how I'm going to be in Year Ten next year?'

I did indeed. Even for one less mathematically gifted than I, the addition of nine and one was somewhat less than a total challenge. As Patrick, when he bothered to do any work at all, was extremely bright, there didn't seem to be any doubt about the addition taking place.

'Big deal, so what?'

'You may well say, so what.' Patrick took a huge swig of his coffee and spilt it down his front, which detracted somewhat from his air of brooding martyrdom.

The coffee machine was still burbling away,

but there looked to be enough for two cups in it. If you time it just right, you can sort of pinch the jug out and quickly pour your coffee, sort of between squirts, and the machine can't tell the difference if you're quick. Of course, if your timing's the slightest bit off, it goes all over the place, but I was lucky today.

Patrick drank some of his new cup of coffee and heaved a great sigh of pleasure, which I thought was laying it on a bit thick since he almost never drinks coffee, and in fact still has to have milk with his dinner when Father Simpson comes. He screwed his features into a facsimile of heroic bravery.

'Well, you might as well know the worst.'

'Well come on, what is it?' I didn't think it would be anything we couldn't handle, it never had been before. Most of Patrick's problems had to do with illicit cigarettes and pornographic magazines, and I had had considerable experience at dealing with various interesting situations. I felt sure this one wouldn't be beyond me, especially as I was now a Married Woman (i.e., an Earth Mother, full of wise spiritual power).

'Well. You know that Joe Morelli.'

Did I. I had at one time thought that Father Morelli was the most attractive man I'd ever seen, as a matter of fact I still did, but he had annoyed me so much over the course of the last two years, continually catching Patrick in unappealing situations and requiring me to spend untold effort getting him out of trouble, that his massive good looks had sort of lost their charm for me. Not, of course, that I'd have refused to speak to him on a desert island, but then. Ah well. I spared a sigh for lost opportunities and turned to the business in hand.

'What's he caught you at this time?'

'Nothing!' The look of outraged innocence was, so far as I could tell, genuine, but then they always were.

'Come on, confess. God, Patrick, it can't be any worse than that boys' camp last year,' (where Morelli had caught him showing stick books to the other boys).

'Well, you know how I've been doing Latin and Greek.'

'Sure.' Of course I knew. Why else had our father insisted on him going to St Bedivere's in the first place? I waited with interest, surely it wasn't going to be pornographic magazines in the classical languages this time?

Just then there was an almighty banging and crashing at the door. Patrick jumped out of his chair and looked furtive. As he well might, having wagged off school on the flimsiest pretext.

It was Gloria at the door, falling on my neck, screaming for coffee, and lighting a black cigarette, all at the same time. She did a massive double take when she saw Patrick.

'What the hell are you doing here, aren't you supposed to be at school?'

'I've run away from home.'

❧CHAPTER EIGHT☙

Thy children like the olive-branches:
round about thy table.

Psalm 128, 4

For the next few minutes there was general pandemonium, like the opening chorus in one of those Italian operas, with everybody screeching and waving their arms. Moses, upset by the general mayhem, forgot himself and sprayed on Gloria's handbag; fortunately she didn't notice. Well, of course she was bound to notice later, but that was another problem for another day, as my grandmother always says.

Eventually Gloria got her cup of coffee out of the machine and everyone subsided into a sort of heaving calm. I mopped up the coffee the machine had squirted out, and sat back at the table, where Patrick was now also smoking one of the black cigarettes. I'd

121

have to open some windows, I thought, and wished these crises wouldn't always happen when I was in my dressing gown. I decided the best approach to this one would be Calm Reason.

'Okay, Patrick, what have you actually done, so far, besides miss school?' I was really proud of my self-restraint, what I was actually dying to know was what he'd packed, he only had his usual school bag with him.

'God, Fiona, why do you always think I've done something?'

'Because you nearly always have. What is it this time?' I knew I was on safe ground. The minute he'd mentioned Father Morelli I'd smelled big trouble.

'Well. Um.' He actually looked nervous. Horrible cold chills raced up and down my spine.

'Well, you know, I thought Mum would be really upset if I ran away. So it's better if she doesn't know.'

I was speechless.

Gloria, who is never speechless, let out a piercing shriek.

'Holy mother of God, now why didn't I think of that when I was your age? If you don't tell her, she'll never know, will she? Jesus Christ on a skateboard.'

Patrick was affronted. Like Moses, he can't stand ridicule.

'Well, she won't know, will she, unless somebody tells her.' He took a huge drag of the black cigarette and turned faintly green.

I wondered if he'd gone stark staring mad. Best to humour mad people, I remembered from Psych One.

'What a good idea. However did you think of it?'

Gloria had majored in Journalism and had no truck with modern psychiatric principles, or with humouring anyone.

'Christ, Patrick. I thought Fiona was the fuckwit of the family. Don't you think she's going to notice after a while, when you don't come home?'

'Well, that's why I left the note.'

'Oh, you left a note! God save us. What did you say in it, at all?'

I thought that was going it a bit strong. You can't be all that Irish when your name's Jackson.

'I said it was all too much, and I'd decided to kill myself.'

Even Gloria was momentarily silenced.

***

After a long pause, during which Moses jumped onto my lap and settled down, purring loudly, I took a deep breath and asked the question that had to be asked.

'What were you planning to do about the body?'

'Body? What body?'

'Well, if you kill yourself, generally there's a body left behind, you know?'

'Jesus, you're thick, Fiona. I'm not really going to do it.'

'Yes, but who's going to believe you're dead, if there's no body? Stop it, Gloria, it's not funny.' I felt the day was somehow slipping out of my control. Gloria was doubled up, snorting. Moses, who believes everything is about him, and is right more often than he deserves to be, woke up and jumped off my lap in a huff, digging in all his claws on the way down. Presently we heard a furious scratching and banging from inside his new Booda Box, which seemed to be designed to magnify sound, like the Opera House. Patrick took another puff of the black cigarette, turned a really interesting colour and raced off to join him. I was left in the kitchen with my friend Gloria, from whom I knew I could depend on some penetrating and compassionate insight.

Presently Gloria straightened up, spluttering faintly, and took a deep breath.

'Look, honestly, Fiona, it's really not all that funny.' She looked faintly reproving, as if I'd been the one having hysterics. 'Your mother's going to be out of her mind when she reads that note, God only knows what he actually said in it, we've got to do something.'

'What?'

'Well, persuade him to go home or something.'

'How?'

Gloria thought for a moment.

'Well, there's only two ways to persuade anyone to do something. You'll have to either bribe him or threaten him.'

'What with?' I still felt stunned and totally incapable of dealing with anything at all. If I acted really helpless, perhaps Gloria would figure it all out for me.

'I don't know. Look, I've got to go, I'm having lunch with Mike. Let me know how it comes out, hey?'

She was gone before I could stop her.

I brooded for a few minutes on the unfairness of life in general, and my family in particular. Just when I was trying to get it all together and make a stunning impression as an immaculate housekeeper, all these crises had to keep happening. You'd think I could have had a few days to settle in after my honeymoon, I thought bitterly, remembering guiltily the great pile of wedding presents in the spare bedroom.

The ghastly heaving sounds had finally subsided. I poured myself another cup of coffee and waited. Presently I heard water running, and Patrick came back into the kitchen looking sheepish. I decided to give him a Piece of my Mind, it would relieve my feelings, and was in keeping with my new role as a Married Woman (guardian of public morals, etc).

'Serves you right, you're much too young to smoke those things. What on earth's the matter, anyway, you've been smoking for years.'

'Oh, come on, Fi, don't give me a hard time. I never really smoke much, I just sort of hold it and wave it around and take these little sips, never did the drawback before, yuk!'

Well, here went nothing (whatever that means). I

was about to Put my Foot Down. I sat up straight, squared my shoulders and took a deep breath. Then I let it out again.

I had no idea, absolutely not a clue, of what to say. I thought longingly that Tim would know exactly what to say. Perhaps I should just leave it all until he got home. But it seemed a bit disloyal, after all Patrick was my brother, and Tim was such a grownup. Also, the longer I waited before doing anything, the more likely our mother was to find the note, in which Patrick had written God Knew What. I had visions of her hanging around the City Morgue, wailing and beating her breast, and spraying disinfectant.

***

I left Patrick watching the educational programs on the ABC while I had my shower. At least he wouldn't miss any of his education while I got everything sorted out. Moses sat companionably in the basin, taking an occasional swipe at the shower curtain, which had cute little fish printed on it in murky shades of brown. It would definitely have to be one of the first things to go, I reminded myself. And the sheets, which were also brown. I don't know what it is about men, that they seem to have this obsession with having everything brown.

While I was debating with myself about whether

to have lavender sheets or white ones with broderie anglaise trim, and whether to have matching towels or go for an entirely different colour scheme in the bathroom (I rather fancied green and yellow, with lots of ferns) the telephone rang.

And rang.

And rang, on and on, it just about drove me crazy. Why didn't Patrick answer it, I wondered, finally giving up and getting out of the shower. It was true that we'd both been brought up not to answer the telephone in other people's houses. But did this count as someone else's house? I couldn't remember if it did or not.

Patrick was curled up on the sofa, right next to the telephone. Giving him a filthy look, which was totally wasted as he was immersed in one of Tim's computer magazines, I snatched it up just in time for it to stop ringing.

'For God's sake, Patrick. Couldn't you have answered the phone?'

'No. I'm a fugitive from justice, remember? That was probably the police, or the truant officer or something. Just remember, you haven't seen me since the wedding.'

He heaved a contented sigh and stretched out on

the sofa, leaving a black mark from his school shoes.

'Leisure, what bliss. Just about now I'd have been going in for Religious Studies.'

'Patrick. Look. We have to talk sensibly about what you're going to do. You can't just run away like this, what about your VCE? What about Uni?'

'Tough. I'll get a scholarship.'

He would too. It's hell when your little brother is smarter than you are. But not as cunning, I thought gleefully, as the one telling argument cascaded into my brain.

'Dad'll stop your allowance.'

***

There was a long silence.

Then there was another long silence.

Patrick shifted uncomfortably on the sofa, pulling himself upright and putting his feet on the floor. I knew I'd won.

But of course, there was a long, hard road to plough still, as one of those depressing people in Patrick White's books might have said.

'What are we going to do, Fi?'

***

Well, there were several options. Actually, leaving the country looked pretty good to me, except that we didn't have any money. Leaping into a Tardis and going off to have interstellar adventures was a close second. I imagined for a moment that I was Dr Who. What were these petty human matters to me when I had Daleks to slay? I dragged my mind back to the present and tried the obvious, but hopeless solution. They always are, aren't they?

'Look, why don't you just go home, confess everything, and say you're sorry and won't ever do it again?'

Patrick looked shifty, reminding me that I still didn't know the full extent of what there was to confess.

'Just what did you do at school, anyway?'

'Well, nothing, really. I mean, I didn't really do anything. Not as such.'

I was just about ready to scream when the phone rang again. I snatched it up, glaring at dear little Patrick.

'Yes? Hello?'

'I don't see any reason to bark like that, Fiona.

This is your father speaking.'

'Oh.'

'I don't wish to alarm you, Fiona, but is Patrick with you?'

'Um. Well. He did sort of pop in, sort of on his way to school.'

'Oh, good.' My father's voice dripped with heavy irony, the kind you could build chariots out of. 'Tell me, Fiona, has he sort of popped out yet?'

'Well. Not as such, actually, no.'

'Well then, perhaps I could have a word with him. As such.'

It's really hell, having parents. I handed the phone to Patrick, who assumed an air of breezy confidence.

'Oh, hi, Dad. Gee, is that the time? I should be at school, see ya, bye.'

He would have got away with it too, except that our father has developed his vocal cords from years of lecturing. The roar caught Patrick just as he was about to hang up the phone.

'Um. Yes, Dad. Right. I'll be right there.'

Ulp.

And with that he raced out of the door without even telling me what our father had said.

***

I thought about it quite a lot during the rest of the day, although I was frantically busy. It had been nearly lunchtime when Patrick had rushed out, and I hadn't even been dressed. I had managed to prise some housekeeping money out of Tim in between him droning on about Our Relationship (whatever that means) so I wanted to go shopping. He had given me $600, but without saying how long it was supposed to last, so I assumed it was for the week.

When I finally found the supermarket, I was amazed and delighted to find out how cheap everything was. Most things didn't cost more than a few dollars. I hadn't actually been grocery shopping before, not by myself, although I'd been with my mother a few times after Tim and I got engaged.

'It will be Good Practice for when you're married,' she kept saying. I couldn't really see the relevance at the time, but now I rather wished I'd paid more attention, because the supermarket was absolutely huge, and I had no idea of where to find anything, or even of what sort of anything I wanted to find.

After chewing it over for some time, I decided the best thing to do would be to go up and down all the aisles; the sight of everything would, presumably, prompt me to get what I needed. That was the way my mother always did it, although I seemed to remember that she generally had some kind of list, which she consulted at frequent intervals, frowning and shaking her head. I would start at one end of the store, and go up and down each aisle, finishing at the other end with the comfortable knowledge that I hadn't missed anything.

It worked, too. This is really quite easy, I thought, passing the washing stuff and putting in a box of Drive. I was getting all the brands we had at home, but after a while I noticed that some things had little red stickers indicating that they were on sale. Wouldn't it be a good idea to stock up on those things while they were on special, taking advantage of the low prices, rather than just waiting till things ran out and then having to pay full price? Yes, I decided, it would. We could save a fortune, some of the special prices were only about half the regular price. Tim would be so impressed with my careful budgeting, and with the money we saved we could buy the new sheets and towels, so they wouldn't really cost anything and Tim wouldn't have an excuse not to get them. I knew he was going to resist parting with all his chocolate brown linen, it was so horrible that he must be really attached to it to have it in the house. Probably one of his old girlfriends had helped him pick it out, or something. The sooner it went the better I'd be pleased.

I attacked the rest of the shopping with great zeal, and spent all the money Tim had given me. It was amazing what I was able to get for it.

❧CHAPTER NINE☙

Thy wife shall be as the fruitful vine: upon the walls of thine house.

Psalm 128, 3

'What the fuck is this?'

I could hardly understand the words, he was shouting so much it was all distorted. Once again I wondered why Tim had such funny moods. I'd expected him to be pleased with the huge bargain I'd got.

'Twenty-eight frozen chickens, for Christ's sake! What the fuck did you think you were going to do with them, hold a black sabbath?'

'But they were only –'

'I don't want to hear it! Whatever they were it

135

was totally fucking wasted.'

This stung me to the core. One thing I knew I had been was economical.

'Now you listen here, Tim. Those chickens were only $4.99 each, they were marked down from $10.54, so don't you dare tell me it was a waste. They'll keep forever, it's not like they were going to go off –'

'Where are they going to fucking keep, Fiona, in the fucking bathtub? Jesus Christ...'

Such language, and all because I'd bought a few chooks. Perhaps I ought to hang up the telephone. As he rabbited on I wondered again whether getting married had been such a good idea. Then I remembered what my boss used to be like, back when I was working, and stifled the thought. I just wasn't assertive enough, that was the trouble. People walked all over me just because I was nice. No doubt St Francis had had the same problem, and that's why he preferred animals.

Tim was still going on without pausing to draw breath. I put the phone down for a few seconds while I put the kettle on. When I picked it up he seemed a little calmer.

'...Fiona? Hello, are you there? Fiona?'

'There's a lot of background noise on this line, Tim,' I shouted, holding the phone at arm's length. 'I can hardly hear you. Why don't we talk when you get home?'

'Look. Fiona. Just look in the freezer and tell me how much room there is, okay? I'll hang on.'

He seemed to be breathing heavily.

'Are you feeling alright, Tim? You sound funny.'

He sort of grunted, which I took to mean that he was okay, so I put the phone down again and opened the freezer. It was quite empty, of course; that was why I'd been shopping in the first place. I reported back with a nice warm feeling of total vindication.

Tim wasn't as crushed as I'd expected, though. In fact, he was quite nasty, in a smug, superior kind of way.

'Okay, Fiona. Look, I want you to put the phone down again and go and put all the frozen chooks in the freezer. Go on, I'll hang on.'

'Okay.' I'd teach him to patronise me, the smug little creep. I opened the freezer compartment and started loading it with the chickens, neatly and methodically. I didn't hurry; let him wait.

Six chickens fitted nicely on the bottom shelf. Another six chickens fitted nicely on the top shelf. That was twelve.

On the other hand, there were still sixteen chickens to go.

I managed to fit four more in by wedging them in between the others. Sixteen down. Twelve still to go.

I sat down for a moment and imagined how nice life must have been before refrigerators were invented. I remembered my grandmother reminiscing about the iceman coming around in his horse-drawn wagon. Of course, in those days you had maids in little caps and aprons, so you wouldn't be having to paddle around with dead hens anyway.

I wondered what Mrs Beeton would have done; I had a depressing feeling that she wouldn't have been having this problem. I thought of ringing my mother, after all it was really her fault since she taught me how to shop, but Tim was still on the phone. Well, that was something I could deal with, at least.

'Hello, Tim?'

'Well?'

'They're all in, no problem.'

'Oh.' He sounded really deflated at not having anything else to scream at me about. He did grumble a bit about eating chicken solidly for the next six months, but I countered that easily by pointing out that there were so many different ways to cook chicken. It was true that I didn't actually know any of them, but, uneasily conscious of twelve frozen chooks making puddles on the counter, I felt that was another problem for another day.

Having got Tim off the phone, I reviewed the situation, sparing a moment to congratulate myself on remaining so calm. There were sixteen chickens in the freezer and twelve not in the freezer. The freezer looked full.

Of course, I reflected that it might just look full because there was a lot of stuff in it. Sometimes my handbag would seem to be quite full, but then I could usually manage to get a lot more into it. I thought I could certainly force in a few more chickens, and perhaps all of them, if I really put my mind to it.

There was a small gap in one corner that looked promising. I couldn't actually fit a chicken into it, but I thought that with some leverage I might be able to make it go in, especially as the chickens were no longer quite as hard as they had been. I had noticed a large screwdriver in the knife drawer the day before; really single men are quite disgusting.

It wasn't as easy as it looked. Pushing hard on the screwdriver, I slipped and made a great deep scratch in the side of the freezer, only just missing my hand. The gap still wasn't any bigger.

It was time for Plan B.

***

Plan B did work, sort of. By frantically rushing up and down stairs, I managed to place out ten of the twelve chickens with various neighbours. It was after five-thirty by the time I'd been to all the flats. I breathed a sigh of relief that Tim worked such long hours. There were still two chickens left, but I could roast them both and have cold chicken in the fridge, it always comes in handy when you're hungry in the middle of the night. I got them in the oven and did the table up all nicely with pink candles. Well, as nicely as I could. Tim didn't seem to own a tablecloth or any napkins. There was a set of cork placemats with views of various public buildings in New Zealand, but in the balance I thought it was better to manage without. First thing tomorrow I would go shopping for some linen.

***

Tim had managed to get into a better mood by the time he got home. He actually seemed quite impressed by the table and the smells coming from the oven.

Dinner was really quite successful, when you consider that I'd never cooked a chicken before. They looked great when I took them out of the oven, well the wings were a bit black, but pretty good really, and by planning it all out on paper I'd managed to get the peas and potatoes all finished at the same time, which I always think is the hardest part of a roast, with everything taking different times to cook. Tim did a great performance sharpening the carving knife and attacked the chook. I watched him in the candlelight, thinking once again how incredibly handsome he was. Moses took up his usual position under the table, swiping at my ankles. For once everything seemed to be going well.

So well, in fact, that Tim carved second helpings.

'Jesus Christ! What the fuck is this?'

'What?'

'This!' On the end of the carving fork Tim was brandishing what looked like a small, steamed-up plastic bag full of something. It had come out of the inside of the chicken.

'Jesus, Fiona, you didn't even take the fucking giblets out!'

I thought that was a bit hard.

'Well, how was I supposed to know they were in there? What are they, anyway?'

'Giblets, for chrissake. Don't you know what giblets are?'

'Well, of course. Um, what are they exactly?'

'Its fucking insides, Fiona. Jesus!'

Oh.

Tim stormed off and threw himself down in front of his computer. Moses enjoyed the giblets very much, and looked quite pleased when I told him I had another twenty-seven packets of them.

***

I managed to sleep through the alarm, and all Tim's crashing around, the next morning. It was a bit after nine when I woke up, and the sun was streaming into the room. Moses was curled up under the doona with me. Life, I thought, could hardly get much better.

Except for the brown sheets, of course. I remembered that today was the day I'd planned to buy new linen.

I rang Tim at his office. The receptionist sounded very off, as though she was having what at Marsh and Spacknall used to be called an Attitude Problem.

Thank God I'm out of all that, I thought smugly.

'Fiona. What's the problem?' Tim sounded very tense.

'Oh, no problem, but I need some money. I've got to buy a tablecloth, and some sheets and things.'

'WHAT? I gave you $600 yesterday, what did you do with that?'

'Well, that was for the groceries, I spent that.'

'You spent $600 at the supermarket? Jesus, I don't believe this.'

I couldn't see what was so hard to believe about it. After all, if he didn't expect me to spend $600, why did he give it to me? I tried to point this out calmly and reasonably.

Perhaps that was a mistake. It seemed to upset Tim, anyway. Then we came to the other question.

'Why the fuck d'you want to buy sheets, anyway?'

'Look, Tim, those brown sheets are just too disgusting, we've got to have some decent ones. And there isn't a single tablecloth in the place, or any napkins, you must have noticed that when we were having dinner last night.'

'Well, why don't you open the fucking wedding presents then, you lazy bitch? Christ, don't you ever think about anything but spending money?'

'I haven't had time to open them. I'll do it after I get our house properly equipped. And I wish you wouldn't say fuck all the time.'

I couldn't believe his attitude. Night and day I'd been devoting my entire energies to his comfort and well-being, and all he could do was shout at me.

'God, Fiona, how can you be so fucking dumb? What the fuck d'you think's in the goddam wedding presents, the fucking Holy Grail?'

'I don't know what's in them, how can I, I haven't opened them. One of them was a copy of Mrs Beeton. Why don't you open them, they're your presents too.'

Tim really exploded then. In between the furious shouting and expletives, I gathered that he wasn't going to give me any money for new linen, and that he thought the wedding presents might contain sheets, towels and tablecloths. I also gathered that the $600 he'd given me for the housekeeping was supposed to last a month.

I managed to get off the phone without shouting back at him, although it was difficult. Then I had a good cry, which made me feel a lot better, it always does. Really the thought of all those gorgeously wrapped presents was quite exciting, now that I came to think of it, although I knew I'd have to write the thank-you letters. What a pity I didn't have Grace Kingsley here, I thought, for once she could have been useful.

I had had a big lecture from my mother before getting married about how to open wedding presents. Apparently you have to open them one at a time and write down what everything is and who it's from, so that later on when you write the letters you thank everybody for the right things. I thought I could go one better by writing the letters as I went; this, however, meant that I would need my fountain pen which, I remembered guiltily, was still at home with all my other stuff. I decided that I would make an heroic effort today, and go round and pack everything up. Then I could do the letters, unwrap the presents, etcetera, on the following day.

It took me pretty well the whole day to get everything packed up, I had to keep stopping to look for eye drops and fix my mascara. My old room looked so empty without Moses. Leaving behind the innocence of girlhood, I reflected miserably, looking at my old armchair where we'd spent so many hours curled up together. It was all ripped down the side where Moses always used to sharpen his claws. I wondered if Tim would let me bring it too, thinking about the square white furniture in his flat I thought probably not. On the other hand, once I had finished redecorating the flat in French Provincial, we wouldn't have the white sofa, or the nasty glass coffee table, either. I thought about the argument we were going to have when I explained about decorating styles. Perhaps it would be better not to say anything. I could redecorate a little bit at a time, and he probably wouldn't even notice.

I got all my things packed up eventually. How lucky that I'd never gone in for hoarding things, I thought smugly. There really wasn't much. All my clothes went into two big cardboard boxes. Another two full of books, and one with all the miscellaneous things, and that was it. How sad, I thought. A whole life, fitting into five cardboard boxes. Then I had to unpack the miscellaneous box again to get at the eye drops. I didn't really mind; the closer I came to finally leaving, the more depressed I got. I felt as though my last hold on real life was slipping through my fingers.

My mother cried buckets too, which didn't help. We kept setting each other off, like a pair of those drinking birds you see in the chemists' windows. Finally I called a cab and got moving, I knew once I got home to Moses I'd feel better. There, for the first time I'd thought of Tim's flat as home. I supposed it must be the effect of having removed Arnold, my beautiful old teddy bear, from my bed.

The taxi driver didn't speak any English, which in a way was a relief, as it took my mind off my troubles having to give him directions to Tim's flat by shouting and gesturing. He carried all my boxes up for me, so I gave him a big tip with the last of the housekeeping money. I was now totally broke again, I reflected gloomily. Tim had been so cross about the chickens that I really didn't want to ask him for any more money just yet. Perhaps I could pinch a few dollars out of his wallet while he was in the shower.

I put on a pot of coffee and watched Moses disapprovingly investigating my boxes in the middle of the sitting-room floor. Surely I couldn't be expected both to pack and unpack on the same day. I decided to have a nice long bath and do my nails instead. Tomorrow would be soon enough for everything.

***

I must have been really tired from all my hard work, because when I woke up it was nearly seven-thirty. Tim wasn't home yet, but he would be any minute. Thank God we had the cold chicken from last night, all I had to do was make a salad, which I knew how to do. I shoved all the cardboard boxes from home behind the sofa and poured myself a cup of coffee, thinking that I still hadn't had that bath. Perhaps I'd have it after dinner, while Tim mucked about with his home computer. Opening the fridge to get out the salad stuff, I noticed the little light didn't go on. I'd have to get Tim to pick up a new bulb for it in the City.

***

Tim didn't get home until nearly eleven. He was full of apologies, apparently they'd had some sort of enormous crisis at the office that was too technical to explain, and hadn't had a moment to ring me. I pointed out that, as I had made cold chicken and salad for dinner, it was still quite okay, but he wasn't hungry. Funny, I would have thought he'd be ravenous after working all night and missing dinner. I decided not to worry him about the light in the fridge.

***

'Bloody, fucking hell!'

I could hear Tim roaring from the bedroom, presumably all the neighbours could also hear it. Dislodging Moses, I grabbed my dressing gown and rushed out to the kitchen.

Tim was standing in a big pool of water, looking furious. He had absolutely no clothes on. I wished he wouldn't wander round with nothing on, since we didn't have any curtains.

'The fucking fridge isn't working, goddam it. It's leaked everywhere. What the hell have you fucked up now?'

I thought that was a bit hard. Why would it be my fault? It was his fridge.

'Maybe the power went off.' I tried the light. 'It's on again now, anyway.'

'Fuck.' Tim banged off to have his shower, shaking his head and muttering. I raced after him to get some towels to mop up the water. Actually I was quite pleased, now I wouldn't have the trouble of defrosting the fridge with all those chickens.

***

With a warm glow of achievement, I sealed the sixteenth thank-you letter. So far we had acquired three toasters, a set of dark green towels, a beautiful set of flowered coffee cups, an Italian espresso coffee thing, some green and white striped sheets, some pink floral sheets, a real down doona, a handmade patchwork quilt (from my grandmother), a copy of *The Joy of Sex* (from Patrick), a dozen silver coffee spoons, a crystal vase, a lace tablecloth, three wooden salad bowls, and an enormous dildo plated in gold, which I was sure was fake (from Peter). Dear Peter, I had written. Thank you so much for the lovely dildo. It is very decorative. We will think of you every time we use it. With love from Fiona and Tim.

I decided to leave the rest of the presents for another day, my system couldn't stand another shock like the last one. I had found some decent linen anyway, which was the main thing. I threw all Tim's brown sheets out in the rubbish, but thought I had better keep the towels; housekeeping seemed to require so much mopping up of water.

I made our bed with the green and white sheets and Gran's quilt. It looked sensational, especially after I'd unpacked Arnold and propped him up against the pillows; he was the perfect finishing touch. I put the lace tablecloth on the kitchen table. It looked great too, I wondered if further unwrapping might reveal some curtains among the presents. I put everything else neatly away in the appropriate places. I wasn't sure what to do with the dildo, so I put it on the mantelpiece.

Having unpacked Arnold reminded me about the cardboard boxes lurking behind the sofa. Perhaps I ought to do something about them, the weekend was coming up and I didn't want Tim discovering how slack I'd been.

There wasn't much room left in the bedroom closet, but then most of the clothes I'd packed from home were stuff I used to wear to work, so I hung them in the spare room wardrobe, which was empty. All the miscellaneous stuff found suitable niches, although I had to empty some of Tim's stuff out of one of the dressing-table drawers; I knew he wouldn't mind, though.

When I came to the last two boxes, I realised I'd hit a snag. Tim's flat had absolutely no bookcases.

***

I switched off the vacuum cleaner and straightened up with a sigh. My back was killing me. I had been at it all morning, scrubbing the bathroom and cleaning everything. This attack of hard labour was occasioned by the fact that Tim had commented unfavourably on the state of the place the previous evening. I was determined that he wouldn't be able to find fault with anything tonight.

There was only the kitchen left to do. I'd get dinner started before I tackled it; since it was Friday I was planning to make a tuna casserole, for which I had obtained the recipe from my mother. I still hadn't managed to prise any more housekeeping out of Tim, so I had no money to buy fresh fish. It was still early, but I would make the casserole now, and then heat it up that evening. I really felt I was getting into the swing of things.

Getting the vegetables out of the fridge reminded me that I still hadn't told Tim about the little light not working. I must remember to mention it, it was really quite hard to find things at the back.

I made the casserole and got it in the oven. That left only cleaning the kitchen. Fortunately I didn't have to worry about cleaning the oven, as it was in use. I was tired anyway, so I just did the bits that showed. After all, it wasn't as if anybody was going to inspect under things. Then I ran myself a nice hot bath. Dismally inspecting the state of my hands after all that scrubbing, I wished I'd thought to buy a pair of rubber gloves while I was at the supermarket.

***

By the time Tim was due home everything was in place. I had even lit some scented candles. He could hardly fail to be impressed with my stunning housekeeping. I turned the oven back on to heat up the casserole. It smelled wonderful.

I was just putting the finishing touches to the table when the phone rang.

'Hello?'

'Oh, Fiona.' Tim sounded vaguely disappointed, as if he'd been expecting someone else. 'Look, a few things have come up at work, I'm going to stay and finish it tonight, rather than come back in tomorrow, okay?'

I couldn't think of anything to say. I'd just spent most of a whole day scrubbing and polishing, and cooking a delicious and nutritious casserole, and now he wasn't even coming home. I felt like kicking him. I took a deep breath and counted to six. I've never been patient enough for ten.

'What time do you think you might be home, then?' Perhaps it wouldn't be too late; I could wait dinner and we could still eat together.

'Oh, God, I don't know. What is this, the fucking Spanish Inquisition?'

'Well, I was just thinking about dinner, you know, whether you'll be home in time –'

'Look, just go ahead and have dinner without me, okay? I'll probably be really late, there's no point waiting.'

'What's all that noise in the background? It sounds like a party.'

'Noise? I can't hear anything, it must be a crossed line. Listen, I have to go, I'll try not to wake you when I come in.'

Well, that was that, I thought miserably. All my

work was wasted. Moses and I would have dinner by ourselves and go to bed early. I remembered earlier, pre-wedding Friday nights, with beer and dancing and silly jokes. I wondered sadly if being married was always going to be like this.

Wait on, though. I knew Peter and Sean would be at the Dead Rat, they always were on Friday nights. Why didn't I just pop down there and join them? I could even ring Gloria and see if she wanted to come too. Tim could hardly complain if I went out with my friends, if he was going to spend the whole evening at the office. I could leave him a note, in case he came home early, and there was the casserole in the oven.

But I didn't have any money. I remembered my plan to extract some out of Tim's wallet while he was in the shower, and wished I'd had the sense to carry it out. Perhaps there was some forgotten cash in one of my other handbags, I often found little windfalls that way.

There wasn't any little windfall this time, though, although I did find several fancy lace-trimmed handkerchiefs that I thought I'd lost. I chucked them in the washing basket and sat down despondently.

There was absolutely nothing on television that I wanted to watch. I was really going to have to have a little talk with Tim about money. And bookshelves too, I remembered, thinking guiltily about the two cardboard boxes still hidden behind the sofa. It was, after all, a husband's duty to provide for his wife, as Tim had pompously pointed out on several occasions, and I was sure that included bookshelves. Well, if it didn't it ought to, I thought crossly, and going to the pub, too. Come to think of it, there was a possibility of finding a little windfall in one of Tim's suits. I'd start looking right away, I thought, feeling instantly more cheerful, and if he didn't like having his privacy invaded it would just serve him right for being so mean. He'd probably never find out anyway.

Tim had a lot of clothes, for a man. He was really extremely vain, and spent hours in the bathroom each day. I often wondered what he was up to in there, with no water running or anything, and had concluded that he was probably admiring himself in the glass.

Methodically I started going through the pockets of his suits, starting at the right hand end. If he arrived home suddenly I'd quickly shut the wardrobe door.

The first three suits yielded nothing except a lot of biros. I was starting to wonder if it wasn't a waste of time looking in the others, when I slid my hand into a coat pocket and encountered something that felt really strange.

After the first excited thrill of discovery I knew it wasn't money. It was too bulky, and sort of scratchy. Cautiously I removed it from Tim's pocket and spread it out on our bed.

It was a black lace garter belt.

❧CHAPTER TEN☙

...and, forsaking all other, keep thee only
unto her, so long as ye both shall live?
Book of Common Prayer

I suppose I must have sat there staring at it for nearly half an hour. Somehow I couldn't get my mind around it. It was like looking at some alien hieroglyph, that you know is just bursting with important meaning, but you don't know the language.

Finally I got my legs to work. I went into the kitchen and turned off the oven. Moses was crying for his dinner, so I mechanically dished up some of the tuna casserole for him. I was flying on automatic pilot, as Patrick would have said. I wished I had him to talk to. Perhaps I ought to ring him up. After all, he was hardly innocent, I didn't have to worry about corrupting him. But it was nearly eight o'clock, and I knew if I rang our house and invited him over suddenly, so late, I would have all sorts of questions to answer from our mother.

What I really needed, I decided as my knees started to shake, was a good stiff drink. That would get me functional again. There was no gin or vodka in the place, but I had got a dozen bottles of Pinot Grigio when I did the grocery shopping. I had also bought a bottle of sherry, I remembered gratefully. I found the bottle and poured myself a stiff shot, in an ordinary wine glass. Tim didn't have any sherry glasses. Perhaps there would be some in the wedding presents. I started to giggle and found I couldn't stop. I must be hysterical, I realised fuzzily. You were supposed to slap people in the face if they became hysterical, I knew. I could hardly slap myself in the face, though, could I?

The next minute the problem was solved for me, as I raced for the loo and threw up endlessly. By the time I'd finished losing everything except my toenails, I was calmer.

I made myself a cup of tea, with no milk, and brushed my teeth. I turned the heater on to full and crouched in front of it. Moses was delighted, we hadn't been putting the heater on at all because it was really quite warm for July, but I felt chilled to the bone. Perhaps I was getting 'flu. A bright thought occurred to me. Perhaps I was really sick and had hallucinated the whole thing. I went into our bedroom. The closet door gaped sinisterly open and the garter belt stared balefully back at me from Gran's patchwork quilt.

Back in front of the heater, with Moses clutched on my lap, I tried to consider the situation calmly. I was able to stay calm, but the considering part of it seemed to be eluding me rather. My brain had gone like a blank sheet of paper. Presently I took a sip of my tea and found it had gone stone cold; it was after eight o'clock. I had lost nearly an hour. My legs had gone to sleep from not moving, as also had Moses, who grumbled frightfully when I shifted him onto the sofa.

I hobbled about the sitting room, getting the circulation going. Actually, now that I was up and moving I felt marginally better, as if I were doing something about my problem.

By some extraordinary piece of luck, Gloria was at home. I explained the problem, and my need for advice, clearly and concisely.

'Gloria, thank God you're there, Oh God, I don't know what to do...'

'Fiona? Is that you? What's the matter?'

'Well, of course it's me, how could I be talking to you if it wasn't?'

'What? What are you talking about, for Christ's sake?'

'Look, there's a garter belt in my closet!' I could feel myself edging towards hysteria again. 'Gloria, a garter belt, don't you understand?'

'God, Fiona. I think you must've overdone it on the honeymoon. I've heard of people bonking their brains out, I didn't realise it actually happened.'

We weren't getting anywhere. Gloria can really be quite stupid sometimes.

'Look, can you come over here? Please? I really have to talk to you.'

'How about tomorrow? I really have to finish this piece.'

'You're working? On Friday night?'

'Yeah, well I haven't got a rich husband like you.'

Hearing her refer to Tim that way just about finished me off, and I was unable to say anything else for several minutes. By the time I was at the hanky-searching stage, I noticed Gloria was shouting down the telephone.

'...always fucking crying. Jesus! Just tell me what's happened, for Christ's sake. Holy Saints and Martyrs! Fiona! Are you there? Christ! I'll be right there, don't do anything till I get there, alright? Ten minutes, fifteen max. Jesus!'

***

Gloria arrived inside a quarter of an hour, wearing a striped caftan and boots. This didn't startle me, as I was used to her weird outfits. She strode into the flat, yards of ethnic material flapping.

'Alright, where is it?'

'What?'

'The holy garter belt of Antioch, or whatever. Come on, let's see it.'

I started crying again at her callous attitude.

'Oh, Jesus, Fiona, don't be so wet. Stop snivelling and tell me what the problem is, will you? I nearly killed myself getting here. Look, just sit down and start at the beginning, okay?'

Gloria shoved me and I fell backwards onto the sofa. Obviously I wasn't going to be allowed to get away with any more crying, so I took a deep breath and started at the beginning.

'Tim's having an affair.'

'WHAT! Jesus, Mary and Joseph, have you gone insane? You've only been married a couple of weeks!'

'He is, I know he is. Look, come and see this, look, I'll show you.'

I led the way to our bedroom. Moses pranced along behind Gloria, batting gaily at the tassels on the hem of her caftan.

The garter belt lay where I had left it, the embodiment of sin. I wondered if it would leave a mark on Gran's patchwork quilt, sort of a scorch mark or something.

'There, you see?'

'Well what, Fiona? Did you drag me over here just to look at your sleazy underwear?'

'It's not mine.'

There was a short silence, followed by a longer silence.

'Holy suffering saints!' Gloria edged reverently towards the bed. 'Where on earth did you find it at all?'

'In one of his coat pockets.'

'Oh. But you've only been married a few weeks, couldn't it have been from before, you know, his bucks' night or something?'

'He wore that suit on Wednesday. That was the night he had a crisis at work. He didn't get home till eleven o'clock.'

'Oh, fuck. Oh Fiona. Shit.'

'Well don't just stand there saying fuck. What am I going to do? He could be home any minute. What am I going to do, Gloria? I mean, should I confront him with it, or what?'

'Jesus.'

Gloria seemed to have become hypnotised by the garter belt. She had advanced right to the very foot of the bed, and was leaning over it, peering intently.

'Look at this. It's from Target. And a size sixteen, the fat slut. Holy Infant Jesus.'

Appearing suddenly to reach a decision, she snatched it up and scrumpled it into a little ball.

'Which suit? Which pocket? The right?'

'Um, I think so. It was the one on the outside.'

'Okay.' Gloria stuffed the garter belt back into my husband's pocket and slammed the closet door. 'Right, now I need a stiff drink, where's the booze?'

***

In the kitchen we formulated a plan of attack. That is, Gloria formulated and I poured.

'Look, the thing is to not let him know that you know.'

'Why?'

'Well, misdirection of your enemy, you know? It can't do any harm, can it? You can always change your mind whenever you like, and pretend you just found out.'

'Not if he gets rid of the evidence. Then I wouldn't have anything to discover.'

'Oh. Well, you could take it out and hide it somewhere.'

'But if he knows it's there, he'll know I took it, won't he?'

'Oh. Yeah. Oh, hey, brilliant, I've got it!'

'What?'

'We'll hide the whole suit!'

I thought about this for a minute.

'He'd notice it was gone.'

'Would he? He's got at least a dozen suits in that closet. What's the bet he just grabs one at random? He probably wouldn't notice it was gone for months, and if he does, you could always look innocent and say you took it to the dry cleaners. If he doesn't notice it's gone, and I'll bet anything he won't, you can haul it out any time you like, shove it back in his closet and find the garter belt in it. It can't fail.'

I thought some more. If I did say that, yes, I could still produce the garter belt and say the cleaners had found it. If I wanted to. It would be my choice. Just the thought of having an actual choice of what to do made me feel quite a lot better. It's always better to be the perpetrator than the victim, as my grandmother says. Contemplating doing something evil, I felt instantly stronger and more in control.

'Where could we hide it?'

'It's got to be somewhere he won't look. Somewhere he never goes.'

I tried to think of somewhere, in Tim's own home, where he'd been living for years, that he never went. I couldn't.

'What about under the mattress? That's where

Patrick hides all his stuff.'

'No good, it'd get creased, and then it won't look natural when you stick it back in the closet.'

'Well, maybe I don't want to stick it back. Maybe I should just get some scissors and cut all his clothes into tiny pieces.' The idea seemed pretty attractive, actually. I got up to pour us some more wine and noticed that Moses had bitten several tassels off the bottom of Gloria's caftan, but it didn't seem like the right moment to say anything. I kicked them under the table and sat down again. I was feeling a little dizzy, having just belted down the better part of a bottle of wine on an empty stomach.

Gloria looked at me critically.

'Shit, Fiona, you look terrible. You're as white as a ghost, have you eaten anything?'

'How could I eat at a time like this? Honestly, Gloria.'

'Yeah, well if you're going to all this trouble to hide the suit and everything, you might as well do things properly. You should be looking totally fantastic when he gets home, as if you didn't have a care in the world. Go and wash your face and put on some makeup, and I'll set the table. What were you making for dinner? It smells alright.'

At this reminder of domestic bliss I burst into tears again. Gloria, of course, was kind and sympathetic.

'Jesus Fiona, will you stop it! Get into the bathroom and fix yourself up. And get that suit packed up, I'll take it to my place.'

'You're not leaving?'

'Go!' She made shooing motions, and I went.

***

I actually did feel better with my face fixed. I sprayed on some Joy for good measure and sniffled back to the kitchen, where I could smell Gloria reheating, yet again, the tuna casserole I had made. I wondered how many times it was safe to heat something like that up, and whether we'd all be dead of botulism by morning.

Gloria had lit the scented candles on the table again, and straightened out the tablecloth and everything, which I had shoved out of the way when we sat down to open the wine. The candlelight softened the room and I had to admit the casserole smelled good. Moses certainly thought so, he was winding around Gloria's ankles, yelling. About half the tassels were left on her caftan. I handed her the suit on its hanger.

'Here you go. I hope you're right about this.'

'Right? Of course I'm right, I'm always right.'

We sat down to dinner and a session of Tim-bashing. I felt definitely better after I'd eaten something.

'Listen, Gloria?'

'What?'

'Do you think I should look for a job or something? Just in case?'

'In case? Oh, come on, you're only just married, you don't think he'd leave you, do you? Naaah. What would he marry you for at all? It's probably some old tart came on really strong and he just...'

'Just what?'

'Well, you know. Look, she might have been just taking off her underwear and stuff, you know, like in a sort of drunken thingy, and he just shoved it in his pocket to, like, get rid of it while somebody was stuffing her in a cab or something. You know?'

'Sure. That's why he's out tonight, I suppose. Visiting the poor old dear in the alcohol rehab centre.' I knocked back the rest of my drink. 'God, yes. He's probably moonlighting with the Salvation

Army. Why didn't I think of that? He didn't tell me about it because he prefers to do his good deeds in secret.'

Gloria giggled. 'What a prince! Oh, hey, that reminds me, Fiona, I've got a bone to pick with you.'

'What?'

'Fixing me up with your bloody uncle, you bitch. You must have known what he's like.'

'Don't tell me you went out with him? Yuk, Gloria, how could you?'

'God, it was awful.' She shuddered and took a massive swig of her drink. 'All through dinner he raved on about his boring bloody reality show, and he expected me to know all about it, Jesus, only a moron would watch that shit. Then we went back to his place and watched about eighteen hours of tapes of it. Christ! When you think about the fact they cut about ninety percent of it out and only use the best bits in the show, and he kept pausing it to explain things and say how clever he'd been. God, I couldn't think of anything to say. I thought once I could get him into bed it would be better –'

'Oh, YUK! You didn't!'

'Well, I did, but I might as well not have bothered. Gross! I mean, he looked so gorgeous, but with his clothes off he was so white and flabby, floundering about with his great beer gut flobbing everywhere. Honestly, Fiona, I'll kill you.'

'Me! It's hardly my fault. Oh yuk, how could you do it with Uncle Mike? I feel sick.'

'Well, don't worry, I didn't, he couldn't get it up.'

***

By the time we'd had a few more drinks I felt much better. It's funny how drinking always seems to cheer me up. Things never seem so serious after a few stiffies, and I was pretty well getting to think of the whole thing as some kind of bizarre practical joke, when I heard Tim's key in the lock.

'Shit! There he is!'

'Holy Jesus, the suit!'

'Quick, get it in your bag. Quick!'

'It won't fit. Christ!'

'And how is my lovely wife?'

Yuk. Tim had the worst of his cute little-boy smirks on his face. I hate that look. Americans call it 'shit-eating', and I can really see why. I threw myself on his neck so he wouldn't see the look of fury on my face, and also to check out whether I could smell perfume.

I couldn't smell anything but garlic, though. This put me in a real dilemma. Should I mention it or not? Just act natural, I thought frantically, taking my cue from Gloria, who had stuffed the suit up her caftan at the last possible second, and was sitting at the table looking incredibly relaxed and natural.

'Yuk! What on earth have you been eating?'

'Oh, a bunch of us stopped off for pizza after work.' Tim looked carefree and innocent. I looked at my watch. It was after midnight. Would it look natural to quarrel with my husband in front of Gloria or not? I decided it would, and anyway I wanted to.

'You could have called, Tim, it's way past twelve. I was worried.'

'Yeah, it looks like it.' Tim looked meaningfully at the table with its detritus of melted candles, empty cigarette packets, full ashtrays, half-dead wine cask, etcetera.

'For God's sake, Tim. If you had time to go out for pizza, you could have made one phone call, don't you think?'

'Look, I'm sorry, but it was nearly eleven by that time, I thought you'd be in bed and I didn't want to wake you up.'

Sure, I thought sourly. He never minds waking me up in the middle of the night when he wants to have sex.

'Well,' said Gloria brightly. 'I really must be going, now that Tim's home safe. You see, Fiona, I told you there was no need to ring the hospitals.'

I thought she was overdoing it a bit, but Tim didn't seem to notice anything. She was walking all sort of hunched over and clutching her stomach, so the suit wouldn't slip out, so I thought I might as well heap some more coals on Tim's head.

'Poor Gloria, the cramps are really bad, aren't they? I'm so sorry I dragged you out for nothing.' Damn right I am, I thought furiously. He should have been run over by a tram and buried in unconsecrated ground.

We managed to get Gloria out the door without the suit falling out or the coat hanger poking through her dress or anything. I went back into the kitchen and started tiredly picking up the tassels. There seemed to be an awful lot of them. I put them in the bottom drawer in case I ever got the nerve to give them back.

***

My husband and I got ready for bed in almost total silence. I was sulking, and Tim seemed to be a bit ashamed. He might well be, too, I thought furiously, trying to get a good look at him without seeming to. Was that a love bite on his neck? I couldn't see properly by the forty watt bulb which was all we had in the bedroom.

I just couldn't believe it when he wanted to have sex. I really couldn't believe it. Straight from the arms of his disgusting size sixteen mistress, and he wanted to make love to his virtuous and beautiful wife. I knew it wasn't the right thing to do, but my natural feelings got the better of me, and I just couldn't help myself.

I said I had a headache.

CHAPTER ELEVEN

*Wilt thou love her, comfort her, honour
and keep her in sickness and in health...*
Book of Common Prayer

I thought I would be able to relax over the weekend
– God knew I had had enough to put up with
during the last week to age a rock, as my
grandmother says. And, after all, everything that
could go wrong, and a few things that couldn't,
already had, so I looked forward with confidence to a
few days of untroubled calm. Of course, there was
still Tim's affair to cope with, but as he would hardly
be seeing her over the weekend, I felt I had a few
days' grace before I really had to do anything.

Tim liked to sleep in very late on Saturdays and
Sundays, so I was very very careful not to wake him
up. Part of the war plan Gloria and I had worked out
the previous night was to be a really perfect wife, so

as to heap coals of guilt on his head. I thought I was already doing pretty well in that area, but it wouldn't hurt to be extra careful. I tiptoed out to the kitchen and started a pot of coffee.

I sat at the kitchen table while I waited for the coffee to finish dripping through – no sense in disturbing Tim any more than necessary by constantly jumping in and out of bed, I thought, pleased with my good sense. It also took care of the possibility that he might want to have sex first thing when he woke up. Once again I wondered if other men were like that, or if Tim was some kind of pervert. I wished I had enough nerve to ask my mother, but I didn't. I couldn't ask Gloria, because then I'd have to admit that I'd never actually Done It with anyone else. I couldn't very well ask Patrick.

The coffee was well under way, so I sneaked myself out the first cup while it finished going through. Once again it was Fiona 1, coffee machine nil, as I suavely whipped the pot out, poured a mugful and slid it back in just in time for the next jet to come spurting out. The machine didn't notice a thing, sometimes it gets angry and spits a mouthful of boiling coffee at you when you try to steal a cup before it's finished.

I settled down to use the time in constructive thought. I thought about getting pregnant and having a sweet little baby and Laura Ashley smocks. Then I wondered if there was any other way to get pregnant than by having sex. Then, for a horrible few minutes, I worried in case Tim got The Woman pregnant. Then I realised it would be her problem, and stopped worrying. I worried briefly in case I was barren, but then I remembered that I knew a cure for that. I'd learnt it in primary school, you had to write the Lord's Prayer on a piece of paper, then soak it in water until all the writing dissolved off, and drink the water. One of the kids' mothers had got pregnant that way. Of course it only worked if you were a good Christian, but I thought I was pretty safe there. Surely all the times I'd been to church counted for something.

The coffee machine had finished belching and hissing. I poured two mugs full, added milk to Tim's and took them into the bedroom.

Tim was awake, sitting up reading one of his computer magazines. He seemed to be in quite a good mood after his night of debauchery. I smiled sweetly as I gave him his coffee. He really was amazingly good looking. He took a sip of his coffee and spat it out.

'Jesus Fucking Christ, what the hell is this?'

I couldn't imagine what was the matter. Hastily checking the quilt, I breathed a sigh of relief that he'd still had the mug up to his mouth and it hadn't got all over Gran's beautiful patchwork.

'What on earth's the matter?'

Tim was glaring into his coffee mug and scowling horribly.

'The fucking milk's off.'

'It can't be, I only bought it on Tuesday.'

'Christ. I bet you didn't check the fucking use-by date. Christ, Fiona, you're so fucking dumb.'

I was speechless, it was like watching Dr Jekyll turn into Mr Hyde. Tim thumped the coffee mug down on the bedside table and leapt out of bed, storming into the bathroom and slamming the door viciously.

I went carefully round the bed and examined Tim's coffee. Sure enough, there were little white flecks in it, the milk was definitely curdled. I went back out to the kitchen and looked at the milk in its carton; the Use-by date was the 22nd of July, six days away. The carton didn't seem to be very cold, though. In fact it wasn't cold at all. I opened the fridge. The little light still didn't go on, but I had got used to that. I reached in and felt a few things. Everything was at room temperature.

There seemed to be only one conclusion I could draw from that. I knew the electricity was on because of the coffee machine. Therefore the fridge had to be broken. Congratulating myself on having my coffee black, I went back to bed.

***

Tim seemed to have got a grip on himself when he came out of the bathroom half an hour later. He always took ages in there, I often wondered what he was doing. Perhaps one day I'd look through the keyhole and find out; now that he was having an affair I no longer felt under any obligation to respect his privacy.

Anyway, he seemed to be in quite a good mood, despite his earlier outburst, and received with equanimity the news that the refrigerator repair person refused to make an appointment, and we would therefore have to stay home and wait for him. He plugged himself into his computer, where he claimed to be designing a clock, and for all practical purposes ceased to exist.

Moses and I had a nice quiet morning. We watched some cartoons on the television, which Moses loved, and then I had a bath and did my nails while Moses rested from his exertions. After several hours the refrigerator man arrived with his box of tools. I thought it would be sufficient to show him the kitchen and leave him to it, but Tim emerged from his computer and greeted the man with cries of rapture and extreme chumminess. Perhaps they were old friends? If so, the refrigerator man didn't seem to share Tim's enthusiasm. He grunted and opened his tool box while Tim danced around yapping like a terrier.

Presently he opened the freezer.

'Holy Moses! Well, that's one problem. Yez can't fill a freezer up like this and expect it to work prop'ly. The air's got to circulate, like. Look, we'll have to take all this stuff out before I can get a look at 'er.'

I don't know who was more upset by the ensuing process, me or Tim. One the one hand, Tim was extremely squeamish, and handling the now soggy chickens seemed genuinely to upset him. On the other hand, I was mortified at the fact that they were all wasted, and that I had not managed to save any money after all. In fact, by the time we had paid the refrigerator man, I would have cost us quite a lot, a fact which Tim pointed out with some force. It was also quite obvious that there were fewer than the twenty-four chickens there ought to have been if I had been telling the truth about fitting them all in. My feeble reply that at least we still had the ones I'd farmed out with neighbours was not well received.

The chickens we removed from the freezer didn't smell very nice, either, which didn't help matters.

Tim, of course, was far too well-bred to raise any of these issues in front of the repair man.

'...and then you have to fucking lie about it! Why the fuck can't you just admit it when you've done something totally fucking stupid, why do you have to fucking cover it up like your fucking smelly cat! Jesus!'

I couldn't think of anything useful to say, especially as we seemed to have had this identical conversation before. An uncomfortable silence fell, during which Tim sighed theatrically, the refrigerator man shone a torch into the freezer compartment, and I wondered if it would be a good time to ask Tim to take out the garbage, which was extremely full after receiving sixteen chickens.

'Aha!'

We both jumped guiltily and looked at the repair man, who was putting his things away.

'Yez've pierced through the gas pipe. Nothing I can do for yez now, yez'll hafta wait till Monday.'

'Can't you fix it?'

He looked at me pityingly.

'See, what yez've done is, yez've broken the gas pipe and let all the gas out. Yez can't fix that in the customer's home, like, we'll have to load 'er up and take it to the shop, right? Prob'ly take, like, two, three days, then we bring 'er back good as new with a twelve month warranty, right?'

Right.

***

Tim was furious. Absolutely mad with rage, he was almost like Goebbels, my old boss, the psychopath, on a good day. He shouted insults, he paced around the flat and threw things. Moses, who had never seen this kind of behaviour before, was frightened and ran under the sofa. This made me lose my temper too.

'Stop it! Don't you dare frighten Moses!'

This, of course, gave Tim instant pause, calming him down and filling him with remorse.

'Oh, of course, we mustn't upset the fucking cat. Christ, I sometimes wonder if you've got a thought in your head besides that fucking smelly animal. Fucking Moses this, Moses that, stinking up our bed and shedding hairs everywhere and his fucking smelly Booda Box...'

Mentally I thanked God for my experience at Marsh and Spacknall. If it hadn't been for working for Mr Goebbels I could never have stood this. I would have either burst into tears or started laughing hysterically, but now I was able to let it wash over me with comparative calm, and even use the time for some constructive thought.

There wasn't much I could do about the refrigerator. It was broken and that was that. Yes, it was true that I was responsible but I had meant well, after all. Thus absolved of guilt, I could proceed to catalogue my other problems, which went something like this:

1. Tim was having an affair.

2. I still hadn't unpacked the last two boxes from home, which were hiding behind the sofa. There were no bookcases at all in the place, and it wasn't the time to ask Tim to buy some.

3. I couldn't buy anything myself because my credit card was still maxed out. Again, it hardly seemed like the time to raise the matter.

4. Patrick had some unspecified problem with Joe Morelli, which was likely to make him do something utterly terrible at any moment. Guiltily I realised that I had forgotten about this until now. I'd better get him over here straight away and find out what the problem was. But I didn't want to involve Tim in it, it would make him rant and rave even

more. So I had to get Patrick over here one day when Tim was at work. But he was at school then. Well, after school. Tim never got home before seven at the earliest, so we could talk about whatever the problem was and then Patrick could stay for dinner, and Tim could drive him home.

I felt better with a plan of action, and tuned back in to Tim. He was still rabbiting on.

'Blah blah blah always in the fucking bathroom blah blah blah never do a stroke of fucking work blah blah blah blah blah blah if you're even fucking listening!'

It sounded so familiar, it was just the way Goebbels, the axe murderer, used to carry on. I knew from experience that conciliatory behaviour just didn't work with these people.

'Blah Blah Blah!' I shouted, and went into the bathroom.

***

My dramatic exit was a bit spoiled by the fact that I had to open the door again to let in Moses. Never mind, I comforted myself, at least in here he'll have to leave me alone. I ran a nice hot bath, with some strawberry flavoured bath salts, and settled into the water. It was true, I supposed, that I spent a lot of time in the bath these days. But it seemed to be the only place I could rely on nothing going wrong. I thought about how happy I'd been such a short time ago, and started to cry.

A long time later I pulled myself together. Moses was sitting on the corner of the bath patting anxiously at my face; at least someone loved me, I thought mournfully. I wished passionately that I could just get out of the bath, get dressed and go home and forget the whole thing, Tim, our marriage, everything that had gone so wrong.

But then everyone would know. I imagined them all laughing at me, saying that I couldn't even hang onto my husband for a month. And my parents would be so disappointed, they'd been so proud at our wedding, and gone to so much trouble to arrange everything, and now that I thought about it, it had probably cost a fortune too. I couldn't possibly let them find out it had all been a farce. And it had to have been, didn't it? People don't suddenly start having affairs for no reason a few weeks after they get married, so he must have been carrying on with The Woman before we got married. I started crying again. I felt as if I would never be able to stop.

Eventually, of course, you have to stop crying. The human system just can't keep it up. I lay in the cold bathwater, feeling utterly drained. I didn't even think I could rake up enough energy to run in more hot water. My mind had turned into an endless expanse of dark grey cotton wool, and my body seemed to be going the same way. I thought vaguely about killing myself, but that would take a lot of energy.

Moses was crying and poking at my face, I had to get out. I dried myself, after a fashion, and fell into bed. Perhaps I was getting 'flu. Whatever the cause, I dropped into sleep like a stone, Moses close behind me.

***

It was about mid-afternoon when I woke up, I could tell from the light, although I wasn't really sure what day it was. I didn't feel like getting up or moving at all. I wondered what was wrong with me; I had thought earlier that I might be coming down with something, but could detect no trace of sickness in myself. No fever, no pains, not even a dull ache anywhere. It was a bit worrying, but I didn't feel energetic enough to do much worrying. Curled around Moses, I fell back into a light doze.

After some time, I was awakened again by the smell of coffee. Tim was sitting on the edge of the bed holding a big mug full. It was real coffee, too. I sat up carefully and held out my hands for the mug. Tim was smiling encouragingly. Something about the whole scenario didn't ring true, somehow. Could I have been asleep for several days or something? No, I couldn't, I decided. They never mention it in books, but if you were asleep for that long, your bladder, let's face it, would certainly let you know about it.

'Are you feeling a bit better?' Tim really seemed concerned. Had I been shouting deliriously in my sleep, I wondered. I sat up carefully and had some coffee. It tasted wonderful. I thought about what to say. Tim was obviously worried about me, who knew why, but it seemed to be making him behave better, so the thing to do was clearly to let him go on worrying about whatever it was.

'I don't know. I just...' I let my voice trail off hopelessly and sank back against the pillows. I really didn't have to act much, I did feel sort of hopeless. I allowed a tear to trickle out of one eye.

'I hate it when you shout at me like that.'

Tim really seemed to be paying attention and immediately launched into a flood of apologies and promises not to do it again, etc. It seemed a good idea to bring up the other matters that needed attention.

'And I haven't got anywhere to put my books, and it doesn't feel like home when I can't finish unpacking.'

'Why didn't you say so? We could have gone shopping today and got you a bookcase. We'll get one next week, okay?'

'I was going to get one, but my credit card's full and I haven't got any money.'

'Well you'd better give me the bill and I'll fix it up. Why didn't you say something before? Christ, Fiona, I'm not a fucking ogre.'

'I don't know. You always seem so cross.'

I really thought Tim was on the verge of crying himself. He was off again on a tide of self-recrimination, I cast my mind back to see if there was anything else I needed while he was in this mood. Oh, yes.

'Tim, would you mind if I asked Patrick for dinner one night this week? I miss him so much, I'm used to seeing him every day and I've hardly seen him at all since we got married...'

'Of course, invite him. Would you like to invite your Mum and Dad too?'

That didn't fit my plans so well.

'Maybe later, when I've had a bit more practice

with the cooking.'

'Sure, whatever you want, darling. Just let me know what night and I'll come home early.'

I smiled vaguely.

'Look, you haven't had any lunch, I didn't like to wake you. What if you get dressed and we'll go over to the park? We can get a late lunch at that new twenty-four hour place.'

'I ought to do something about dinner, we lost all those chickens...'

'Don't worry about that, we'll go out. Can't have my beautiful wife worrying.'

Tim looked so pleased with himself that I had to smile. He always got this really queer expression on his face when he said anything sloppy. He probably thought it was a Tender Expression, but actually it looked as if he was going to be sick.

***

Having finally managed to get my way about a few things I made a big effort to be perfect for the rest of the weekend. We went to Chapel Street on Sunday afternoon and got a lovely rosewood bookcase, and I rang home and arranged for Patrick to come for dinner after school on Monday. Tim wrote a cheque for my credit card bill, although he grumbled and muttered a lot about how expensive I was. I couldn't see what was so expensive, it was only just a little bit over $5000, and I shouldn't need any more new clothes until next winter. It was true that we went out to dinner on both Saturday and Sunday nights, but, as I pointed out, we'd saved so much money by getting sheets in our wedding presents that it was almost free.

On Sunday night I finished opening the wedding presents while Tim played with his computer. I was determined not to let them drag on into next week. If I was going to be a Perfect Wife I would have to make the effort, and get everything done on time. I gritted my teeth. I wasn't entirely sure I wanted to be the Perfect Wife. Perhaps Perfect Schmuck would be a better description for what I was doing – half killing myself with fatigue and boredom just to provide ultimate comfort and well-being for someone who screwed around behind my back. My grasp tightened on the scissors as I stared at the back of Tim's head.

I imagined him laid out in his coffin, a waxy smile and peach-coloured blusher on his face. I, the grieving widow, gazed sorrowfully out from a black lace veil. I imagined the hollow thuds as the clods of earth dropped onto the coffin. Of course, as the widow, I would get to throw on the first shovel full. I imagined the grave after it had been filled in, a grassy mound in the sunshine. I imagined coming back, alone, and dancing a little jig on it.

Tim turned around and said something. I jumped guiltily.

'Sorry, what did you say?'

'What were you thinking about, darling, you looked so happy.'

I smiled lovingly back at him.

'Oh, I was just thinking about you, darling.'

❧CHAPTER TWELVE☙

...that this woman may be loving and amiable, faithful and obedient to her husband...

Book of Common Prayer

Having decided that my husband would be better dead than alive, I had a lot to think about that night. Fortunately I was able to account for my absent-mindedness by remarking from time to time how much I was in love with him. Tim accepted this without the faintest hint of suspicion, which, I thought, just went to show what a creep he was. He was so vain that he couldn't imagine anyone not being as much in love with him as he was with himself.

Still, I mused as I lay in bed after the usual matrimonial activities, the big problem was really whether I could get away with it. Poison seemed to be the obvious solution, but I had no idea what kind of poison would be best, or where I could get some. And would it be better to make it look like a lingering illness, or pretend he'd drunk it by accident? Children were always dying from drinking kerosene that was kept in soft drink bottles, or so I remembered my mother saying, but would it look realistic to have a lemonade bottle full of kerosene in a flat in the middle of the city? And where did you get kerosene from, anyway? I never remembered seeing it for sale anywhere.

Of course, I could tamper with the brakes on his car so he'd have a fatal accident, but somehow I doubted that a car accident in the middle of Melbourne would be fatal. It works well in the movies, but then the hero is always going terribly fast down a winding mountain road with a five thousand foot cliff on one side. And even then they always manage to escape by doing something clever with the handbrake or something. And there was just the tiny detail that I didn't know anything about cars, or even where the brakes were. I sighed and snuggled up to Moses. How else could people die?

Well, of course people were sometimes killed by falling under a train. There had been something about it on the news just the other night. Perhaps I could get him on a crowded platform and just sort of give him a quick shove? But someone might see me doing it and tell the police. Well, I could pretend to stumble and sort of push him accidentally, but then he was a lot bigger than me, somehow I couldn't really see it working.

Of course, given that he was sleeping with some bimbo, he might easily die all by himself, by catching Aids. That would be the best way, I thought sleepily. I could go and see him in hospital and gloat. I imagined taunting him. 'See where your disgusting behaviour has got you,' I'd say as he was gasping on his deathbed. Best of all, I wouldn't have had anything to do with it, so I wouldn't have to worry about getting caught. I could go back home and resume life as if the wedding had never happened (but keep all the presents) or I could keep the flat. I imagined myself as a widow, pale and elegant in my black draperies, giving off that faint aura of mystery that widows always have in books. Perhaps I would take up embroidery, it always looks so virtuous when you see people doing it. That would give me something to do while I was visiting Tim on Death Row, and take my mind off the ugliness of it all, and I'd be making all kinds of beautiful cushion covers and things to do up the flat with once he was dead. A thought struck me – I could even start a glory box! After all, I was only twenty-two, I was bound to meet someone else sooner or later. Probably sooner, after all, as anyone who's ever watched television knows, hospitals are just crawling with handsome and single doctors selflessly dedicating their lives to the care of the dying. No doubt there'd be one or two hanging about when I went to see Tim.

I was just dropping comfortably off to sleep when it hit me. An icy blast of realisation slammed into my spine and I shot upright, clutching the doona.

Aids was catching.

And I'd just been sleeping with someone who had it.

He might be the one visiting me on Death Row.

***

First things first, I thought as I scrubbed myself under the shower. I must go first thing and get a blood test. Then somehow persuade Tim to get one, make sure he didn't already have it. Then, somehow, I was going to have to find a way to practise safe sex with my lawfully wedded husband. How on earth could I justify the use of condoms in the marital bed?

Bang, bang, bang.

'Fiona? What the fuck are you doing, for Chrissake? It's fucking one o'clock in the morning!'

I thought frantically as I dried myself.

'Um. Well, I was just–'

'What? You're having a goddamned shower, for Christ's sake, at fucking one o'clock in the morning. What the fuck is going on?'

I wished he wouldn't swear so much. God would get him for it. Then I remembered that I wouldn't mind as long as I wasn't involved. 'Go for it, God,' I whispered. God didn't do anything, though. Perhaps he was Biding his Time.

Tim was practically dancing up and down with rage. He had nothing on and I suddenly noticed how ridiculous he looked. His head was slightly too big for his body. Why hadn't I ever noticed that before?

'Fiona, I'd like an answer. What the hell are you doing?'

What a stupid question. Couldn't he see I'd been having a shower?

'I was having a shower.' I headed back to bed. Tim followed me, bitching and complaining every step of the way. I curled up with Moses and pulled the covers over my head.

'Your hair's all wet. Jesus.'

It was imperative to do something constructive before I got Aids. I tried to tune out Tim's pestering and concentrate. He kept rabbiting on and on, usually I could tune him out, but I fell asleep before I could manage it.

***

'Miss, MacDougall, is it? What can we do for you today?'

The doctor was nice, I'd been going to him for years, but now that I was in his office it was a bit hard to think of what to say.

'Um.' I could feel myself going bright red.

The doctor looked encouraging. He was quite good at that. I decided to make a clean breast of it. After all, he couldn't tell anyone else.

'Well. Um. It's my husband, sort of. He, well...'

'Oh, I didn't know you'd got married. Congratulations.'

The doctor beamed at me in a fatherly sort of way and it was all too much. I burst into tears.

***

After drinking some water out of a paper cup (why?) and using a number of tissues from a box that appeared, after some excavation, from under what looked like several years' worth of random paper, we got down to business. The doctor seemed quite surprised when he learned what I'd come for.

'But why on earth?'

'Well, Tim, that's my husband, he's been sleeping with God knows who, and I just thought, well, you know...'

The doctor looked thunderstruck, but pressed on bravely.

'Well, of course, if that's how a couple wants to live, of course that's perfectly okay, there's nothing wrong with having an open marriage...'

I couldn't believe my ears.

'What! Of course there's something wrong with it, it's disgusting. Marriage is a sacrament, how would you like it if your wife was jumping into bed with people all over the place? And bringing home God knows what diseases?' I grabbed another tissue in case I gave way again.

'Oh, dear. Well, it's really not worth testing for Aids, I'm assuming, of course, that your own sex life with your husband is fairly normal... it's virtually impossible, you know, for a woman to catch Aids from normal sexual intercourse. Unless there was some anal penetration, or...'

I waved frantically at him to stop, I really didn't want to hear any more. There's something wrong with the world when your kindly old family doctor starts talking to you about anal penetration.

'I just want to make sure. It's easy enough, isn't it, just a blood sample?'

The old man sighed. 'Well, if it's going to make you feel better. We'd better do syphilis as well.'

I had a cold feeling in my stomach, and felt as if I was getting out of my depth. Slowly and carefully I asked him what he meant.

'Well, syphilis is far more of a risk, you know, when people are sleeping around. It's far more common than Aids and much easier to catch. So if we're testing for Aids, it's only sensible to test for syphilis as well, they can do both tests on the one sample.'

I felt faint. Everybody knew only dirty people and prostitutes got syphilis. Oh, and sailors. And kings, of course, but nobody normal.

'Well, we might as well check you out for the other nasties while you're here. How long since your last Pap smear?'

My last what? What on earth was he talking about? Did he mean sex? No, I'd heard all the words for that at the office. Bonk, screw, etc. He must be talking about periods and was too delicate to say the word.

'I had one just before I got married, about four weeks ago.' I couldn't actually remember, but I had to have had, since I hadn't had one since, and we'd been married for over three weeks.

'What, you've only just got married? I assumed it must have been some time ago. Are you sure about your husband? Not many people have extramarital affairs in the first month of their marriage, you know.'

The poor old man really looked quite shocked.

'Yes, I am sure. I found the evidence of it in his coat pocket.'

'Evidence?'

'Yes, a black lace garter belt. I found it when I was, um, going through his pockets. You know, before sending it to the cleaners.' I didn't like to tell respectable old Dr Sanders that I'd been looking for money in my husband's pockets.

'Good grief! What did he say about it?'

'Nothing, I didn't tell him I'd found it.'

'Well, why on earth not, child? There may be a perfectly innocent explanation, and here you are having all these blood tests...'

I just looked at him.

'A perfectly innocent explanation. For a black lace garter belt in my husband's coat pocket. And him working late till all hours and ringing me up with sounds of a party in the background.' (It was all coming together now.) 'Face it, Dr Sanders, the man's an adulterer.'

'Yes, well... oh, well. I'd better give you a bit of an examination. Just hop up on the table... let me know when you're ready.' He busied himself with some papers on his desk. Really, I thought, the old dear was getting quite senile. How long did he think it took one to heave oneself up on the examination table? There were even little steps. Perhaps a lot of his patients were really old and infirm, but then you'd think he'd give them a hand to get up there, wouldn't you?

I climbed the little steps and sat on the examination table, being careful to keep my knees together.

'I'm ready, Dr Sanders.'

Dr Sanders turned around, saw me, and froze. He settled back in his chair.

'Ah, Fiona, didn't you say you'd had a recent Pap smear?'

'Yes.' I couldn't really see what that had to do with anything.

'Where did you have it, may I ask?' He seemed troubled about something, but even so I could hardly believe my ears. Was the old devil totally insane? Perhaps I should ring for the nurse. On the other hand, it might be best to humour the old dear.

'Well, in the usual place.' Good Heavens, did he think I was going to get my period in my ear?

Old Sanders was still frowning and shaking his head.

'Look, come and sit back down here, I think there are some things I need to explain to you.'

I went and sat back down and looked at him expectantly. He cleared his throat and harrumphed several times. He looked at me and sighed.

'Well, look. When we examine a patient...'

***

I was never more shocked and disgusted in my life. Like that famous guy on the television, I was shocked and horrified and appalled. He really expected me to... oh, yuk! It was worse than sex.

How I got through the next ten minutes I will

never know. It was the nastiest experience of my entire life. The whole disgusting process was made even worse by the fact that Old Sanders insisted on calling his nurse in to witness the whole thing, which made it all even more embarrassing. She kept making remarks like, 'What do you think it'll be like when you have a baby?' I made up my mind that the minute I was a widow I would swear celibacy forever.

Dr Sanders seemed quite unembarrassed by the whole thing. Being a doctor must coarsen one's sensibilities, I suppose. He whistled jauntily as he stripped off his disgusting plastic gloves and tossed them in the waste paper basket.

'Well, we can rule out gonorrhoea and Herpes. In fact we can rule out all the common STDs, and I'll just take a bit of blood for the other tests, if you could just roll up your sleeve... close your fist, if you would... just relax, this won't hurt at all...'

I shut my eyes, I hate needles. It didn't really hurt, but I screeched a bit anyway, just to make old Sanders feel bad after all the nastiness he'd inflicted on me.

***

I left the surgery feeling cross and disgruntled. I had thought he'd do the test straight away, and had braced myself for the result, but apparently he didn't have the facilities (probably didn't have the brains, I thought crossly) and would have to send it away to the pathology lab, where it would take about ten days. I was extra cross that he sealed the little bottle of blood into an evil-looking black and yellow plastic bag with a skull and crossbones and 'CONTAMINATED BLOOD' in big black letters. He had a nerve saying my blood was contaminated, the old fart, when I'd been a virgin less than a month ago.

Still, the sun was shining and it was a beautiful day. I had prised some more money for housekeeping out of Tim, so I decided to go grocery shopping and get all Patrick's favourite things for dinner that night.

When I got to the supermarket, though, I found I couldn't remember what Patrick's favourite things were, so I settled for getting all my favourite things. Well, up to a point, anyway. The butcher didn't have any Carpetbag steak. He tried to cover up for his deficiency by pretending that you have to make it yourself out of ordinary meat, but I was wise to his little tricks. Honestly, tradespeople are so evil. They'll rob you blind if you don't watch yourself.

**

Back at the flat Moses threw himself on me with

cries of love. I had bought his favourite things too, so I fixed him a little snack before going to have my bath. It was astonishing how doing just a couple of things could eat up the day, I thought as I poured in some of my favourite bubble bath. It was nearly three already, and hopefully Patrick would be there by four. I'd told him to come straight from school, which I calculated would give us at least three hours to thrash out whatever problem he was having at school. Once again I debated whether to tell him about Tim's affair. I knew that, in principle, one shouldn't burden young teenagers with adult problems, but it was hardly possible to corrupt Patrick any more than he was already. And the habit of a lifetime was hard to break; I'd confided in him about practically everything almost since he was born. I knew he was totally discreet, about my confidences anyway – apart from anything else, he had too much to lose not to be.

Of course, if Tim came to his senses and became a model husband, it might be rather galling to have Patrick muttering about garter belts all the time. Perhaps it was better to say nothing. Realistically, though, how much chance was there of that? And did I, really deep down, want to know? I thought back over the past few days. Hadn't I stopped thinking of Tim as someone I loved already?

Moses, having finished his snack, came in and

sat on the corner of the bath.

'What do you think, Moses? Is he worth worrying about?'

Moses evidently thought not. He shook his front paw delicately and started washing his face.

'Well, if he's totally R.S., what am I doing staying? Wouldn't I be better off leaving him?'

But there was the embarrassment to consider. And all the wedding presents, although since we actually had got married and lived together, perhaps it wouldn't be necessary to return them.

There was also having my credit card bill paid, and not having to be lectured about hygiene every day by my mother. There was not having to sit through dinner with Father Simpson every week.

On the other hand, there was the garden at home, and here there was only a balcony. Moses hadn't actually complained, but I was sure he must miss going out and catching the occasional bird. And climbing trees and things.

Moses yawned, reminding me that I'd got off track. We were supposed to be discussing whether or not to tell Patrick about it all. The trouble was that, deep down, I couldn't really imagine having a problem like this that I didn't talk to Patrick about, whether it was too grown-up for him or not.

Shit! Was that the door? Surely Patrick couldn't be here already? I jumped out of the bath, grabbed a towel and raced dripping to the door. Looking through the tiny glass hole, I saw that it was indeed Patrick. He must have skipped out early from school. I hoped they wouldn't blame me.

Patrick erupted into the room, dropping his schoolbag noisily on the floor. It sounded like a ton of bricks.

'What on earth have you got in there, the Holy Grail? And why are you so early, you didn't wag off did you?'

'Yes, hello Fiona, yes it is lovely, isn't it, but I think it might rain later. And may I say how lovely you look in that...um, whatever it is.'

'It's a towel, don't be stupid.' I eyed the bag uneasily. If Patrick didn't answer a direct question, it had to be at least a nuclear bomb or a consignment of illegal substances. I supposed there was no point worrying. If the police came, maybe we could chuck whatever it was over the balcony and deny everything. 'Look, why don't you find something to drink while I get dressed. I got some Coke, it's somewhere about, have a look in the fridge.'

I raced off to get dressed, leaving Patrick howling in an outraged way, I supposed because I'd offered him Coke instead of whisky or whatever. He should count his blessings, I thought virtuously, it might have been milk.

I didn't worry too much about what to wear since it was only Patrick. I wouldn't have spent more than five minutes getting dressed, and yet I was still trying to get my jeans done up when Patrick burst into the bedroom.

'What the hell's going on, Fiona?'

'Don't come in here while I'm getting dressed.' I threw a pillow at him, but it lacked conviction as I'd been telling him the same thing for the last fourteen years – well, ever since he could walk, anyway. 'What's the matter with you?'

'Where's the bloody fridge?'

Oh.

'Oh, yes, well, I'd sort of forgotten about that, it kind of broke down and we had to send it to the repair shop.'

'No shit, I thought Cedric must have flogged it to pay your Mastercard bill.'

'Well, I don't see what you're so upset about,' I

pointed out reasonably. After all, if Tim and I could manage, why should Patrick have a problem for one evening?

'Christ, Fiona. How can I live in a place with no fridge?'

ૹCHAPTER THIRTEENૹ

...assist with thy blessing these two persons, that they may both be fruitful in procreation of children...
Book of Common Prayer

There was a long and horrible silence. I tried to contemplate what I had just heard while also doing up my jeans. This was a pretty complex mental exercise, as I had also to worry about breaking my fingernails. On the principle that it's always best to take care of the major risk first, I lay down on the floor to get the buttons done up. This always works, thank God.

'Shit, Fi, you must have really put on a lot of weight.'

I didn't say anything. It's hard enough to maintain your dignity when you're squirming around on the floor on your back without getting into an argument with a precocious schoolboy. My air of calm control of the situation wasn't really enhanced by Moses wandering in and jumping on my stomach just as I was about to get the last button done up, either.

Moses turned round a few times and settled down, apparently for a nap. This left me unable to get up off the floor; on the other hand I didn't have to worry about the last button, since he was lying on top of it. I turned my attention to the other matter, being careful to stay very very calm.

'What the hell d'you mean, how can you live here? You don't live here. You haven't run away from home again, have you?'

Patrick assumed an air of wounded dignity, at least that's what it looked like, although it was hard to tell from underneath. People's facial expressions always look so different if you can see up their nose.

'Well, no. Not really, not as such.'

Dear God, it was worse than I'd thought. From my vantage point on the floor I could see his feet shuffling. I wished I could sit up and confront him.

'What the hell d'you mean, not as such? Have you or have you not run away from home again? I want a straight answer, Patrick, none of your bullshit.' I hoped I sounded convincing. It's really hard to be assertive with someone who's standing up when you're lying on your back on the floor.

'Well, it's a bit complicated.'

'Complicated?' I was practically blacking out from the effort not to scream. I took a deep breath. I took another deep breath, watching Moses rise and fall gently on my stomach. 'Look. Just tell me what happened, okay? No, on second thoughts, go in the kitchen and get me a stiff drink, then come back and tell me what happened.' Then, somehow, I would have to fix it. Dear God.

Patrick was gone for quite a while, which gave me an opportunity to notice how dusty it was under the bed. Really Tim wasn't much of a housekeeper. But then he wasn't much of a husband either, apparently. I wished I'd married Colin Firth instead. He was better looking too, I thought spitefully. Tim was too pretty to be really masculine. Perhaps he was a repressed homosexual. Perhaps The Woman was really a man. Don't think about that now, I warned myself. You might start crying again in front of Patrick. I will if I want to, I replied. Bugger Patrick.

'God, Fiona, you're always crying. Don't you think you ought to cut it out, now you're an old married woman?' Patrick lowered himself to the carpet, balancing two huge glasses of wine.

I grabbed one of the glasses. 'Never mind changing the subject. What have you been up to this time?'

'Well, the thing is, you know...'

I nearly screamed with frustration. I couldn't hit him because I was flat on my back with a cat sleeping on my stomach. I wished I could just go to sleep at will in stressful situations, like Moses. On the other hand, Tim would have been really ratty on our honeymoon. On the other hand, who cared? I dragged my mind back to the immediate problem. Must concentrate. Perhaps, if I was really careful, I could get my glass to my mouth and take a sip, just sort of sideways.

'...so I really had to get out of there. I mean, really, Fi, you should understand, you know what he's like.'

I had got the glass up next to my face and was stuck. If only I had one of those bendy straws they give you in hospital.

'Fiona. Are you listening?'

'What? Of course I'm listening, don't be stupid.' Bugger. Now I had no idea what he'd been saying. 'But I don't quite understand...'

Patrick heaved a huge sigh, as if he was

humouring a moron. I decided to let it pass.

'Well, look. If I'm not living there, they can't make me go to these extra classes, can they?'

'What extra classes?'

'Honestly, Fiona. The ones I've just been telling you about, I knew you weren't listening. Joe Morelli is giving these extra classes after school to all the kids who're doing Latin or Greek next year. Dad, of course, put me down for both, you know what he's like. I mean, most kids get to pick their own subjects, but you know Dad, he just goes... HRRRMPH!'

'So what? I didn't get to pick my subjects either. He made me do six years of French, besides the Latin. And Ancient History. That's just what he's like.'

I thought I had finally managed to raise my head up enough to get at the top edge of my glass, but Moses, ever watchful even in sleep, took umbrage at the movement of my stomach muscles and jumped off, kicking me in the solar plexus and spilling half my drink. He also exposed, in passing, my dark secret, viz:

'Couldn't you get your jeans done up?' snigger snigger. 'I wondered what you were doing lying on the floor,' snigger snigger. I ignored him and licked wine off my arm.

***

It was great having Patrick there. I had worried a bit that after I was married things wouldn't be quite the same between us, but before long it was just as if nothing had ever changed, the only difference was that here we were in Tim's flat drinking wine, instead of being at home pinching Dad's whisky. My flat, I reminded myself sternly. I was having such a great time that we were opening the pizza we'd ordered in before I remembered about the other matter.

'Um, Patrick?'

'Mmmmffmhh?'

I waited a little while till he appeased the worst of his hunger. It's pointless to ask Patrick questions until after the fourth slice.

'Patrick? What did you mean about not living there?'

'Oh. That.'

I narrowed my eyes into little slits and glared at him. That didn't work, so I snatched the rest of the pizza out from under his nose and held it out of his reach.

'Hey, come on, Fi, put it back, I'm starving.'

'What did you mean?'

Patrick sighed. 'Well, you know, just about living here and that.' He took a swig of wine. 'Christ, this stuff's disgusting warm.'

'What d'you mean, living here? You can't live here, what would Mum say?'

'Well, she said quite a bit, actually, but then Dad went that it was a, you know, some kind of sociological thing or something, and then he went on and on about some people in Peru or something, you know what he's like, and by the time he ran down, it was kind of a done deed, you know?'

'Well – what, you mean they actually said you could come and live here?'

'Yeah, kind of. Well, they just sort of accepted it. I think they felt kind of sorry for you, you know, being on your own all the time and that.'

'What being on my own? What are you talking about? And don't you think you could have asked me first? What's Tim going to say, for heaven's sake?'

Patrick looked injured. 'Well, of course I didn't need to ask you. I knew you'd want me to come.'

He was right, when I thought about it. Life would be much more fun with him there. Although God only knew what Tim would say. I put the pizza back on the table.

***

'He fucking WHAT!'

'Calm down, Tim, it's not a big deal, we've got a spare room.'

'Not a big deal? We've only been married ten minutes and you've got your fucking brother moving in? How can you say it's not a big deal, for Christ's sake?'

'Sssh, he'll hear you.' I had sent Patrick off to have a shower while I explained things to Tim. I could hear the water running, but I knew he would actually have his ear glued to the keyhole. I didn't really care if he heard, but I felt the warning added a realistic touch. I lowered my voice meaningfully. 'It's Mum, she's had a nervous breakdown. The doctor said she's got to have absolute rest and quiet.'

'Bullshit, that old bag's never been sick a day in her life. No germ would dare to go near her.'

The story we'd made up wasn't working. It was time for the ultimate weapon.

I burst into tears.

***

It wasn't easy. I sobbed and howled for what seemed like hours before he gave in, not very graciously. I was actually quite shocked at how strongly he resisted having Patrick to live with us, although I'd been prepared for some resistance. It made me wonder a bit about his basic character, although really I should have had enough evidence of that by now. Then he was cross all over again because Patrick had used all the hot water. I supposed he must want to scrub off traces of his mistress. I don't know why he blamed me for it, after all there wasn't any hot water for me either. Then he was cross yet again because I refused to have sex with him. But what else could I do? I hadn't yet figured out a way to insist on safe sex without admitting that I knew what was going on.

***

I dreamed that I was an heroic adventurer, questing after a magic stone that would cure all the world's evil and end war. For weeks on end I poled a tiny raft through underground caves of ice, drawing ever nearer to the sacred cavern of Aparna, where I would battle unbelievably horrible monsters before returning in glory to the desert city of my birth. It was a pretty average dream, really, but having got used to sleeping until I woke up, I was really annoyed when a horrible monster landed heavily on my stomach, catapulting me rudely back into my life.

'Fuck off, Moses,' I screamed, or perhaps mumbled, swatting at him with Arnold, my teddy bear. This usually calms him down – well, at least it makes him leave me alone for a few minutes – but the weight remained solidly on my stomach.

'Come on, Fi, wake up, I've got to go to school.'

School? Moses? I decided I must be in one of those multi-level dreams. Wriggling out from under the monster, or whatever it was, I burrowed my head under the pillow. If I was careful, sometimes I could get myself back into the same dream at the point where I'd left off.

The monster settled firmly on my back and started tickling my ribs. I recited the Lord's Prayer from under the pillow. It didn't work.

'Shit, fuck, bastard, piss off,' I shouted experimentally. This had no discernible effect. It must be a fairly hard core monster, and I couldn't escape it by waking up because I was already asleep. No, that didn't seem quite right. I could go to sleep and get away from it if I was already awake, that seemed fairly sensible, and then if it was one of those multi-layered dreams, I could still get away from it by going to sleep one layer down. Yes. Wherever I was in reality, I could escape torment by going to sleep. The thought settled into my mind with all the comforting weight of a universal truth, and I drifted away down the dark tunnel, my tickled ribs receding into a distant point of discomfort.

I was almost fast asleep when the thought hit me.

What if I was awake and the thing was real?

!!!!!!!!!!!!!!!!!!!!!!!!

I exploded up out of the bed in truly heroic style; as I launched myself desperately across the bed I felt the back of my skull collide sharply with something. An unearthly screech shattered the early morning quiet. Off balance, I fell over on top of whatever it was.

MMMMMMMMMPH!!! ARRRGH!

The thing under me was making terrible sounds. I struggled to regain my balance and get away before it bit me. Oh, dear God, it already had bitten me – there was blood all over the sheets. Hardly daring to look, I checked that I still had both feet.

Investigation revealed that I did, in fact, still have both feet. I also had a brother.

Reality trickled back as I sat in my ruined bed and watched blood drip from Patrick's nose. Patrick didn't say anything, just kept looking at me sort of reproachfully like a dog I'd kicked. Not that I ever would, of course.

Well, whatever was going on there was obviously a crisis on hand, and emergency measures were called for. There's no time to be lost in situations like this, that was one domestic thing that I definitely knew.

Patrick howled at me when I tipped him off the bed, but it really was necessary to hurry.

Once I had the sheet soaking in cold water in the bath, I came back to survey the rest of the damage. Patrick was sitting on the floor in his pyjamas, the front of which was also covered in blood, but his nose was hardly bleeding at all now, just a sort of trickle. I raced to the kitchen for some ice before I realised the fridge wasn't there. Tim was so inconsiderate, he could at least have arranged for a temporary rental or something. I soaked one of the old brown towels in cold water and hurried back to the bedroom. Patrick was lying on his back groaning.

'God, Fi. You broke by dose. Bitch.' He continued mumbling in this vein from behind the towel. This started me worrying rather – what if it was broken? Clearly the best thing would be to get him to a hospital. Patrick had a lovely nose, straight, perfect and Grecian, I couldn't stand to think of it with a bend in it like some grubby old footballer. I went to the phone and dialled 000.

It wasn't easy to make myself understood on the telephone, with Patrick bawling like a wounded elephant in my other ear, and Moses, who had woken up and decided he wanted his breakfast, swiping at my ankles with his claws out. But I did manage, finally, to get the message across.

Sort of.

'Alright, help's on the way. Don't move him at all, and don't give him anything to drink if he wakes up.'

What an extraordinary thing to say, I thought as I hung up. Why would he be going back to sleep now?

๑CHAPTER FOURTEEN๛

...till death us do part...
Book of Common Prayer

The ambulance men didn't take Patrick to hospital. They weren't very nice about it either. I must say I thought that was a bit unfair; how was I supposed to know it was only a slight nosebleed? Given the state of the sheets, it had looked pretty serious to me, but when I tried to point this out to the ambulance men, they marched out saying that they were not a bloody laundry service.

By this time it was after nine o'clock. I realised I would have to ring up St Bedivere's and let them know he was going to be late. Quite late, since the sheet was still soaking in the bathtub, and he couldn't have a shower until I got it out. Also, I was worried about the possibility of concussion. The ambulance men had said he was perfectly okay, but after all, what did they know? He had lost a lot of blood, and would probably be far better off for spending the day at home.

The thought had a ring of truth to it; I was sure I'd heard my mother say something like it once. Besides, it was easier to let him stay home than it would be to get him to go to school when he had the slightest excuse not to. It's no use spitting into the wind, as my grandmother often says.

Besides, I wanted to talk to him. In the fun and excitement of seeing him after such a long absence, I hadn't thought at all about my own problem, but now it loomed back again. I needed advice, because I could see I wasn't going to be able to stall Tim off forever. If anything, his libido seemed to be increased by having a mistress.

I rang up St B's and informed them that I was keeping Patrick at home for the day, due to a head injury. The woman seemed a bit puzzled, perhaps they thought a True Manly Schoolboy ought just to soldier on regardless. Well, to hell with what they thought, I told myself as I hung up. I'm in charge here.

Patrick didn't think it was worth while having a shower as he'd had such a big one the night before. I knew he hadn't got under the water at all, but had let it run for camouflage while he eavesdropped on me and Tim, but it didn't seem worth while to argue about it when I had more important things on my mind. I made him wash off all the blood though, despite his squeals of agony; you can't just have people sitting about the place covered in blood, it's not nice.

'Listen, Patrick.' I turned the television off. 'There's something I have to talk to you about.'

'Can't you talk about it after Captain Disgusting? I never get a chance to see it.'

'Cartoons rot your brain.' I knew he wasn't allowed to watch television in the mornings at home, not that anyone in their right mind would want to, surely? The few times I'd stayed at a friend's place and seen it first thing, it made me feel quite seasick.

'Bullshit. It's an important facet of our cultural heritage.'

I didn't pay any attention to this inane remark, as I knew he was just repeating something our father had said, probably out of context and without any idea what it meant.

'Look. It's about Tim.'

'What?'

That stopped me. What, indeed? I hadn't

thought past telling Patrick what was going on and getting his input, but now that it had come to the crunch, I wasn't quite sure what to say. Patrick was only fourteen, I didn't want to shatter all his boyish illusions, assuming he still had any left, and also I was embarrassed.

'Come on, what? It must be something juicy, you've gone all red. Does he tie you up and beat you or what?'

I shook my head frantically.

'Oh, come on. Hey, I bet I know what it is. He likes to dress up in your underwear, right? I knew there had to be something suss about him, with a middle name like Cedric. Christ, wait'll I tell Tony. A real live pervert in the family! Mum'll have kittens!'

'Patrick Aloysius MacDougall! Don't you dare say anything to anybody, I'll kill you!'

Patrick looked awestruck.

'God, you mean it's true? He really does –' He dissolved into a fit of giggles. I didn't see what was so funny about it, myself. Neither did Moses, who hates anybody laughing in case it's at him. He stalked out of the room lashing his tail; presently we heard him scratching furiously in his Booda Box, scattering kittyflakes all over the loo floor.

'Look. I'm trying to tell you, okay? This is serious, Patrick. Life-threateningly serious, okay?'

'How could it be life-threatening? He's hardly going to accidentally strangle himself with your pantyhose, is he?' Patrick started giggling again. Really, I thought, perhaps it had been a mistake to bring it up at all.

It was too late now though. I had brought it up, and unless I wanted to be tormented about Tim dressing up in my underwear for the rest of my life, it seemed I would have to go through with it. I imagined the veiled references to underwear that would constantly come up at family dinners, and shuddered. Anything was better.

I took a deep breath.

Then I let it out and took another deep breath.

Nothing magic happened. Patrick was still sniggering faintly. People in books always seem to take a deep breath and then be able to do whatever it was they were trying to do. It doesn't work in real life, though. I tried a few shallow breaths instead, but it made me feel dizzy.

'For Christ's sake, Fi, what are you doing? LaMaze breathing? Oh Jesus. You're pregnant!

Christ, you didn't waste much time, did you? Or were you already...'

Dear God, things were getting worse and worse. I had to stop him before he had my reputation in tatters.

'Tim's having an affair.'

There was a sort of silence. Well, quite a long silence actually. Neither of us seemed to be able to say anything, so we just sort of sat there and listened to Moses scratching and thumping in his Booda Box.

'Fiona. This is real, isn't it?'

I understood his problem. It was probably the first time he'd ever encountered a problem that demanded to be taken seriously. I had felt exactly the same way. Remembering how I'd sat in a sort of fugue for hours, I decided it was best to leave him alone for a bit, to let it sink in. I'd go and see if our coffee was ready.

I took as long as I could pouring coffee, wiping the counters and so on, but I must have overestimated Patrick's sensitivity, he followed me into the kitchen while I was still putting in the milk. Fortunately the milk from yesterday was still alright, although I didn't think it would last the day. Perhaps our refrigerator would come back today.

'Fi, for God's sake, you can't be serious. You've been married, what, three weeks? Four? Even Cedric couldn't be wandering yet.'

Why did I feel I'd had this conversation before? Was there something in society's expectations that meant when you told people your husband was unfaithful you were expected to justify it? I had a dismal feeling that every person I told would be counting days and weeks on their fingers like some kind of matrimonial accountant. And was there just a faint hint of disapproval? As, 'you should have been able to keep him faithful longer than that'? I was nearly sure, although I only had Gloria and Patrick to go by so far. Oh, and Dr Sanders, who had had the same reaction. Almost as though I were tainted by association with someone so promiscuous.

Well, I wouldn't let it worry me, I decided. It was just silly.

'Why does everyone keep saying that? It's not my fault, for God's sake.'

Patrick sat at the table and hunched over his coffee. He looked oddly smaller and less colourful than usual, I hoped I hadn't stolen his childhood innocence. But it was too late to worry about that, and anyway it was sure to be all the blood he'd lost out of his nose that made him look so frail. And the shock of almost having a broken nose, that might heal with a bump in it. I shivered in sympathy. He really should be in bed.

'Look, why don't you get back in bed for a while?'

Patrick looked at me disgustedly.

'God, Fiona, I'm not a cripple. A nosebleed isn't a big deal, you know. I mean, what a wank calling the ambulance, they thought you were a total jerk.'

He had been the one screaming that his nose was broken before they arrived, but I let it pass.

'You've got to keep warm and have plenty of fluids when you've lost blood.' I had seen it on the television. 'Anyway,' I played my trump card, 'if you're living here then I'm your guardian, and you have to do what I say.'

The minute the words were out I realised how weak it sounded. Patrick, however, to my surprise, seemed to accept this state of affairs. He shuffled off to bed, grumbling spitefully. Well, there was no reason he had to be in there alone. I went in and made myself comfortable on the end of his bed. After all, there was a reason I'd told him about Tim, although what it was eluded me for the moment.

Comfortably propped up on three pillows, Patrick stared at me over his coffee.

'Well, I must say you seem to be taking it well, Fi. I'd have thought you'd be hysterical. How did you find out?'

Oh, Lord. Well, in for a penny.

'I, um, found a... well, a garter belt, in his coat pocket. A black lace one, actually.'

'No shit, really? What was he doing walking around with it in his pocket? Have you got it there, give us a look.'

'No, I haven't, Gloria's got it.'

'Gloria? Why?'

'Well, it's a bit complicated. You see, I didn't want him to know that I know, but I want to be able to produce it later, as evidence, you know, in case I want to confront him with it, so I gave it to Gloria to keep for me. You know, so he can't find it and get rid of it.'

Patrick chewed this over for a second or two.

'But what happens when he notices it's gone? He must have already, you couldn't just forget something like that.'

'Well, I don't suppose he left it in his coat pocket for me to find on purpose, Patrick, he must have already forgotten it was there. Anyway, he can't notice it's gone, we took the whole suit.'

'Jesus, Fiona. A whole suit? How the hell can he not miss it, for God's sake? What is he doing, going to the office in his underpants? Hasn't he said anything?'

'Don't be silly, Patrick. Of course we didn't take his only suit, I'm not stupid. He's got about eight, all practically identical, he'll never miss one.'

'Eight? What's he want eight suits for?'

'I don't know. Is that a lot? I'd have that many clothes.'

'Yeah, but you wouldn't have eight dresses all the same, would you? What is he, Imelda Marcos? I've got to see this.'

He put down his coffee and lurched out of bed. Presently I heard shrieks coming from our room.

'Fiona! Come and see this!'

Oh, God. What had he done? I rushed after him, visions dancing in my head of 'CEDRIC PINKPANK IS AN ADULTERER' written on the walls in red crayon.

Patrick was standing in front of Tim's wardrobe,

laughing.

'What is it? What have you done, you creep?'

'Look at his ties!'

Well, I could see his point. Hanging in the wardrobe were three sort of rack things, each laden with what looked like a million ties.

***

Of course we had to count them. I mean, Patrick did jump up and down a bit and insist on it, but he didn't really have to insist very hard. I mean, here was a unique sociological whatsit, right in my own bedroom. We wouldn't be our father's kids if we didn't take the opportunity to gather some statistical data, would we? Really it was a sort of intellectual duty, like acknowledging sources.

There were eighty-seven.

'And you know something else, Fi.'

'What?'

'Every one of those ties was pure silk.'

'Well, ties are. Silk, I mean. Dad wears silk ties.'

'Yeah, I know, but he's got maybe six ties, ten

tops. He's only got that many because of all the ones we've given him for Fathers' Day. Anyway, most of those were Christian Dior. That's got to be more expensive than normal ones.'

Well, yes indeed. I had checked out some Dior ties in George's last Fathers' Day, but I nearly fainted when I saw the price tag. There had been no way I could afford it, although of course solicitors get paid more than trainee programmers. I pointed this out to Patrick.

'Sure, but why eighty-seven? The guy's compulsive, for God's sake. He's a sick man.'

I thought about it. Really, if Tim were the victim of some kind of mental illness, that would explain everything. Who, after all, could really be so deliberately and cold-bloodedly vicious as to be running around with other women just a couple of weeks after his wedding? It would explain his violent outbursts of temper too, and why he seemed to be jealous of Moses. Perhaps he was more to be pitied than censured, as it were.

'Patrick, d'you reckon he might be? Mentally ill, I mean? And he sort of can't help himself?'

'Shit, I don't know, Fi. Having a middle name like Cedric's bound to warp a person.'

'No, really. What if he needs help?'

'Fiona. Come on. The guy doesn't need help, he needs a fucking suicide pill. He cheats on you before you've been married a month, then he goes and buys all these designer ties. What a lowlife, look, you can't just let this go, you've got to do something about him.'

'Well, I know what I'd like to do. Come on, we've got to get all these ties back in the right order.'

'Just shove them back on the racks, he'll never notice.'

We put all the ties back on the racks and shut the wardrobe door. Immediately the room seemed lighter, as if an evil presence had been removed.

'So, look, Patrick. I am going to do something about it, I'm just not sure what. Yet. I mean, there are a lot of options here, a lot of things to consider.'

'Like what?' Patrick jumped onto the bed and bounced up and down.

'I really don't think you ought to do that with a head injury.'

Patrick fixed me with a look of withering scorn. 'Hey – I wasn't the one that cried wolf to the ambulance. Head injury!' snigger snigger. He could be so infuriating. I wondered whether this was what it would be like when I had teenage children of my own. Not that that seemed likely ever to happen.

'Come on, Fi, what are the options? As you see them.'

'Okay. Well, I can just leave him and go home. Or I can confront him with it and try to beat him into line. Or I can just hold out and try to be better than she is and wait until he comes to his senses. Or I can kill him.'

ಐCHAPTER FIFTEENೞ

Blessed are all they that fear the Lord:
and walk in his ways.
                              Book of Common Prayer

Patrick looked at me as though I'd just laid an egg or something.

'Jesus, Fi. None of them's exactly a quality solution, is it?'

'I don't know about that,' I said defensively. 'Anyway, what would you know about quality solutions?'

He looked at me pityingly.

'Fiona, everyone knows that stuff except you.'

I compressed my lips at him and said nothing. One day I'd definitely strangle him, but right now I needed an ally, however useless.

'Alright, let's take the alternatives one by one. Have you got a pen and paper?'

'What for?'

'God, Fiona. To write to the editor of the Financial Review. Sometimes I wonder how you keep breathing. Look, chuck my school bag over here, would you?'

I could hardly lift it. I dragged it over to the side of the bed. Patrick dived in and threw out a great heap of jeans, socks etcetera, several pornographic magazines and a Walkman.

'Where's all your school stuff?'

'Didn't have room for it. Ah, here we go.' He withdrew a spiral notebook and a chewed biro from the very bottom of the bag. 'Okay, let's bring some order into this situation.'

I was speechless at his nerve. Patrick had to be the most chaotic person I knew, I had spent my life extricating him from one awkward situation after another, and now he was patronisingly talking to me about order. And quality solutions.

'Right. The first option was to leave him.' He wrote it on the pad. 'Now we identify all the fors and againsts, and write them underneath.' He looked at me expectantly.

'Well, go on then.'

'Go on what?'

'Jesus, Fiona. Go on with the pros and cons. Of leaving him, for Christ's sake. Pros first – go!'

He was starting to sound like a basketball coach, or one of those television game show ladies. Why such terminal enthusiasm, I wondered, in the circumstances it hardly seemed decent. However, he was really trying to help, so I'd better give it my best shot.

'Well, er. Um.' Actually I had immediately thought of one, but it was too embarrassing to say in front of my little brother.

'Well, come on. God, it shouldn't be too hard to think of some reasons in favour of leaving Cedric. I can think of at least a dozen without even trying.'

'It's not that I can't think of anything, it's just... well, you know.'

Patrick has absolutely no delicacy. I may have mentioned this before. While he was still pestering me Moses wandered in, jumped on the bed and started licking his bottom. Really they were about on a level.

Patrick, apparently feeling that I needed assistance, started offering me multiple choice alternatives.

'He snores.'

'He picks his nose during breakfast.'

'He buggers the cat.'

This finally stung me into response. In front of Moses, too.

'Patrick, stop this minute! He doesn't do any of those things!'

'Well, he must do something pretty bloody awful, you aren't game to say what's good about leaving him.'

'Alright! I wouldn't have to sleep with him any more. There!'

'Aha! I knew he was a pervert! Or is he such a pathetic lover you can't stand it any more? Can't he get it up or what? I bet he can't, after exhausting himself all night with his dusky full-bodied mistress.'

'Don't be so disgusting! And how d'you know she's dusky and full-bodied? She might be skinny and a blonde. Well, a peroxide blonde, anyway. And for your information, it's not that at all anyway, I'm just afraid of getting a disease or something.'

Patrick shrugged and wrote something on the pad, I stretched my neck around.

'Exemption from Matrimonial Duties,' it said.

Well, alright. What else was there? I cast my mind back over the last few weeks.

'Well, I wouldn't have to listen to him always complaining about Moses. And I wouldn't have to wake up at six o'clock every day with his stupid radio clock. On the other hand, I suppose I'd have to go back to work.'

'Not really, you could go back to Uni instead.'

I supposed that was true. I could live at home and finish my degree. Okay, then, that wasn't really a con.

'Well I can't think of any cons then.'

'Good. Three for, none against. The next option is to confront him with it.'

'No, hang on, wait. If I leave him and go home it'll be so embarrassing, I mean everyone would know.'

'You could tell them he was dead.'

'Not Mum and Dad. They'd expect to go to the funeral and everything. I don't think I could face everyone knowing I couldn't even keep my husband for a month.'

'Well, okay, I'll put it on the list. God, Fiona, why you couldn't think of it before. Now you've messed up my spacing... Okay, now the confrontation. You drag out the garter belt, it's probably dripping with spoof, and shove it in his face. Then you break a few plates and stuff and he grovels and swears never to do it again. Is that the general idea?'

'Don't be so disgusting. It's not dripping with anything, I told you it was in his coat pocket.' I fished around for my handkerchief. Patrick was so insensitive, I felt totally bruised that he could take such a horrible incident so lightly.

'Christ. Don't start crying. Honestly, Fiona, you're so wet. I was only joking.'

Having made my point, I put my handkerchief away and thought about confronting Tim with the garter belt.

'Well, it would be very, I don't know, sort of satisfying, you know, to stop pretending that everything's alright and just scream at him. I mean, I'd really like to do it. And then I could relax about the sex thing, I mean I could just be totally open about it and refuse to sleep with him until he's had a blood test and everything.'

'Right, that's two for. Anything else?'

'Well, yes. I could do some revenge. Like I read about this woman that cut up all her husband's suits into tiny pieces. I could chop up all his ties or something. I'd like that. I mean, I can't do anything like that now, because I wouldn't have an excuse for it.'

'Okay. Three for. Any against?'

'He might leave me. I mean, that's really what I'm afraid of. And then, you know, that would be so embarrassing, just like if I left him, only even worse. And what if, you know, he just refused to stop seeing her? Having it all out in the open like that, I'd really be forced to leave him, wouldn't I? I couldn't go on living as his wife with that going on.'

'I don't see why not, you are now.'

'Yes, but I don't know about it now, or he doesn't know that I know, oh shit, you know what I mean. Having it out in the open would be totally different. I mean, it's one thing to turn a blind eye, but if I knew about it and stayed, it would be like I sort of didn't care about it. And then he could do whatever he wanted, and I'd just have to accept it. He might even bring her home or anything.'

'Okay. Well, all that's sort of conditional, isn't it? He might just as easily be totally ashamed and behave himself forever.'

'Well, I don't know. I mean, if the only thing stopping you from something you want to do is getting caught, wouldn't you just be more careful? At least at the moment I know what's going on. What if I had a baby and it was someone else's?'

Patrick stared at me for a long moment.

'Jesus, Fiona. Do you actually know the facts of life? I mean where babies come from and that?'

'Of course I know. More than you, anyway.' How outrageous. As if I, a married woman, wouldn't know more than a grubby little schoolboy!

'Well just think about what you just said.'

Oh.

'Well, anyway, I still might get a disease or something.'

'Yeah, sure. But what I'm saying is, you don't know. None of that might happen.'

'But I'd always be suspecting that it might be

happening, and I'd never know, would I? So it might as well be happening.'

'Okay, so look, what d'you want to write down as the against for this?'

'Well, all of it.'

Patrick sighed. 'I've only got one biro, you know.' He scribbled a few words. 'Okay, the next option is pretending to be a perfect wife.'

'Pretending not to know anything, and being a perfect wife. You haven't written everything down yet.'

'Yes, I have.'

'No you haven't, you've only written a couple of words. Give me that.' By lunging suddenly I was able to snatch the pad. I turned it around.

Under Against, Patrick had written 'pox, bitches, no more Cedric.' I opened my mouth and closed it again. There didn't seem to be much point in arguing about it.

'Right. Pretending to be a wife. Sorry, a perfect wife.'

'Patrick. Pretending not to know.'

'Sure, okay. So what's this got going for it?'

'Well, Gloria thinks I can keep my options open that way. I mean, as long as I don't know about it I haven't burnt any bridges, and I can always confront him later if I change my mind, that's why we hid the garter belt. And while I'm being a perfect wife, he can't, you know, I mean he's got to be feeling guilty about what he's doing, and the better I am, the more sort of guilty he'll feel, you know? I mean, it must be really making him suffer.'

'Oh, yeah, he must be really in agony boffing his mistress and coming home to a nice hot supper and all the housework done. Seems to me he's in clover, why would he change anything?'

'Well, because he'll feel more and more guilty about being such a creep. And an adulterer. And eventually he might, you know, see the error of his ways.'

'And in the meantime you're a nervous wreck and could be catching a dose at any moment. And how would you know if he stopped, anyway? You'll always be thinking he's off having a bit on the side even if he really is working late.'

'He couldn't go on forever, could he? He'd have to give it up sometime.'

'Why would he? He must like screwing around or he wouldn't be doing it. And if he wasn't too guilty to start screwing around two weeks after your wedding, what makes you think anything you do is ever going to make him feel guilty enough to stop? More likely he's congratulating himself on having his cake and eating it too.'

'Don't be disgusting. Anyway, what would you know about it?'

'Obviously more than you if you think a hard-core adulterer is going to change his ways just because you whip up a batch of your rock-hard granite scones.'

'Tim is not a hard-core adulterer! You take that back.'

'What is he then?'

I had to think about that for a minute. Actually the best description of Tim that sprang to my mind was Slime Bucket. I didn't say anything.

'Well, on the pro side you keep your options open. On the con side, A it won't work, B you probably can't do it anyway, and C why bother.'

'Wait on, you can't put that.'

'Why not?'

'Well, who says I can't do it?'

'Well, look, it's not going to be easy, is it?'

'Well, no. Not exactly easy, no. I mean, what I'd really like to do is stick nails in his eyes. But I can do it if I want to.'

'Yes, but how much do you want to?'

I thought about that for a minute.

'When you put it like that, not a lot, actually. But if it's my best option...'

'Yeah. And the last one was to kill him. Well, that's not a serious option, is it?'

'Why not?'

'God, Fiona. You can't kill him. Jesus.'

'I wish you'd stop blaspheming. Anyway, why can't I kill him? I can if I want to.'

'You want a list?'

'I don't see why I couldn't kill him. Not that I mean I want to, but, you know, it is an option.'

'No it isn't. You just can't go around killing people all over the place.'

'I'm not talking about killing people. I'm talking about killing Tim.'

'Jesus, Fiona, will you listen to yourself? You're not rational. One minute you're going on about being the perfect wife and baking scones, the next minute you want to stick a fucking axe in his head. I mean, don't you see a problem here?'

'Well, maybe, but you're the one that wanted to list all the options. I'm just saying that's one of the options. And I never said anything about scones, that was you that said that.'

'Look, is it really worth spending the rest of your life in jail?'

'I wouldn't, you only get about five years for murder, if it's a first offence.'

'A first offence. Jesus, Fiona.'

'Look, just write it down, will you?'

Patrick heaved a martyred sigh. Kill Cedric, he wrote.

'I wish you wouldn't keep on calling him that.'

'God, Fiona. You want to kill the guy, and you're worried because I'm calling him Cedric? Don't you think things are getting a little out of proportion here?'

'I didn't say I wanted to kill him. I just said it's

an option.'

'Oh, alright. Againsts. You go to jail.'

'Only if I got caught. I could make it look like an accident. Or suicide. Or something. Anyway, that's a detail.'

Patrick gave me a slitty-eyed look. 'Well, how about this? You'll go to Hell.'

I could beat that one, easily.

'Not after I've been to confession.'

There was a long, long silence. Then Patrick sighed and picked up the biro again.

'I guess the againsts are obvious on this, but are there any actual fors?'

'Well, he'd be dead, wouldn't he?'

&CHAPTER SIXTEEN&

*...and may ever remain in perfect love
and peace together, and live according
to thy laws...*

Book of Common Prayer

We looked at each other for a long moment, the words hanging in the air. Then Patrick got a worried look on his face. He frowned, and flipped back through the notes he'd been taking. Several minutes passed as he flicked back and forth, frowning more and more and occasionally scratching his head. At length he looked up in a baffled sort of way.

'Has Cedric got life insurance?'

'What d'you mean? How would I know?'

'Well, it's just that... I mean, when you look at it... the thing is, it's not so...'

He was dithering. If there's one thing I can't stand, it's a person who dithers. I snatched the pad out of his hand.

Reading over our list, I started to see what he meant. Two of the options involved extreme embarrassment, and one carried the risk of Aids. Really killing him was the only viable solution.

My head spun and my vision clouded. There were just too many things to think about. I had no idea how to go about murdering a husband, although I had entertained some daydreams on the subject. But none of the things I'd thought of had seemed remotely possible. On the other hand, now I had Patrick helping me.

I took a deep breath.

'What did you mean about life insurance?'

Patrick still looked a bit pale and shaken, but of course that could just as easily have been due to the blow to his nose and all the blood he'd lost. Guiltily I realised that it had been at least half an hour since I got him the cold towel, which was lying forgotten in a heap on the bed, making the doona damp. Well, that was something I could take care of. I went to the bathroom to freshen it up with some more cold water.

In the bathroom I examined my face to see if I suddenly looked like a murderer. I was a bit pale, and slightly freckled, but then that was because with all the alarms and emergencies I hadn't put on any makeup. Other than that, I couldn't see any difference from how I normally looked, I certainly hadn't turned into a steely-eyed killer, anyway. I wrung out the cloth and went back to put it on Patrick's nose.

By the time he'd finished screeching and ouching and I'd finished yelling at him not to be such a baby, we both felt more normal. Armed with fresh cups of coffee, we sat down in front of the sitting room heater to consider our plans. The wet towel had made Patrick's bed a bit nasty, so I spread his doona out over the sofa to dry out.

'Okay, so how are we going to do it?'

'Whoa, wait on, what d'you mean we?'

'I mean we, us, you and me, Patrick.' A horrid thought struck me. 'You are going to help me, aren't you?'

'Jesus, Fiona. You're really going to do it? Kill him?'

'Well, you said yourself it's the best solution.'

'I didn't say that.'

'Oh, yes you did. You said... well, anyway, all the other things are impossible. So there really isn't any other way.'

'Shit, Fiona, I'm sure there must be other viable alternatives than first degree murder. Like, how about, I don't know, blackmailing him or something?'

'That's just silly, Patrick. How could I blackmail him when he's not ashamed of anything? Anyway, it's against the law.'

'Oh, what! I suppose killing him's just a slight misdemeanour, like a parking ticket. God, Fiona.'

'No, you know what I mean. If he's dead, he can't very well complain to the police, can he?'

Patrick lay down on his back and started groaning. Fortunately, however, I knew exactly how to deal with that. I poked him gently in the ribs.

'Ow, stop it, piss off, pax pax pax.' He hitched himself into a sitting position considerably farther off.

'Look, we just have to make it look like an accident, then there won't be any problems. That's what I need you for.'

'What?'

'Well, to figure out how to do it so that it looks natural, stupid. You're always going on about how you're so clever. I mean, if it was just killing him, I could just stick an axe in his head or something, but it has to be special.'

'Special! God, Fiona, you're making it sound like a fucking Christmas present.'

'Look, there's no need to swear all the time. Just because you're living here. They expect me to look after you properly, I can't have you going home saying fuck all over the place. Mum'll kill me, you know what she's like.'

'Oh, gosh! Frightfully sorry, Fiona, old bean!'

I let it pass.

'Well, look. I can't shoot him or hit him with a blunt instrument, it's too suspicious.'

'Oh, do you really think so? I think it would be jolly hard to detect myself, old thing.'

I hit him with a cushion.

'What about poison?'

That had its merits. I thought for a moment.

'What kind of poison?'

'Shit, Fi, I don't know. Rat poison? Arsenic? A rare South American poison for which there's no known antidote?'

'Don't be stupid.'

'Funnel web spider venom, Botulism, Strontium 90, your cooking... no, he's probably immune to that...'

'You take that back, there's nothing wrong with my cooking. Bastard...' I grabbed another cushion.

'Cut it out, Fiona, I'm injured already, stop it, you bitch, pax pax pax pax pax...'

I stopped. I had had an idea.

'Look, Patrick. The thing about poison is that you're supposed to think the person died of a natural illness, right? Well, what about poisoning him with a natural illness?'

'Huh?'

'Don't grunt, it's vulgar. Look, all we'd have to do is get hold of some really deadly germs, diphtheria or something, from a hospital and stick it in his coffee or whatever, and bam, shazam! Then when he starts to get sick I just call the ambulance or whatever, and look really surprised when he dies.'

'Yes. Yes, I can see a lot in that. But where are you going to get the germs?'

'Um... a medical supply house?'

'They probably keep records, though, don't they? Wouldn't it look a bit suss, this housewife suddenly rings up out of the blue and orders half a pint of Cholera germs and two days later her husband pops off?'

'Oh. D'you think they keep records?'

'Well, it stands to reason, doesn't it? They keep records of selling poison, it's in all the Agatha Christies. You have to sign the poison book.'

'Oh. What about getting it off a sick person, then?'

'Where would you find one?'

'Well, there're plenty in hospitals, that's where they all are, all the really infectious people.'

'Yes, but most of them have got Aids. There's no point giving him Aids, he's probably got it already, anyway it'd take him years to die and in the meantime he gives it to you.'

'Not necessarily. The doctor said it's almost impossible for women to get it from normal... well, you know.'

'What doctor?'

Damn. I hadn't meant to say anything about that.

'I went to see Dr Sanders, for a blood test, just in case, you know... well, you never know... it's just a blood test... will you stop looking at me like that?'

'God, Fi. You mean you could have...'

'Look, it's not likely... I just wanted to be sure.' Had it really only been yesterday morning? It seemed as though years had passed. 'I should have the results back in about ten days.' Suddenly the ten days seemed like an eternity. Seeing Patrick's white face, I realised what I'd been too busy to notice before, that having the test meant admitting the possibility of having the disease.

Patrick must have really had a shock. Instead of yelling at me for crying all the time, he patted my shoulder and offered me a not very clean handkerchief. I had to admit he was taking it all very well, but even in the middle of my crying fit, I couldn't help feeling a bit bad about him even having to know about this kind of stuff at his age.

The trouble was, I just couldn't seem to stop.

***

'Come on Fiona, fucking snap out of it.' Someone was shaking me roughly by the shoulder. I couldn't see who, because I had curled up on the sofa and pulled Patrick's doona over my head.

'Jesus, Mary and Joseph, how long has she been like this at all?'

Well I knew who that was alright. I poked one eye out of the doona, flinching at the bright light. Gloria was leaning over the sofa looking extremely threatening. She had on what seemed to be a set of skin-tight bike leathers, dripping chains and studs everywhere, and high heeled boots. As soon as she saw me, she grabbed one end of the doona and ripped it away, disturbing Moses, who at some stage had crawled under it with me.

'Jesus, Fiona, you're a mess. What happened?'

I don't know why other people have nice, sympathetic, caring best friends, and I have Gloria. Still, at least she was bracing. I felt marginally better already.

'She went for an Aids test yesterday.'

Gloria looked more shocked than I'd ever seen her look before, which was not very.

'Well, it can't have been positive, surely? What would you be wanting an Aids test for anyway? You haven't been letting Tim bugger you, have you? I hope you know that sodomy is one of the four sins crying out to heaven for justice.' She frowned disapprovingly. I sniffed.

'What are the others?'

'Depriving workers of their fair wages, oppressing widows and orphans, and, oh yes, wilful murder. Shit, I wouldn't want to be Mr Howard, would you? He's nearly got Bingo. Look, go and wash your face, you look terrible. Patrick, see what there is to drink.'

We both headed off meekly to carry out Gloria's instructions, while she prowled menacingly around the sitting room. The leathers looked as though they might be so tight she couldn't sit down in them. Moses looked a bit disappointed that there were no tassels.

I washed my face. The dried tear marks went, but I couldn't do anything about my red eyes, even a double dose of Visine didn't seem to help much. I soaked a flannel in cold water and wambled back to the sitting room, where Patrick had produced some more glasses of the disgusting warm wine. I took a big slug, and felt it burn its way down my throat like battery acid.

Gloria emptied half her glass and made an awful face.

'Dear merciful God, what is this crap? It tastes like cat piss. Right, Fiona, what's the story? Was the test positive?'

'I haven't got the results yet, it takes ten days.'

'Well, what are you so upset about? Jesus Christ on a bicycle, you're practically catatonic. Don't you think you're overreacting?'

'No, I don't,' I said crossly. Didn't she have any sensitivity?

Apparently not.

'For fuck's sake, Fiona. What good is creeping under a blanket and howling for three hours? Get a grip. Now, what are we doing about it?'

'There isn't anything I can do, except wait for the results. Dr Sanders said –'

'Fuck Dr Sanders. Jesus, that's a pseudonym if ever I heard one. He probably sells crack to little boys on the streets of St Kilda. What I mean is, what are we doing about Fuckface?'

'Well, you know...'

'Look, all I know is I've got some tart's

underwear and a suit of your husband's stashed in my wardrobe. That isn't really doing anything, though, is it? What have you done so far to make the creep feel guilty?'

'Well, it's a bit difficult, he's hardly here, and then when he is he's always cross about something.'

'Cross about what?'

I drank some more wine. Patrick wasn't saying anything, his head was going back and forth like a tennis match. I wondered what warped ideas he was getting about Adult Life.

'Well, I sort of broke the fridge. And then he was cross with me for having a shower in the middle of the night. And now Patrick's living here, he wasn't very happy about that either...' I noticed Gloria was sitting down. Maybe it was some kind of new stretch leather.

Gloria looked at me as though I'd grown an extra head.

'You broke the fridge? Christ Almighty, how can you break a fridge at all, they're solid steel! I'm not even going to ask why you were having a shower in the middle of the night.'

I knew what that meant. She would pester me until I told her.

'Well, we'd just... you know. And I got to thinking, what if he's got a disease? So I just got up and had a shower, I don't see what's so wrong about that.'

'Christ, Fiona. I thought you were supposed to be pretending to be a perfect wife. Is leaping out of bed the minute you've finished bonking and racing to the bathroom to scrub it off, is that your idea of caring behaviour? Is it? Jesus, how d'you think he must have felt, like you thought he was contaminated or something? Holy Mary!'

I thought this was a bit unfair. Whose side was she on, after all?

'Well, he is contaminated. I've just had a blood test, God, Gloria, he could have anything.'

Gloria sighed patiently. I hate it when people do that.

'Look, Fiona, the whole point is you're not supposed to know anything. Now is that loving sexual behaviour, to rush off and scrub yourself as if your partner was disgusting? You've got to have a little more discipline if you're going to make this work.'

'Well I'm not. Your plan sucks, I could get a fatal disease any minute doing it. Or even crabs. I hate him and I'm going to kill him.'

Gloria relaxed slightly. 'Oh, okay, so you're going for the confrontation now? Why didn't you say, you'll be needing the garter belt back then.'

'What for?' I had a feeling I was getting out of my depth. Across the room I could see Patrick shaking his head frantically.

'God, Fiona. It's the only evidence you've got, isn't it? Unless you've got something fresh?'

'Well, no. The idea, basically, is not to have any. Evidence, I mean.'

Gloria looked baffled. 'You're going to confront him without evidence? He'll just deny everything.'

'I'm not going to confront him, what are you talking about?'

'But you said you were going to kill him.'

There was a long silence.

'Fiona, for Christ's sake shut up. She's just upset, she doesn't really mean it, don't pay any attention.'

Gloria turned around and fixed Patrick with a gimlet stare.

'What happened to your nose?'

'Fiona did it, it was an accident. She's just not herself, it's the strain of it all, living a lie...' he tailed off uncertainly.

'Bullshit. What's going on that I don't know about? Did Tim hit you? What's this about killing him? You're not really planning to murder him, are you? Murder is one of the...'

'Four sins crying out to Heaven for justice, yeah, yeah, but have you got a better idea?'

Gloria had to think about that, but not for very long.

'Well, no. Actually, no, I haven't.'

CHAPTER SEVENTEEN

God be merciful unto us, and bless us:
and shew us the light of his countenance,
and be merciful unto us.

Psalm 67, 1

I sometimes think Gloria should have been in the Army. It wasn't long before she had us all organised for what she called a brainstorming session. The brainstorming session required a fresh pot of coffee, a large ashtray, and a pad and pen, in Gloria's possession of course.

'Right. Now the first thing we have to decide is whether to make it look like an accident, or suicide, or to go for the street violence type of thing. Personally, I reckon that's got a lot going for it. You don't have to worry about evidence, for one thing.'

'What street violence, what d'you mean?'

Gloria looked at me pityingly.

'Holy sacred virgin, don't you ever read the papers at all? People are always getting killed. Armed robbery, muggings with violence, satanist ritual murders, cults, political protest – it goes on forever. All you have to do is be in the wrong place at the wrong time. Look at that guy that they found his penis cut off in the men's public loo, he was probably someone's husband. Actually, you know, that wouldn't be a bad way to go – mutilate the body so it can't be recognised, then wait a couple of days and just declare him missing.'

'But he has to be dead or she can't collect the insurance.'

Gloria turned her look of scorn on Patrick.

'Well he will be dead, won't he? You can't really mutilate someone beyond recognition without a little bodily insult. Jesus!'

'No, but he's got to be provably dead, so as to get a death certificate and things.'

'Provably? Provably! Jesus Mary and Joseph, what sort of a word is that at all? Where is it you're going to school, Patrick, just so I know not to send my kids there. Jesus God Almighty! Provably!'

Patrick got a sulky look on his face. 'Well,

anyway, it's no good mutilating him.'

I felt a calm voice of reason was needed. 'He's right, Gloria, anyway, who'd do the mutilating? I couldn't do it, it's bad enough cutting up liver for Moses once a week.'

'You can hire a hit man, they're not even very expensive. You could probably get him killed for about twenty, or put in the hospital for, say, ten. Well, don't look at me like that, I'm a journo, for God's sake, you get to know these things.'

'I haven't got twenty dollars. I mean, I could hardly ask Tim for it, could I?' A thought struck me. 'Wait on, do they take Mastercard?'

'No, Fiona, they don't take Mastercard. Holy saints, I sometimes wonder how you stay out of an institution. We are talking about twenty thousand, not twenty dollars.'

'Don't be horrible. What about suicide? He could leave a suicide note all about how he couldn't go on leading a double life, you know, with his mistress and that.'

'Well, it's tricky. You'd be the prime suspect, and the police aren't really as dumb as they are in detective books. I could see you getting five to ten, easily, and the insurance wouldn't pay out either.'

'Five to ten what?'

'Christ, Fiona. Years in prison. Probably in a maximum security one, and believe me, you wouldn't like it.'

I thought about that for a minute. Would it be worth five years in prison to get rid of Tim? They hadn't let me have Moses in the residential college at Uni, so I supposed I probably couldn't have him with me in prison either. Five years without Moses, oh help. He'd probably pine away and die without me. It struck me that he might even die of old age while I was in there, especially if I got life. Gloria had said five to ten, but I knew it was possible to get life imprisonment for murder.

'No, look, the only safe way is to make it a real accident.'

'What d'you mean, a real accident?'

'Have him fall down the stairs and hit his head, something like that.'

'But what if he didn't die? Then he'd know I tried to kill him, wouldn't he?' I wondered whether Tim would dob me in to the police if I tried to murder him. He probably would, I decided; if he was disloyal enough to be having an affair a few weeks after our marriage, he was capable of anything. It all seemed a bit risky to me. There had to be a safer way.

'What about magic?'

'MAGIC! Christ, Fiona, are you taking this seriously? He's your husband, after all.'

'I mean, pointing the bone at him, you know, Aboriginal people can do it, they sing you and then you just die. In a few days.'

'Jesus, Fiona. Assuming it works on Europeans, assuming it even works at all, how the hell d'you think you're going to persuade some Aboriginal person to sing your husband? I mean, what's in it for them, for Christ's sake? How are you even going to find someone in Melbourne that knows how to do it? Get real.'

'Well, they must have hit men too. Don't you think it's a good idea?' I had a vague idea that a person who was able to point the bone would be some kind of priest, and wouldn't cost much and would also be under the seal of the confessional, well sort of, anyway.

'For Christ's sake, Fiona. Just shut the fuck up if you can't be more constructive. Look, go and get us some more coffee, Patrick and I'll work it out.'

I went to the kitchen in a bit of a huff. It's

annoying to have a really good idea that nobody will take seriously. For a second, I wondered if killing myself might not be a better option, but then I remembered that I was the good guy. I could hear Gloria and Patrick talking together in the other room. Well, to hell with them, I'd just drink all the coffee myself. I poured myself a mug full and sat down at the kitchen table. The room seemed much bigger, I noticed, without the fridge in it. There was a horrible grungy patch on the lino where it had been. Of course the stupid fridge had to break down after I'd washed the floor.

I let my mind drift into pleasanter channels. Tim would die of some horrible disease, probably Aids, but without infecting me. Something that wasn't catching, it would have to be. Like leukaemia. No, that took too long. I needed a disease that you died of quickly. Rabies would be good, I decided. As long as he didn't bite me, I'd be safe from infection. I let the scenario unfold in my mind. Somebody smuggles in a rabid dog to the country, let's say from America. I knew they had rabies in America because of *Cujo*. Tim would have to be at the airport when it escaped from the person's hand luggage. He'd probably be meeting his mistress off some plane. Or they'd even have been away on a dirty weekend to Surfer's Paradise, which Tim would have pretended was a business trip. Yes, that looked good. The dog would bite Tim, who would immediately contract rabies, and would die horribly, foaming at the mouth, before any vaccine or whatever could be flown in. I thought about my outfit for the funeral. Deepest black, of course, with maybe a little veil. Yes, then no-one could see me smiling. When no-one was looking, I'd spit on his grave.

Feeling much better, I poured coffee for Gloria and Patrick and went back inside.

'...fuck, no, I'm not doing it, no way. Fiona can do it herself, he's her husband.'

'Look, Patrick, you know what Fiona's like, she's just as likely to break her own neck. Besides, she's sleeping with him. What if he wakes up and catches her doing it? No, you've got to do it.'

'Well I'm buggered if I will. What if he catches me doing it?'

'Why would he?'

'Shit, I don't know, he might be prowling around the place, he might not be able to sleep, anything. He might get up to go to the lav.'

'Fiona'll have to monitor his sleeping habits for a while. Then we'll be able to predict exactly, if he gets up in the middle of the night or anything, and what time.'

They obviously hadn't noticed I'd come back in. I cleared my throat loudly.

'Oh, thanks, Fi. Just put it down here.'

'What is it I'm going to be monitoring Tim's sleeping habits for?'

'Oh, we've got it all worked out, a beautiful plan. See, during the wee small hours, when Tim's fast asleep, Patrick will quietly get up and go and put a whole lot of marbles on the stairs. When he's leaving in the morning, he slips on the marbles, breaks his neck, and dies. It's early and no-one's about, so then you nick out and collect all the marbles again, and it looks as though he just slipped and fell. Accidental death, you get your death certificate, collect the insurance money, and live happily ever after. Everybody's happy.' Gloria was positively glowing, she was so pleased with herself. It seemed a pity to be negative, but I could see one or two flaws in her plan.

'What if he sees the marbles?'

'Patrick can take out the stair light globe when he's putting the marbles there.'

'Wouldn't that be a bit suspicious?'

'No, people in flats are always nicking the lightbulbs out of the common areas. Even in the better buildings. If that worries you, we could remove the bulb a week or so beforehand, they probably don't get around to replacing them all that often, or you could put it back again when you're collecting the marbles.'

'Well, what if he doesn't get killed? Then he'll know someone tried to kill him with marbles.'

'He won't know someone tried to kill him, that's the beauty of it. He'll just think some kid left marbles on the stairs. There must be a few kids in a building this size.'

'Not at six o'clock in the morning.'

'Oh. Look, let me think for a minute. There's got to be a way round this.' Gloria shut her eyes and appeared to go into a trance, except that she kept on smoking her black cigarette. Now that I noticed, the air was getting awfully thick in here. I'd better open a window.

'Hang on, Fiona, what're you doing?'

'Opening a window, it's dreadful in here.'

'You can't, somebody might overhear us.'

'How?'

'Through the window, stupid. Look at Esther.'

Now I was really at sea. 'Esther who?'

'Esther in the Bible. You know, Mordecai overhears the murderers plotting through the window and goes and warns the king. You know.'

'We're on the second floor. Besides, they didn't have glass in those days.'

'We won't have glass if it's open, will we? Look, you've got the other flats right across the courtyard, they could probably hear every word.'

I got a cold feeling in my stomach. What if they already had heard?

'Look, maybe we should just forget the whole thing.'

'No way, it's fun.'

I didn't know what to say. I had expected anything but that. Here was my little brother, at fourteen, wanting to kill someone because it would be fun? Perhaps his teacher had been right and he really did need counselling. But how could I bring it up with our parents, they'd be bound to want to know the context of him wanting to kill someone, and then the whole unsavoury business would be out, which was why we were killing Tim in the first place. Anyway, it wasn't like killing a real person.

I shook my head, trying to clear out the fumes. I couldn't seem to get everything straight in my mind, probably the smoke was getting to me. What I really needed was a nap.

'Look, I'm going to go and lie down for a while, I feel funny.'

Gloria's eyes snapped open. 'Oh, no you're not. I'm figuring this whole thing out for you so you hardly have to lift a finger, the least you can do is stay awake.'

'Look, Gloria, I'm not so sure this is a good idea. I think it's being a bad influence on Patrick.'

'Patrick? It would take Ming the Merciless to be a bad influence on him, I wouldn't worry about that.'

'Look, would you mind not discussing me as if I'm not here?'

'Sorry.'

'Anyway, aren't you forgetting the most important thing?'

'What?'

'Cedric's insurance. Hadn't you better check that he's got some? It'd be a pity to kill him for nothing, after all it'll be too late afterwards, to get him some.'

'Patrick! We're not killing him for the money.'

Patrick didn't seem convinced. 'I just think it'd be a shame. You've got a chance here to be rich, you'd never have to work again, and for someone like you, that's a lot.'

'What d'you mean, someone like me?'

'Well, you know, you're not exactly good at working, are you?'

I was stung to the quick. For Patrick, who arguably might be the laziest and most dishonest schoolboy ever to have lived, to say that about me!

'You little rat! I got that programming job for doing so well on the aptitude test!'

'Yeah, and then you got sacked a few months later for pressing the Emergency Stop. You think people don't remember these things, but it's no use setting yourself up to be some kind of captain of industry, when everybody who knows you knows you're totally useless.'

Totally useless? I thought I might be going to cry again. This was turning out to be one of the worst days of my life. They wouldn't even let me have any input to the plan for killing my husband, and neither of them even seemed to have any feeling for the fact that I was about to be a widow. Really, it was all a bit much.

'Oh, Christ. Don't start crying again. Fiona, stop it this minute. Look, he only meant your talents aren't in a commercial direction.'

'Really?'

'Really, honest, Fiona, that's all I meant. That your talents... what she said.'

'Okay. Just don't be so horrible, okay? What d'you think it's like for me?'

'Okay, look, guys, let's not get off track here. We've only got a few hours now before Fuckface'll be home, so why don't we just search the place and see if we can find anything about insurance?'

'Okay. You take his desk, I'll do the bedroom. Patrick can do the kitchen.'

'Right. Anybody know what they look like?'

We all looked at Gloria who seemed to be the day's expert on everything.

'Fuck, what are you looking at me for, I've never seen one. It'll have to be some kind of papers, though, won't it?'

'But his desk's full of papers.'

That was no exaggeration, either, they were overflowing out of every drawer and all over the top, every inch that wasn't covered with computer stuff, and a few that were. This, of course, was why I had cleverly suggested that Gloria do the desk. I was reasonably sure there were no papers in our bedroom, and I could have a little nap while she was finding the insurance document.

'Yeah, it is kind of stuffed, isn't it? I reckon it's better if we all start with the desk, take one drawer each, then if it's not there we can move on to the other rooms.'

Bugger. Why had Patrick had to open his mouth?

'Okay, there's three drawers on each side. I'll take the top, Fiona you take the middle and Patrick can do the bottom drawers. Try to be careful to put everything back in the same order it was in, we don't want to give the game away.'

Patrick sniggered.

'What's so funny,' I asked crossly, struggling to pull out the overstuffed middle drawer.

'Never thought I'd be getting into Cedric's drawers.'

***

'Christ almighty, he's got junk mail here that practically goes back to the Ark. What's he keep all this shit for, Fiona?'

'God, I don't know.'

'Stupid bastard. What's he think he's going to do, go back in time to get the Target specials of 1988? Prick.'

Patrick sniggered. This time no-one asked him what about. He sniggered again.

'Shut up, Patrick, no-one wants to know your grotty little schoolboy thoughts.'

'I'd be polite if I were you, Fiona. I've got one of your love letters here. Cedric must have treasured it, isn't that sweet? I'm surprised he didn't tie them up with a red ribbon.'

Gloria merely snorted, whether with contempt at Patrick for being empty-headed, Tim for keeping love letters or me for writing them, who knew? I wasn't ready to dismiss the matter so easily.

I had never written any love letters to Tim.

'Give me that!'

'No way, it's really interesting! You just don't

want anybody to see your mush. God, I don't blame you either, how could you write this stuff?'

'I didn't write it, you arsehole!'

'Tut, tut, Fiona, language! You... my God! You really didn't!'

Gloria stopped rummaging and pricked up her ears.

'It's from someone called Kathryn! Listen to this, guys – I will always be your adoring Kathryn! Look at the way she spells it, silly bitch. And then there's all hearts drawn around it, and kisses, yuk!'

Gloria sniggered. 'She'd have been better off drawing penises, that's obviously the centre of Tim's emotions.'

'She probably didn't have a tiny enough pen. God, I think I'm going to be sick.'

'Read it out.'

No, don't, I wanted to say, but the words stuck in my throat. It was obviously ultimately yucky, but I had a horrible sick fascination to hear what some other woman had written to my husband. Although, I supposed, he probably hadn't been married to me when she wrote it, but what was he doing keeping it?

'My darling Timmy.' Patrick paused to do vomiting actions. 'I just had to tell you again how much I love you. Yuk. After our wonderful night together, I couldn't think about anything but you. She's a sick woman. Don't you laugh, Fiona, you're the one that married him. You are the most wonderful lover... can you confirm, Fiona?'

I couldn't think of anything to say, not having any basis for comparison, and not being willing to admit it. But certainly that side of marriage didn't have much relation to what the descriptions of that kind of thing in novels had led me to expect.

'Well, he must have gone downhill a bit.'

'See if there's any more in there, Patrick.'

'Yeah, okay... look, here's another. It's signed "your ever-lovin Kathy-wathy". Christ, I really am going to puke.'

'Well do it in the drawer, he'll never notice in all that mess.'

BANG! BANG! BANG!

Silence fell. Everybody froze except Moses, who dived for cover.

'Dear God, what was that?'

'Someone at the door.'

'Why are we whispering?'

'What if it's the police? Quick, get everything back in the drawers.'

BANG! BANG! THUMP!

We shoved everything back in the drawers as quickly as possible, not worrying too much about which drawer they went in. The middle drawer wouldn't shut.

'It's the police, I just know it is. What are we going to do?'

'We haven't actually done anything. Just deny everything.'

'Oh, God.'

I tiptoed over to the door and looked out through the little spy glass. As usual, I couldn't see anything. I looked back at Gloria and Patrick. They were crouched defensively in front of the desk like wild animals. I tried frantically to gesture to them to look natural.

BANG!

I opened the door. It wasn't the police.

It was my grandmother.

And Euthanasia.

∞CHAPTER EIGHTEEN∞

O Lord, send them help from thy holy place: And evermore defend them.
                    Book of Common Prayer

'Hello, Gran.'

I didn't get a chance to say hello to Euthanasia. He was too busy saying hello to me. His way of doing this was to knock me flat and sit on me, and lick my face seventy million times. Euthanasia's tongue is about a foot square, which makes it hard to say anything while getting a kiss from him, so I concentrated on keeping my mouth tightly closed and not drowning.

By the time Euthanasia let me up, Gran was sitting on the sofa drinking coffee. I wiped my face off as well as I could on my sleeve.

'How lovely to see you, Gran, you're looking

really well.' I stayed sitting on the floor, there wasn't really much point in getting up again with Euthanasia still in his first raptures at seeing me again. He put his great head in my lap and looked up at me adoringly. For a fleeting moment I wondered if Gran would consider swapping him for Tim.

'So, what have you young people been up to? Rifling your husband's desk, Fiona, unless I'm very much mistaken.'

Shit. But she could only be guessing. I decided to brazen it out.

'What on earth do you mean, Gran? We've been playing cards.'

'Tush, girl, don't try to pull the wool over my eyes. All young wives do it, it's only to be expected. I remember when I was first married to your dear grandfather, I found the most interesting things.'

'What did you find at all, Mrs MacDougall?'

'Ah! I mustn't tell you that, my dear, it'd be disrespectful to my dear husband's memory, the old fart.'

Dear God. No wonder Patrick was so evil, spending every summer holidays up there. I'd forgotten how wicked she was.

'So, Fiona, you might not have heard me telling Patrick and Gloria that I've come down to stay for a week or two.'

'Oh, that's nice.' Gran usually came to Melbourne for a couple of weeks every year to do shopping, so I wasn't terribly surprised.

'Yes, and since Mary always has such a conniption fit about Euthanasia, I thought I'd stay with you, now that you've got your own establishment.'

'Of course, Gran, it'll be lovely having you. Tim will be delighted too.'

I suspected that this was an outright lie, since Tim had been so furious at me for letting Patrick move in. I wondered what he would say, and whether he would have the decency to say it quietly. I'd let Gran tell him herself, I decided. Actually, I wasn't so sure I was pleased myself, it was going to be awfully full with four of us in the two bedroom flat. On the other hand, I'd have a huge majority of my own people, and Tim wouldn't dare to scream at me with Gran there, which would be lovely. I wondered how long I could persuade her to stay. I would move Patrick to the sofa and let Gran and Euthanasia have the spare bedroom, then Patrick wouldn't have to sneak past them to put out the marbles.

***

The rest of the afternoon passed quite quickly, what with one thing and another. Euthanasia had to be taken across the road to the park to do Number Twos, and he insisted on swimming in the artificial lake, which was filthy and smelly, so then he had to be rinsed in the bathtub, and he took exception to my rubber duck. By the time we'd got him dry and the bathroom cleaned up, it was nearly time for Tim to arrive home. Gloria had left when we took Euthanasia out for his walk, so there were just the three of us. Moses was still under my bed, sulking. He disapproved of Euthanasia.

'Now, I think we should all have a nice drink. I've been dying to catch up with you two young things.'

'Sure, Gran. Would you like white wine or sherry? The wine's not cold, we had to send the fridge in for repairs.'

My grandmother shuddered delicately. 'You'll ruin your constitution, Fiona, drinking that cheap plonk, and don't bother to pretend it's not, I saw the cask in your kitchen. I'm not even going to ask what you did to the refrigerator. Here, Patrick, you take this, and go and bring back some tonic water. Make sure it's chilled. I came prepared.'

She rummaged around in her travelling bag and produced a bottle of gin.

'Wholesome life-giving gin, there's nothing so good for your circulation. Oh, Patrick, I should change out of my pyjamas first if I were you. Up to you of course, but you know how people talk in flats.'

Patrick reappeared shortly, wearing jeans and a T-shirt with Edward Cullen on it, and disappeared in the direction of the corner shop. The instant the door closed behind him, Gran fixed me with a gimlet stare.

'Right, Fiona, what's the trouble?'

'Trouble, what trouble?' She couldn't possibly know anything. Could she?

'Whatever it is that's wrong with Tim, I can see perfectly well that there's something badly wrong, so it's no use trying to cover it up, and it has to be something to do with Tim, I've never seen you in this kind of state before, you're not normally a tense person.'

'No, really Gran, I couldn't be happier, I'm just getting over a cold, you know how it is, and having Patrick home sick, it's just been rather a full day, that's all. Honestly.'

'Stuff and nonsense, young lady. Also bullshit. One, there's no point trying to lie to an expert, and two, lying to your grandmother is an offence against filial piety. Out with it.'

'Well... it's sort of Tim.'

'I know that, girl, get on with it.' She shook her walking stick at me. 'What's that young devil been up to, I knew he was no good as soon as I set eyes on him. Euthanasia doesn't like him at all, you know.'

'He doesn't?'

'No, I had the devil of a time controlling him at your reception.'

I hadn't noticed her controlling him all that much actually, since he had sent the whole table flying, demolishing the wedding cake and everything else in his path. It didn't seem like the time to mention it, though.

'Well, come on, Fiona, don't dither about. Is it gambling, drink, or women?'

People like Gran really do simplify things.

'Women.'

'Humph. A bit soon for that sort of thing, isn't it? Are you sure?'

'Absolutely.'

'Humph. What are you going to do about it?'

People like Gran really didn't simplify things at all, I thought nervously. What on earth could I say? It was probably best to trot out Gloria's original strategy, I pretty well had it off by heart.

'Well, I thought it's probably better not to confront him with it, but to just, you know, sort of pretend not to know anything, and just be a really good wife and wait for him to feel guilty and come to his senses.'

Gran fixed me with a steely glare.

'What, fancy negligées, cooking all his favourite meals, all that sort of business?'

I nodded.

'Humph. And then at the other end, you've got some little bimbo doing all the same things trying to convince him to leave you for her. He must think he's died and gone to heaven. Can't say I think much of that idea.'

'You don't?'

'Good God, girl, have you turned into a parrot? Show some backbone, for goodness' sake.'

It was easy enough for her to say.

'Well, what would you do?'

'Well, I never had this particular trouble with your grandfather, his faults were in other directions, so I can't say for sure, but I rather think that if I were in your shoes, I'd murder him.'

❧CHAPTER NINETEEN☙

*...that they may see their children
christianly and virtuously brought up, to
thy praise and honour...*
                    Book of Common Prayer

Dinner was rather a strained affair. Tim, for once,
had come home at six-thirty (why?) so there
were four of us, not counting Moses and Euthanasia.
Euthanasia had been fed his dinner at five o'clock, so
he stayed out of the kitchen, leaving the coast clear
for Moses, who sat on my lap and, between receiving
bits of lasagne, which made an awful mess of my
jeans, plucked idly at the tablecloth with his claws.
Patrick, who had had a stiff gin with me and Gran
before Tim got home, was not an asset.

'So, Cedric, how come you're home for dinner?
Secretary got a headache?'

Tim fixed Patrick with what was evidently

meant to be a look of stern authority.

'After dinner, young man, you and I are going to have a little talk about your attitude.'

'Shut up, Tim, he's my brother, and if anyone's going to have little talks with him, it'll be me.' I had had just about enough. I'd just got used to Tim being out all the time, and he had to suddenly arrive home and spoil my nice cosy evening with my family. How were we ever going to figure out how to kill him if he kept popping up like the demon king?

Gran could be faintly heard at the end of the table muttering something about infernal hypocrisy and bad food. I didn't think that was very fair. We'd had to send out for dinner because of the fridge, so it had been professionally cooked by experts. On the other hand, of course, Gran didn't have my cooking to compare it to.

Patrick hadn't fired all his arrows yet.

'You know, Fiona, I think I'd like to be a solicitor. It must be great having a secretary. They sit on your knee and take dictation. What's your secretary's name, Tim?'

Tim gritted his teeth. 'Her name's Kathryn, and she doesn't sit on my knee. She's a very professional young lady.' He glared at Patrick angrily, missing the lightning glance that shot around the table.

I kicked Patrick, hard, and then had to suppress a scream of agony as Moses, unbalanced by the sudden movement, dug in his claws. I couldn't see what Gran did under the table, but from the way he jumped I thought she might have poked him with her stick.

I sighed and got up to make coffee. Obviously the whole evening was going to be like this. Moses wound around my legs. I put down some Snappy Tom for him. He sniffed it and walked away shuddering. Presently I could hear him scratching vigorously in his Booda Box, the lavatory was just across the hall from the kitchen. I sighed and filled up the coffee machine. Behind me, my grandmother coughed and roared into life.

'Really, Fiona, if that's your idea of a sensible dinner it leaves a lot to be desired. While I'm staying here I think we'd better have a few remedial housekeeping lessons.'

Tim froze, staring at her in dismay.

'Oh, didn't Fiona mention that I've come to stay for a few weeks? Try to contain your joy, Tim, you're dribbling on the tablecloth.'

Patrick sniggered.

'Cedric's hardly ever here anyway. He spends all his evenings with Kathryn,' he emphasised the name meaningfully, 'working late.'

It was more than Tim could take.

'Look here, young man, I've had just about enough –' his face was all purple. He was on his feet, leaning over the table at Patrick, who was still unrepentantly sniggering. The next minute we were all silenced, as Euthanasia raced into the room, skidding on the lino, roaring and slavering at Tim. I hardly recognised him, he seemed about twice his normal size and all black, his fur was standing on end and his eyes seemed to glow red as he leaped up and down, booming and clashing his great jaws within a millimetre of Tim's face. Tim shrank back into the corner with a grey face, I thought he was going to faint or wet his pants. His face was collecting bits of foam which were flying off Euthanasia's teeth, which seemed at least six inches long. I had known Euthanasia for years, and he was the world's gentlest and most lovable dog, but he seemed to be in some kind of berserker fit, and I really wondered if he was going to kill Tim and save us all the trouble, until I happened to catch sight of Gran's face.

She was sipping her drink with a quiet smile of enjoyment.

***

I moved back into the corner of the kitchen to be out of the way, and watched carefully. Euthanasia actually never touched Tim, he jumped up and snapped his jaws a fraction of an inch from Tim's nose, but it was all show. It seemed obvious that, if he were really attacking Tim, Tim would be dead, and also Gran would certainly be making some attempt to restrain him. Also, I remembered as my breathing returned to normal, everybody knew what happened to dogs that bit humans, let alone killed one. They were shot by the police. Yes, the situation definitely had to be under control. I smiled to myself. Tim was absolutely terrified, and had started screaming. I reached out and flicked the switch on the coffee machine; it might as well be dripping through while we watched the entertainment. I had a feeling I was going to cherish the memory of this incident for many nights to come.

'Euthanasia. Enough.' Gran's voice was only just loud enough to be heard, but Euthanasia stopped roaring and slavering instantly, and subsided onto the floor, muttering and grumbling. Tim was cringing back against the kitchen cabinets, as white as a sheet and trembling. The look he turned on us all was not nice. I'd better say something, I thought desperately, anything at all, to break the dreadful embarrassing silence.

'Kathryn, Tim. Wasn't she the girl you said got pregnant, and she's not even married?' Across the table, Patrick's eyes caught mine in a meaningful stare. It just had to be the same person, I remembered him bitching about her taking maternity leave after his first day back at work. And those letters in his desk had been signed Kathryn. Did that mean he was the father of her child? I felt faint.

Patrick has a stronger constitution.

'Christ, what a slut. Does she even know who the kid's father is?' From the evil glint in his eyes I knew he had followed the same line of reasoning as I had, and was deliberately goading Tim. Really, it wasn't turning out to be the best night of Tim's life, I thought with some satisfaction.

'Humph! Can't say I think much of the type of young person you're employing in your firm, Tim, if this unfortunate young person hasn't even bothered to keep quiet about it.' Gran had obviously caught on, although she didn't know about the letters signed Kathy-Wathy.

'Oh, don't be uncharitable, Gran, the poor kid's probably from some kind of disadvantaged background or something, and doesn't know any better. I read a book about those kind of people, you know those hill-billies in America, they never even get married until they're pregnant.'

'Yeah, Gran, and those bikie chicks, you know, they have to do it with every member of the gang, she's probably one of those or something. Does she have black nail polish, Cedric – sorry, Tim?'

'She might be one of those Women's Lib types with hairy armpits. I bet that's what it is, she probably thinks marriage is some kind of oppressive institution.' I could sort of see her point, actually. I looked sideways between my eyelashes to see how Tim was taking it. He had started to shake. I added fuel to the fire. 'You've got to respect people's personal beliefs, after all, we live in a free society.' Over to you, Gran.

'Humph! A cheap piece of goods is a cheap piece of goods, free society or no free society. It's probably just as well she's leaving, a young person with that kind of sloppy attitude couldn't be very careful about her work.'

What fun this was, I thought. We could slag off his bimbo mistress, saying the most dreadful things, without even admitting that we knew she existed, and he couldn't do a thing about it. I felt happier than I had for days.

'I wonder what they put on the birth certificate, when they don't know who the father is,' I remarked in a musing tone. 'You could hardly write that you slept with ten people and put all their names down, could you? Does that mean the baby won't have a birth certificate?'

This was too much for Tim.

'She knows who the father is,' he grated out between his teeth.

'Humph! He can't have respected her very much, for her to be in this kind of mess. Mark my words, Fiona, if you don't respect yourself you can't expect other people to respect you. If that unfortunate young person had had any self-respect at all she wouldn't be in the mess she's in now.'

I thought that was going it a bit strong. I mean, any amount of self-respect would hardly stop you from getting pregnant if you didn't have birth-control pills. I didn't see any need to mention this, though, Gran was doing just fine without any assistance from me.

'Well, I feel sorry for her, poor thing, she's going to have an awful time on her own with a baby. She's really messed up her whole life, hasn't she?'

'Oh, I don't know. She could always move to another state and pretend her husband died in an accident. Then her child could grow up without the stigma. Of course, that's assuming she hasn't got Aids, then she'd pass it on to the poor little mite.'

Tim abruptly left the room. We all looked at each other. Presently one of his ghastly pop records filled the air. Under cover of it I quickly filled Gran in on what we'd found in his desk.

When Tim came back in, he had managed to get himself under control (just) with an air of forced joviality that showed only a few slight cracks around the edges.

'Thought we could do with some music, cheer things up a bit.' He rubbed his hands together and sat back down at the table. Gran raised her eyebrows disdainfully.

'Oh, is that what it is? Fiona, isn't that coffee ready yet?'

***

We didn't stay long at the table after that. I had to get the spare room sorted out for Gran and Euthanasia, and the sofa made up for Patrick. Gran got out a new board game from her bag and forced Tim to play it with her and Patrick. From the occasional glances I got as I went back and forth, Tim seemed to be losing. He was not a very gracious loser.

Fortunately I had another set of clean sheets from the wedding presents, so I was able to make the spare bed up for Gran. Patrick would just have to keep the same sheets on the sofa, he'd only been in them for one night anyway. It meant there were none left spare, though. I wished I hadn't thrown out all Tim's brown ones.

Then I remembered our own sheets still soaking in the bath.

Well, there was no help for it, I thought wearily. I'd just have to wash them and get them dry before Tim and I could go to bed.

***

'Fiona, for God's sake. What are you doing washing now for?'

Damn, he didn't miss anything.

'Our sheets, I had to wash them. Um, I spilt a cup of coffee this morning, they've been soaking.' I didn't want to mention Patrick's accident, it might give him ammunition.

'Christ, I suppose we'll have to stay up till bloody two o'clock in the morning until they're dry. Why can't you be a bit more organised?'

I didn't want to get into another argument in front of Gran and Patrick, so I just shrugged my shoulders and went to have a bath. I knew he wouldn't dare to be rude in front of Gran, with Euthanasia curled up on the floor not six feet away, still giving him the occasional glare out of slitted eyes, and growling softly whenever Gran looked the other way. I collected Moses and the latest trashy best-seller from the bedroom, and went to find an hour of peace.

Unfortunately, I had forgotten about the washing machine emptying itself into the bath.

Moses was very cross.

Tim was even crosser.

We ran out of towels.

***

'Well, Fiona, I think it's time we had a little talk.'

I felt a cold shiver race down my spine. All my life, whenever I've heard those words, something dreadful has been coming. Like, your teacher has just noticed you haven't handed in any homework for the entire term. Or your father got your report card. Or your mother discovered that you'd borrowed her pearls. I still shuddered whenever I remembered that. I'd arranged them so carefully back in the box, hoping she'd think when she picked them up that the string had spontaneously broken from old age.

I generally try to get out of it when I hear those words, by saying I'm in a mad hurry to get to church or something, but this time it was Gran, and I knew I didn't have a prayer. Not that it ever works anyway. I sighed inwardly and sat down, ankles neatly crossed, hands folded in my lap. Perhaps if my deportment was really perfect I could offset part of whatever dreadful thing was about to be sprung on me.

'Look here, Fiona, this thing with the marbles just isn't going to work. If one of the other tenants happened to see them, there'd be all kinds of questions asked.'

'What marbles?' I was totally at sea.

Gran sighed and got that patient expression on her face. I hate that patient expression people get, they do it to annoy me. I pretended not to notice it.

'The marbles, Fiona, on the stairs, for killing your husband, remember?'

Oh, those marbles. Right. I looked furtively around to make sure the windows were shut. Perhaps I'd better draw the curtains in case any of the neighbours could lip-read. But we didn't have any curtains.

'Yes. I was thinking about it this morning, after your husband woke me up with his nasty little radio.

I must say, Fiona, he's not a considerate man, is he? You ought to take him firmly in hand. Old people need their sleep, you know.'

'Sorry, Gran. I keep meaning to speak to him about that, he wakes me up with it every morning, but he's always so cross already, it just never seems to be a good time.'

'Well, you're going to have to make it a good time sooner or later, my girl, or make up your mind to be a doormat for the rest of your life. It's very easy to rush around being cross all the time so that nobody ever dares to disagree with you about anything, oh yes. You can get your way practically all the time that way, but it doesn't make you very pleasant to live with, and if people let you get away with it, well the more fools they.'

I sighed and accepted the lecture patiently. What is it about people that they always have to pick on me to lecture? Besides, I thought there was something quite odd about her grammar, but knew better than to say anything. I tried to work it out while she rattled on.

'...leave a mark. So cotton would be better, but I don't think it's strong enough, it would just break. Fiona, do listen. What are you making those silly gestures for?'

I had been trying to work it out; the more fool him? he? the more fools them? I gave up.

'Sorry, Gran. What were you saying?'

'I thought so. You weren't listening at all, were you? Really, Fiona, the least you might do when I'm trying to help you solve your problems is pay attention.'

'Sorry. I will, I mean I am. It's been so...'

Gran shook her stick at me. It was a great nobbly thing, very shiny and glossy. I'd never seen her actually lean on it, she just carried it around to shake at people, and occasionally to poke someone. Really old people get away with murder. I hoped that would be literally true in this case.

'Don't you dare start snivelling, girl, you're not too big for a clout on the ear.'

'Yes, Gran.' I sat up straighter.

'Now, as I was saying, fishing line, black fishing line, is virtually invisible under normal conditions, however if a person were tripped by it, it would almost certainly leave a mark of some kind, possibly even a cut, on the front of the ankle. This might be discovered at a post-mortem, which we want to avoid at all costs. Therefore –'

'Well, that's easy enough, isn't it? We just won't get one.' I was a bit hazy about what happened after a person died, but I was fairly sure a post mortem was part of the burial procedures, an optional part. I'd just tell Tobin Brothers to skip that bit and get on with the cremation. The customer is always right, after all. Perhaps I'd have a big party to celebrate, I could get away with it by calling it a wake. After all, I was half Irish. I wouldn't have Tim on display in his coffin, though.

'I don't think we'll be able to avoid it. When a young man in the prime of his life dies in suspicious circumstances, I rather think there's always a post mortem. To rule out the possibility of Foul Play. So we have to take that into account in our plans. Now, black cotton is also pretty invisible, but not strong enough. So what I was thinking was, if we got several strands of black cotton and plaited them together, we might have something that would be strong enough to trip him but soft enough not to leave a mark.'

'Oh.' I couldn't think of anything to say. I was still a little bit shocked at Gran. I mean, really, it's one thing to sit down over a few drinks with your best friend and your brother, and plan to murder your husband, but it's quite another thing to hear a respectable old lady calmly comparing the merits of fishing line and black cotton as tools of assassination.

'Well, don't sit there gaping like an idiot, girl. We've got to get cracking and do some experiments.'

***

It took me nearly the whole day to plait three lengths of black cotton together. The threads kept getting tangled and I'd have to start again. Gran wouldn't let me have a knot in the middle. By the time I had managed to produce something that would satisfy her, it was after four o'clock and I was just about ready to strangle her with it. Then it was time for my remedial cooking lesson.

***

'Honestly, Gran, I don't see much point in worrying about it at the moment, we still haven't got a fridge.'

'Rubbish, girl. You young people rely far too much on electrical appliances. Now today you're going to learn how to make a decent batch of scones.'

***

The scones were not a success, but Gran quite liked the super-hot Mexican pizza. Once again Tim stayed late at the office, so there were just the three of us. It was a festive occasion, as the refrigerator place had rung up at five o'clock to say that they would bring our fridge back some time tomorrow.

After dinner, I thought I might manage a bit of peace and quiet in the bathroom while Gran and Patrick had another game of whatever had made Tim so cross last night, or watched some television or something.

'Oh, no you don't, my girl. You're not sneaking off to the bathroom again, it's a wonder you haven't washed away down the plughole. It's time for our experiment. Now, you ring up Tim's office and find out what time he's going to be home, we don't want him walking in and seeing anything suspicious.'

'Okay.' I dialled Tim's office. Ring. Ring. Ring.

The telephone rang fifty-seven times before I got the engaged signal.

'It's rung out, there's nobody there.'

Gran looked exasperated.

'Well, of course there's nobody there. I must be getting silly in my old age. We didn't really think he was working late, did we? He'll be out with his mistress, or in bed with her, more likely. Well, that is a problem, now we've got no way of knowing how late he'll be. Patrick'll just have to be a lookout.'

'What d'you mean, a lookout? You mean sit on top of the roof with a spear or something?'

'No, you just go out in the parking lot and keep an eye out for his car. When you see him drive in, you race up here and let us know, and we can get everything out of the way before he finishes parking the car. You can take Euthanasia down with you, then if he catches sight of you you'll have an excuse for being out.'

'What if he doesn't get home till midnight or something?'

'Put on a nice thick sweater.'

ಬCHAPTER TWENTYೞ

...that whatsoever in thy holy Word they
shall profitably learn, they may in deed
fulfil the same.
                    Book of Common Prayer

'Right, let's get cracking. Where's the string?'

'What string?'

'The string you spent all day making, stupid girl.
Really, Fiona, sometimes I wonder if Mary didn't
drop you on your head when you were a baby.
Where is it?'

My head, as usual, was on top of my neck. I
supposed she meant the plaited black cotton. I had
put it away carefully, winding it up neatly so it
wouldn't get tangled. I pointed this out virtuously.

'Yes, yes, but where did you put it? Get it out at

once, how can we do the experiment without the string, you foolish child?' Gran waved her stick at me in a peremptory fashion, although I was getting so used to it that it didn't have much effect.

Fortunately I remembered just then that I'd put it in my jewellery box.

'Calm down, Gran, I'm just getting it. Won't be a sec... damn.'

I should have remembered, I suppose, what happens to things that you put in a jewellery box. Although I had only put the string in there that afternoon, it had already become inextricably tangled with my earrings, chains etc. 'Shit,' I muttered, feverishly trying to get it unstuck. As it always does, this resulted in it becoming so violently tangled that you couldn't even see where to pull.

'Fiona, what in God's name is taking you so long? Can't you even remember where you put it? Dear God, it was only– Oh, for Christ's sake! Of all the stupid places to put it!'

'Well, I thought it was a good place to put it, Tim never looks there.'

'Indeed, for a normal person who keeps her jewellery box in some kind of nice neat order, it wouldn't have been a bad place at all. For you –

really, Fiona, you must know what a mess your things are always in.'

I thought this was a bit hard. I'd always kept my room immaculate, with any mess nicely put out of the way inside drawers, and under the bed. It didn't seem like the time to say so, though, with Gran sitting on my bed patiently untangling the black cotton from a lot of earrings and things that I never wore. I curled up on the other side of the bed. It was amazing how it was always not the right time to say things, I thought, feeling rather annoyed. When was it the right time to say anything, anyway? Perhaps I was too careful of other people's feelings, no-one ever seemed to worry about mine. Perhaps I should just consider myself for a change.

'Fiona, don't you dare go to sleep. Honestly, I have never seen anyone as lazy as you. I really think if you could you'd spend your entire life in the bath and in bed. If you haven't anything to do you can get me a drink while I untangle this.'

I went to get Gran a drink, thinking how much simpler it would be to use the marbles. After all, so what if questions were asked? And we still hadn't found an insurance policy.

***

'Here you go, Gran.' I handed her a glass of sherry.

'What the hell is this?'

'Sherry,' I pointed out reasonably. 'I didn't think you'd want a warm gin and tonic.'

'Sherry, after dinner? Really, Fiona. And what took you so long, may I ask? I've nearly finished untangling this awful mess. What on earth did you do, stir it with a pointed stick?'

'Well, I stopped to have a look in Tim's desk, to see if he's got a life insurance policy. And I found something that might be it. I think.'

'Well, just a moment while I finish the last of this, and we'll see. Get out of my light, Fiona. Go and do the washing up, or something.'

I was a bit stung. Why should Gran automatically assume that I hadn't done the washing up? Not that I had actually done it, not as such, but I had put most of the dishes in the sink, so it was nearly done. Patrick should do it, anyway, it's character building for young people to have responsibilities. I had a look at the thing I'd found. It was quite thick, and all in very tiny print. I couldn't make out much by the light of the mingy forty-watt bulb which was all we had in the room. Hadn't Tim ever heard of lamps, I thought crossly? Didn't he ever read, for heaven's sake? Evidently not, I supposed, since he was never home.

I decided to go downstairs and tell Patrick to come up and do the dishes. I could just as easily keep watch for Tim while he did them.

I was just escaping noiselessly out of the front door when a tremendous roar erupted behind me.

'And just where do you think you're going, Fiona? You get back here and hold the end of this cord.'

I thought it was pitching it a bit strong calling it a cord, you could hardly see it. But what else could you call it? Not a thread, because it was made of several threads, three to be precise. Hardly a rope. A string, perhaps, or –

'Come on, girl, stop shilly-shallying. Here, you hold this end while I pay it out.'

She walked backwards across the sitting room, carefully paying out the – well, whatever it was – until she reached the far wall, where she tied the end of it to the handle of the balcony door.

'Now, just tie your end to something steady, so there's a bit of slack in it. Let's see, we want the middle of it to be at about ankle height.' She looked at me expectantly.

'There isn't anything to tie it to.'

I could tell she was just dying to get into me about shilly-shallying (whatever that was) but there really wasn't anything there, just a blank wall and my new bookcase.

'Well, alright, I'll hold it then. No, don't you move, you'll get it all tangled again, just stay there.'

'Why don't I hold it while you do whatever it is?'

'Oh no, I'm not risking my life. Old bones are brittle, you know.' She glared at me as if I'd just tried to snatch her bag. 'Now, you walk along towards it, and just pretend it isn't there, what we want to see is whether it trips you up.'

'Wait a minute. How can it trip me up? I know it's there.'

'Better shut your eyes, then. If you step over it or something I'll call out. Look, just start over there by the corner, face yourself across the room, shut your eyes and start walking.'

I screwed my eyes shut and shuffled forward a couple of steps, hating it. It's loathsome not being able to see.

'No, no, no! Stop that! Stupid girl!'

I opened my eyes. 'What's the matter?'

'You're shuffling along like a cripple, girl. Is that the way your husband goes down the stairs? God's teeth, if he does I don't see how he's coping with a young piece of fluff. Walk properly, as if you were going somewhere without a care in the world.'

'But what if I fall over it? This isn't a real floor, you know, it's concrete.'

'Tush, girl, what are a few bruises? Where's your sense of adventure?'

In my dreams, I wanted to say, but didn't. I got back into position again. I was just nerving myself up to shut my eyes and walk confidently forward when Moses darted out from underneath the sofa and bit through the string.

***

BANG! BANG! BANG!

'Oh, God!' I whispered, panicked. 'It's the police!'

'Rubbish, girl. What would the police be doing here at nine o'clock at night? They certainly wouldn't come for the cooking.'

Nevertheless, I noticed that Gran was deftly winding up the black string as she spoke.

BANG! THUD!

'Come on, Fiona, let me in, it's freezing out here.' THUD THUD THUD.

'Dear God, it's Patrick! Tim must be back. Oh, help. Hide the thing. Oh, God, where did I put the whatsit?'

'Stop fussing, Fiona, for goodness' sake. You're being sillier than a wet hen.' Gran calmly stuffed the string into her bag and went to the door.

As soon as she opened it, Euthanasia burst through and went into some kind of state, running all over the room and sniffing everything. His little tail was a blur of wagging, but he was making a growling noise in his throat. Finally he got himself into the middle of the room and ran round and round in tiny circles, droning like a jumbo jet on idle. Patrick had slunk into the room looking like a victim of child abuse, and huddled in front of the heater.

'Christ, it's cold out there.'

'Stop it, Patrick, look normal, he'll be here any second.'

'Who?'

'Tim, you deadshit.'

'How d'you know?'

I resisted an impulse to throttle him.

'You were watching for Tim, remember, tiny-brain? You're here, so he's probably on his way up the – Oh, God, quick, get out a board game or something.' I hastily threw myself onto the sofa in an attitude of carefree repose. Gran was already sitting back in the corner chair in her usual attitude of grand and unbending repose, I noticed. For an old lady she's pretty quick on her feet.

'Oh. I didn't come up because of that.'

Gran glared at him scornfully.

'Well, in God's name, why did you come up, then?'

'Well, actually, to tell you that I could hear you both screaming and yelling in the carpark. The neighbours must be in fits. What on earth were you doing?'

'Moses bit through the string. Gran wasn't very happy about it.' I sneaked a look sideways at Gran.

'Humph!'

'Well, and then he sort of bit her. Just in the ankle, you know how he does.'

'Really, Fiona, I do not call being savaged by a Wild Animal being "just sort of bitten".' Gran's voice dripped with outrage. 'I don't know why you don't teach that animal some respect.'

'Well,' I said brightly, hoping to lift the atmosphere. 'It's been a long day, I think I'll be off to bed.'

Amazingly, they let me get away with it.

***

I had second thoughts about the whole thing as I lay in bed listening to the muffled conversation from the sitting room. Tim still hadn't come home, so I had peace to think. Wrapped tightly around Moses, I let my mind range over the events of the day. There had been something I'd meant to think about later. Ah, yes, that was it. It had been when I was shuffling across the sitting room with my eyes screwed shut, waiting to trip over the black string. Suddenly I'd thought, we're testing to see if this would kill Tim. So if I fall over it, it might kill me. That had made the whole thing seem frighteningly, almost disgustingly, real. I don't like things to get too real, they're always nastier when they are. When they do. Anyway, the thing was that I'd made a sort of mental note to myself to think about that when I had more leisure and wasn't in imminent danger of losing my life, and being shouted at by Gran, and things.

So, what was it that had flickered on the edge of my mind in that worrying way? I couldn't think of it at all, probably because I was spiralling gently down into sleep, a natural consequence of lying down in a warm, dark room with a large, purring cat next to me. Of course, you couldn't do much about things if you were asleep, I thought comfortably, in fact...

❧CHAPTER TWENTY-ONE☙

...assist with thy blessing these two persons, that they may both be fruitful in procreation of children...
Book of Common Prayer

I stretched out on the sofa, revelling in the beautiful sensation of being utterly alone, except for Moses, of course. Patrick had gone back to school and Gran had beetled off to the city to do shopping, taking Euthanasia with her. She had wanted me to come with her, but with visions of standing around for hours while Gran satisfied herself yet again that nobody makes linen sheets any more, I had hastily invented a headache. Encouraged by Gran's instant concern, I had elaborated the headache into a slight queasiness of the stomach.

'Of course, it's much too early to be sure yet...' I had murmured demurely, making myself blush, which is a thing I do rather well. For once I had got away with it, a further cause for celebration. I only hoped she wouldn't dash straight around to my parents' place and start ringing up half of Australia. Or at least that, if she did, no-one would tell Tim.

I looked idly around the room, planning the changes I would make. Some of those nice little palm trees in the corners, perhaps? We'd never had indoor plants at home, my mother thought they were unhygienic. But Moses might enjoy lurking around behind them, he'd always had a garden before. The glass coffee table would have to go, of course. I'd donate it to the Salvation Army. And the sofa... well, perhaps if I just got one of those loose covers in a nice chintzy floral? Then I wouldn't have the bother of buying new furniture, and the cover could come off and be washed when Moses shed hairs on it. Peach and a nice soft yellow, I decided, would be the main colours. With pale green cushions. On the other hand, perhaps blue and lavender...

Loud knocking interrupted my contemplation and I jumped guiltily. I carefully checked that the document I'd found last night was tucked out of sight under the sofa cushions and opened the door. I had given up trying to see anything through the little hole.

There were two suspicious-looking men in grey

overalls, and a refrigerator. My refrigerator! I was so overcome with joy I could hardly speak.

***

'Jesus, Mary and Joseph, what's going on at all?'

'Is that you, Gloria?'

'No, Fiona, it's the bloody Aga Khan in drag.'

I thought that was a bit unfair. I couldn't see out very well because the refrigerator was stuck in the doorway. The two men had been puffing and wheezing for half an hour with no discernible result. One of them was inside and the other was outside; I reflected uneasily that I was trapped in my apartment with a maniac. On the other hand, I could always leap to safety over the balcony. We were only on the second floor and there were earth and wood chips in the courtyard; I was sure the drop wouldn't kill me.

'So what are you doing with the fridge sitting in the doorway? It's a bit inconvenient, I'd have thought.'

'Don't be an arsehole, Gloria, you can see it's stuck.'

'But that's just stupid, it came out of that door so it must go in, if it's the same fridge. Look, you there, move your side around to the left so that it's lined up straight. No, left, left, your other left. Left, dickbrain. Right, now just slowly... No left, you moron. When I said right I meant... LEFT, LEFT, dickhead!'

Gloria obviously had things under control, so I left her to it and went to put on a fresh pot of coffee. It was really amazing how she was able to reduce chaos into order, a bit like a steamroller passing over rubble and leaving behind a nice, smooth, uniform surface. Presently the refrigerator arrived into the kitchen in a slow and stately fashion and took up its rightful place in the corner. In its wake came Gloria, who for some reason was wearing a power suit and carrying a briefcase. Being Gloria, though, she had added four-inch heels in scarlet patent leather.

Being Gloria, she got right down to business.

'So, have you found it?'

'Found what?'

'Tim's life insurance, what else? Surely you must have finished going through his desk by now, haven't you? Or is the old lady watching your every move? What you need is a pencil torch, then you can do it at night while everyone's asleep.'

'I can't, if I get out of bed in the night Tim wakes up and gets upset. I can just about manage a quick trip to the loo, but if it's any longer he comes out and gets really shitty.' Anyway, I thought, when everyone's asleep then I'm asleep too, aren't I? Gloria can be quite thick about things sometimes. I refrained from pointing this out.

'Anyway, I found something that might be it, but I'm not sure.'

'What d'you mean, not sure? How can you not be sure? Either it's a life insurance policy or it isn't.'

'Well, it doesn't have Life Insurance Policy stamped on the front in big red letters, you know. That's not the way they do things.'

I felt I had scored a point.

'Well, let's have a look at it.'

I retrieved the document from its hiding place under the sofa cushions. It was a bit creased, I hoped I'd be able to replace it without Tim noticing. I handed it to Gloria and got ready to snatch out the coffee pot between spurts.

Gloria whistled softly.

'My God, Fiona.' Her voice was hushed and reverent.

'What? What is it?'

'Just listen to this. Life insured, Timothy Charles Cedric Alfred Pinkpank.' She paused for the obligatory snigger.

'Policy owner, Timothy Charles Cedric Alfred Pinkpank. One Point Five Million dollars sum insured, plus savings bonuses attaching, is paid on death of Timothy Charles Cedric Alfred Pinkpank.' She didn't snigger.

'What are savings bonuses?'

'Jesus, Fiona, I don't know, who the hell cares? The point is that the policy's here, and it's for a frigging million and a half bucks! You're set for life! Christ, all you have to do is knock the fucker on the head and you're laughing all the way to the bank!'

A shiver ran down my spine. I wasn't used to thinking about large amounts of money. My annual salary at Marsh and Spacknall had been on the cold side of forty-five thousand. Well on the cold side. Of course, we used to report on companies with annual sales figures in the millions, but that wasn't the same thing as real money at all, more like playing Monopoly. I hadn't a clue how much money a million actually was.

'Gloria? How much money is that, actually?'

'Jesus, Fiona. What the hell sort of question is

that? At all,' she added as a kind of afterthought. 'Half a million dollars is five hundred thousand dollars, plus a million, so fifteen hundred thousand, that's how much money it is. It's like asking how many beans make five. God, Fiona, sometimes I really worry about you.'

'Yes, I know that, but how much is it? I mean, you have a sort of gut feeling about how much twenty dollars is, you know you can go to the movies with it, or buy a paperback novel, or three pairs of pantyhose... it's got a sort of real value, you know?'

'Oh. Well, if you invested it at, say, five percent, you'd have an income of seventy-five thousand a year. At ten percent you'd have a hundred and fifty thousand a year. I mean, it's private income sort of money, that's what it is. Or you could, I don't know, well you could buy a shop that was a going concern, and still have plenty left over, if you wanted to have a shop, you could live on the profits and stuff.' Gloria wound down rather lamely. I thought she was a bit overawed by the amount herself.

'The thing that's really important about amounts like this, Fiona, is the danger of it.'

'What danger? You mean from fortune hunters?'

'It ruins people. I did a story on it last year. A lot

of these people that win first division Tatts, they get sort of carried away. The people I did the story on won about three million, so they chucked in their jobs, there were two of them, they had good secure jobs with the government, and they moved up to Queensland and got one of those huge palaces built by one of those Glen Gelding sort of companies, the sort of thing you see in those Art Union raffles, with a jacuzzi in every bedroom, you know? What your dad calls a triumph of money over taste. Then they bought a fanging great expensive car, I think it was a Porsche. No, that's right, they bought two cars. All this they paid for with cash, and that pretty well took care of the money they'd won. So they moved into this Gelding mansion, with no jobs, and pretty soon they were broke. Then the house started to sink, it was built on a swamp. They had to move out, the house was condemned and never mind getting their money back on it, they couldn't give it away. They couldn't get jobs up there, things had started to get tight in the economy by that time, and they ended up selling both cars. When I interviewed them last year, they were on the dole and living in a caravan park. They cursed the day they bought the winning ticket. Reckoned it had pretty well ruined their lives.'

I was silent for a moment, digesting this. I didn't really see how it applied to me. For one thing, I didn't have a driver's license, so I couldn't very well be tempted to buy expensive cars. For another, I loathe housing estates. I didn't have a job to lose, either. It seemed to me that I didn't have any particular worries, I could just buy a nice little house, put the rest of the money in the bank, and maybe get a part time job, one that didn't start too early in the morning.

'So, look, anyway, it doesn't matter. The important thing is that we've found the policy and Tim really does have life insurance, so we can just get on with killing him.'

Somehow it didn't sound like so much fun when she put it like that. I suddenly remembered what had been bothering me the other night – it had been when Gran and I were experimenting with the plaited cotton and it had occurred to me that I could be injured by falling over it on the concrete floor. I had had a sudden vision of Tim, broken and dead at the bottom of the stairs.

It really wasn't a game.

I thought about succeeding in murdering Tim. I thought about waking up every morning with the knowledge that I was a murderer. I remembered my confirmation classes, and someone bringing up the question of why murder is wrong, aside from the fact that it's in the Ten Commandments. Father Simpson had said that in case the person has led a sinful life, and might have repented and obtained salvation in the future, the murderer took upon themselves the guilt of denying him the opportunity of repentance and forcing him to die in his sins. Tim certainly was in a state of mortal sin, I thought, and I was very, very displeased with him, but did I really want to condemn him to everlasting torment in Hell? Of course, I could settle the state of my own soul easily enough by going to confession. But would the priest make me give myself up to the police? I didn't really know, but surely Father Simpson wouldn't be so strict. I could always leave confessing until I was on my deathbed, but then what if I got killed suddenly in a hit-and-run accident? I'd go straight to Hell for sure. No, I would really have to go to confession as soon as I'd done the deed.

Of course, even if Father Simpson didn't make me give myself up, there was the issue of getting caught. I was pretty sure the police would take a dim view of killing one's husband whatever he'd been up to, so that if I got caught I might easily go to jail for years and years. Look at Mrs Chamberlain, I thought uncomfortably, she'd been in prison for ten years or something before she got let out, and nobody even knew if she'd really done anything. I thought about Moses growing old and dying, listening every night for the sound of my footsteps coming up the path, waiting at the window, crying each morning when he woke up in an empty bed. He'd never know why I'd deserted him.

I realised Gloria was shouting at me.

'...sit there staring into space with your mouth open for hours and then suddenly start snivelling! For Christ's sake, Fiona, get with it!'

'I can't do it, Gloria.'

'Of course you can, just get a grip on yourself and pull yourself together. Jesus, Mary and Joseph!'

'No, I mean I can't do it. We can't do it. It's wrong.'

'What's wrong?'

'Killing Tim, it's murder.'

'Suffering saints, you can't just change your mind now.'

'Why not? I can if I want to.'

'But we agreed, Fiona, it's the ideal solution. If you don't kill him, you're back to square one with all the same problems you had before.'

'I don't care. I'm not doing it.'

I felt a strong urge to burst into tears again, but

restrained myself. Gloria was looking dangerously close to losing her temper, and when that happened you couldn't rule out the possibility of violence.

'Look, Fiona, we've got it all worked out. We've all put a lot of effort into this. You can't go round getting all ready to kill someone and then just suddenly say you're not doing it.'

She didn't know the half of it, I reflected uneasily. What was Gran going to say when I announced that I'd had second thoughts and all her experiments were going to be wasted?

✇CHAPTER TWENTY-TWO✇

For this cause shall a man leave his father and mother, and shall be joined unto his wife; and they two shall be one flesh.

Book of Common Prayer

Gran didn't get home till nearly six, and she looked very tired. I gathered that Euthanasia, left outside David Jones, had taken violent exception to the window display, and had subsequently threatened a busker. It didn't seem the moment to upset her further with my change of heart. I'd tell her tomorrow, when she'd had a good night's sleep, I decided.

For once, Tim was home in time for dinner. He was in a reasonably good mood, too, which was further improved when he saw the refrigerator. We all sat down to dinner in as much of a happy family atmosphere as one could hope for, under the circumstances.

This lasted about ten minutes.

'How come you're here for dinner, Cedric? Has your ever-lovin' Kathy-Wathy got a headache?'

My blood froze. Besides having said almost exactly the same thing the last time Tim had been home for dinner, Patrick was now quoting directly from one of those sloppy love-letters we'd found in Tim's desk. He was bound to give the game away, I thought in agony. If Tim found out I'd been snooping through his desk drawers, he'd be bound to suspect I was onto his affair with The Bimbo, and if he mentioned that to anybody else, then when I murdered him I'd be the number one suspect. I kicked Patrick vigorously under the table.

'Ow, that hurt. You bi–'

He froze in his place. From the slitty-eyed look Gran was giving him I gathered she'd kicked his other shin.

'Oh. Um. Sorry, it must have been Euthanasia. Here, old boy, have a piece of steak.'

Euthanasia was not under the table, but fortunately Moses was. It would have been embarrassing to have the floor covered with pieces of meat when we all got up. Fortunately in my family there's very little chance of that ever happening, although I do remember one time when my mother had got onto some health kick and made the most disgusting meat loaf. It was quite awful, just like a kind of medicinal dog food, and both Patrick and I had fed most of it to Moses under the table. He must have not wanted to be impolite, because he had taken everything he was given, but when the cloth was removed the entire floor was covered in spat-out pieces of it. I couldn't convince our mother that it was Manna, either.

Anyway, I didn't have to worry about that here, I comforted myself. There was no way Tim would remain in the kitchen long enough to see the cloth removed, there might be washing up in it. Sure enough, as soon as the last fork went down he was swooping at me and thanking me for a delicious meal, as if he were a dinner guest, and two seconds later we heard the computer starting up.

Gran and Patrick stayed in the kitchen to help me with the washing up.

'I was thinking about grease,' my grandmother said out of the side of her mouth, like a prisoner in one of those Alcatraz movies.

'Yes, well, I generally soak the pots overnight, it's easier that way.' I knew my mother would have had fits, but what's the point of scrubbing when you can soak?

'Fiddlesticks, girl. I'm talking about the stairs.'

'Well, it's not like that in flats, Gran. You just look after your own flat and then a little man comes once a month and does the common bits. That's all included in the rent.'

'No, no, no. I mean, what about spilling a pot full of grease down the stairs, late at night?'

'Well, I suppose you'd have to clean that up yourself, unless he was coming the next day or something. Why would you, anyway?'

'Sssssssssssssst!'

I turned around to see what Patrick was doing. Gran poked me in the ribs with a fork.

'Ow! What'd you do that for?'

Patrick was making frantic gestures. A second later Tim poked his head around the door.

'Can I help you with anything, darling?'

The patent insincerity made me want to vomit. He'd made damn sure we had the washing up well started before he stepped foot near the kitchen.

'Oh, no, darling, you go and rest. You've had a hard day at work.' Behind Tim's back Patrick grabbed his crotch and made obscene thrusting motions, dancing up and down with his tongue out and his eyes crossed. As soon as Tim turned away I tried to quell him with a look. It was a pointless exercise, though. People have been trying to quell Patrick with looks for fourteen years. Most people only try once.

Tim got a Coke out of the refrigerator and went away. We all relaxed. God knew why, we hadn't been talking about anything private. I wondered why Gran was suddenly so interested in the cleaning arrangements of the building.

'Well, that's the lot.' I handed Gran the last fork and pulled out the plug. She looked at me with horror.

'What about the pots?'

'Well, I always just fill them up with hot water and leave them to soak. That way, it's a lot easier to wash them.' I didn't see any reason to mention that usually I left all the washing up till the next day anyway. Old people fret so, and I was mindful of the fact that I already had one piece of upsetting news to break to Gran. Although she hadn't mentioned anything about our murder plans since she'd got home from shopping. Perhaps she'd forgotten all about it, in which case it wouldn't be necessary to tell her anything. I could just let the whole unsavoury business slide gently into oblivion. Yes, that would be best. Just never mention it again. I shook my head and reached for the coffee-pot. Imagine washing up before the coffee. Really, old people could be such a pain.

I measured the grounds and started the coffee, ignoring Gran who had pointedly run another sink full of water and was banging away at the saucepans. I wasn't going to let her make me feel like an inferior housewife. If it amused her to scrub things, I was sure I could find plenty more for her to do. Like the patch under the fridge, for instance. I had meant to give it a good scrub before the fridge went back into position, but somehow I had never quite got around to it. Of course, I had been living under a great strain recently, I reminded myself. A house full of relatives at the same time as an adulterous husband would probably have upset even Mrs Beeton.

In fact, I reflected as I curled up on the sofa, I had coped with it all remarkably well. A lot of people would have panicked when confronted with this situation, but I had kept my head and remained calm and in control of the situation at all times.

'...off in never-never land again. Honestly, Fiona, sometimes I worry about you. I've been speaking to you for the last five minutes.'

'Oh, sorry Gran, what did you say?'

'Patrick is going to come out and help me take Euthanasia for a walk. You'd better come too, I'm quite sure you haven't had a breath of fresh air all day, lying around sleeping and sitting in the bath. I don't think these flats are a healthy way to live. Come along, get your coat.'

I shuddered. I could hardly think of anything I wouldn't rather do than drag around Albert Park Lake in the middle of the night in the dark, with Euthanasia leaping in and out of the water and covering everyone with slime.

'You go ahead, Gran. I've got some ironing I want to do.'

'Oh, alright, please yourself. But I still think a nice brisk walk...'

Her voice tailed away down the stairs, counterpointed by Euthanasia's clicking toenails and Patrick sycophantically agreeing with her. What a little sleaze-bag he was.

I sighed and looked at my husband. He was absorbed in his computer and didn't notice me watching him. I couldn't remember ever really looking at him like that before, when he was concentrating on something else. He probably didn't even know I was in the room, and somehow because of this he looked different, smaller and more weedy. What I had been accustomed to think of as elegant slenderness now revealed itself as a puny lack of muscle development, probably resulting from cowardice on the playing fields as a boy. His head was definitely too big for his body and his posture was extremely bad, I now noticed with surprise. Another thing I'd never noticed before was how funny his casual clothes always were. Every night when he got home from the office, unless it was so late that he was going straight to bed, he immediately changed out of his suit, and his casual clothes all seemed to be bigger versions of what children wear. Why had I never noticed this before? Probably, I thought, because when we'd been dating I didn't see him in his casual stuff very often. Usually we were going out somewhere, and he'd either be in his business suit or, if it was at the weekend, smart sports clothes not all that different from what I was used to seeing my father wear. Now I wondered if all that had been an act put on to impress me.

Suddenly I noticed that Tim had got up from his desk and was coming towards me with an amorous look in his eyes. Horrors, surely he wouldn't want to...

'Well, thank God we've finally got some time to

ourselves.'

Oh, yuk. Frantically I cast about for an escape.

'Um, Tim, I think I will go with Gran and Patrick after all. I can just about catch them up if I hurry. I'm afraid they might get mugged...' Desperately I hunted around for my jacket. Keep talking, that was the thing.

'Christ! You're never in the fucking mood, are you? You think more of that fucking smelly cat than you do of me.'

'No, I don't, Tim, don't be silly.' I had found my jacket behind the sofa. Were my keys in the pocket? I felt frantically around all the pockets, discovering three tissues, a few toffee papers and an old tram ticket.

'Christ! You're not even fucking listening to me, are you? I'm standing here talking to you, and you're rummaging around hauling tat out of your fucking pockets.'

It was a bit like a litany the way Tim started all his sentences with 'Christ!'.

'Oh, God, come to our aid,' I murmured reflectively. This seemed to goad Tim to an absolute white-hot rage. Perhaps he was in the service of the Evil One and couldn't bear to hear prayers. It seemed a bit far-fetched, but I made a sign my grandmother had taught me against the Evil Eye, just in case, and got out of there fast, having remembered that Patrick had the spare key and so I had given mine to Gran that morning.

***

They hadn't actually said which way they were going, but I assumed they would have gone over to the lake since they only had to cross the road. The problem was which way they had set off around the lake. If I went in the other direction I might not find them for hours. It takes over an hour to walk around Albert Park Lake, I knew because I had done it once, for a bet.

I started off in a clockwise direction around the lake, on the principle that it was farther away from the highway and therefore a more attractive walk. Sure enough, before long I caught the sound of their voices carrying across the water.

'...the grease. It looks so natural, and even if they suspected, nobody could ever prove a thing.'

'Yeah, but Gran, it's just the same as the marbles, I mean they're bound to wonder where this great lot of grease came from, and that.'

'Young man, just pull up your socks and stop

murdering the King's English. There is absolutely no need to add the words "and that" at the end of every sentence. And there won't be any need for anyone to wonder anything, you're missing the whole beautiful simplicity of it.'

I was fascinated. I wondered if I could sneak up on them around the edge of the lake. I walked a bit faster, trying to keep as quiet as I could.

Patrick said something in a low voice, which I missed, and Gran continued in her old, carrying, beautifully enunciated voice.

'This is where we take advantage of as much of the truth as possible in order to create a really artistic lie. Goodness knows I've explained these things to you often enough, Patrick. In this case, the fact of which everyone who knows her is well aware, is that your sister is extremely clumsy. She's always dropping things, and it will therefore be no surprise to anyone when she drops a saucepan full of cooking oil on the stairs.'

'Well, it sort of will, a bit. I mean, what's she doing on the stairs with a big pot of oil?'

'Ah, that's where the diabolical cunning of it comes in. You must have heard me warning Fiona about putting grease and oil down the drains. Everybody knows how it can clog them up, and since

I've just been staying with her and giving her a few little pointers on household management, it's only natural that she would be carrying it out to dispose of it harmlessly.'

'As if it were nuclear waste.' Patrick giggled.

'Quite. You must admit the whole thing is very plausible. After all, that's Fiona all over, isn't it? Something goes wrong, her first impulse is to cover it up, no matter how innocent it is. The girl is naturally furtive.'

I couldn't believe my ears. Me, furtive! How dared she? I slipped back behind a tree. I had been planning to overtake them and join them on their walk, but I certainly didn't want Gran knowing I'd heard her saying all that about me. I'd wait a few minutes, and then jog along and overtake them as if I'd only just come out.

I never quite figured out what happened next. One minute I was standing firmly under a young poplar tree, listening to the receding voices of my traitorous and ignoble relatives and fuming at their unfair remarks, and the next minute I was immersed in freezing, stinking, slimy water, with no idea at all how I'd got there. I suppose it's possible that some creepy character was lurking about in the bushes and pushed me in. Or perhaps there was a tiny landslide on the edge of the lake. In any case, before I really knew what was happening or could get my feet under me, someone had me, rather painfully, by one arm, and was pulling me firmly to the edge.

It was some time before I was able to get up. For one thing, I had swallowed some of the filthy lake water and was being sick. For another, Euthanasia was so pleased with himself for having rescued me from drowning, that every time I tried to get up he leaped on me and knocked me down again. In between this, he was jumping back and forth over the top of me, apparently expressing his jubilation at a job well done.

I prefer to draw a veil over the remarks made by my brother and grandmother on the way back to the flat.

There was one good thing about it, though. When Tim saw me stagger in the door, festooned with slime and dripping lake water, he went right off the idea of sex.

&CHAPTER TWENTY-THREE&

Those whom God has joined together let
no man put asunder.
                    Book of Common Prayer

By the time I'd finally satisfied myself that the last trace of lake slime had gone from my person, everyone was asleep. Not that I was really completely satisfied, but there was no more hot water, and Moses was running out of patience, and kept leaning over the edge of the bath and raking at my hair with his claws. I had refilled the bath three times, scrubbing the tub in between, and used an entire bottle of gardenia flavoured bath crystals. I sniffed suspiciously at one arm. Was there a lingering trace of swamp? I shuddered. Perhaps it was in my imagination, after all the water had been very cold and I might well have caught a fever. I was sure there was some connection between fever and swamps. I'd better take my temperature before I went to bed, I decided. Then I'd know the worst.

I knew there had been a thermometer somewhere in the stuff I'd packed up from home.

***

...blah blah blah always fucking waking me up blah blah blah in the middle of the fucking night blah blah blah why can't you do anything like a normal person blah blah blah have to get up in the morning blah blah blah haven't even ironed a fucking shirt blah blah blah socks blah blah blah fill up the house with all your fucking indigent relatives blah blah blah sexual deviates blah blah blah SLAM.

***

This left me at even more of a loose end, as I now had no idea where I could sleep. Tim had slammed the door to our bedroom so definitively that I just didn't dare open it. Not that I'm a coward, of course, but if Gran and Patrick had managed to sleep through his outburst I didn't want to risk waking them up with another dose of it. And tense situations are always so upsetting for Moses, they tend to make him spray. Fortunately Moses had been on the outside of the door.

'Patrick? Are you awake? Patrick!'

'Mmmmmmff. What? For God's sake, what?'

'I said, are you awake?'

'Well, I am now.'

'Move over.'

'Why?'

'Never mind, just move, I'm getting in at the other end.'

'No way, you're not sticking your feet in my face all night. What's wrong, had a tiff with Lover Boy?'

'He's shut me out of the bedroom. Move over.'

'I can't move over, God, it's only a sofa. What are you doing, rack off, there's no room.'

'Yes there is, I'm freezing.'

By wriggling and pushing and a bit of discreet elbow work, I managed to get almost enough room on the sofa for Moses and me to be comfortable. One of Patrick's feet seemed to be wedged into my left ear, but at least it was warm. Moses wasn't too thrilled, but settled down after considerable grumbling and walking round and round on my stomach a few million times, digging in his claws.

***

I dreamed that I was back home and everything was alright. In the dream, my mother and I were making a batch of chocolate chip cookies. Sun streamed in through the window, and Moses sat on the corner of the kitchen table, washing his face and purring. Then Patrick came in from school, and we took the biscuits out of the oven. The dream wasn't very exciting, not at all like my usual ones, but it had such a flavour of peace and quiet happiness. Naturally, when I woke up and found myself back in Tim's flat, scrunched up on the sofa, with Tim shaking my shoulder and glaring into my face from six inches away, I burst into tears.

***

By the time I got Tim out of the door, it was time for Patrick to get up for school. I wondered wearily if I would ever have five minutes to think about how I would get myself out of this dreadful situation. That's the trouble with dreadful situations, they take up all your time just coping, so that you can't think straight enough to plan your way out. I knew I desperately needed what Patrick had called a Quality Solution, but I was so tired, and things kept cropping up. Like Tim, who'd shaken me rudely awake at the crack of dawn. He had looked as if he were about to start shouting at me again, but when I'd started crying, he had insisted on having one of those frightful Deep and Meaningful conversations in the kitchen. Really I'd have rather he'd shouted, it's far less draining, and you don't have to listen all the time. This particular Deep and Meaningful was about Our Relationship (aren't they all?) and went on for an hour and a half. By the time Tim looked at his watch in horror and scuttled out of the door, I was starting to think perhaps I'd murder him after all.

Patrick was cross and sleepy and didn't want to go to school, which isn't all that far out of the norm. I made him coffee and soothed him with the reminder that there was only one more day till the weekend. What I actually felt like doing was clouting him, but I was grateful to him for letting me have half the sofa, so I restrained myself heroically.

By the time I got Patrick out of the door, Gran was up and demanding coffee and bowls of milk for Euthanasia. My life seemed to have become an endless procession of people with their wants, I thought dismally, as I hunted around for a big enough bowl. No doubt as soon as Gran was taken care of, someone else would magically pop up, demanding something else. I was still in my dressing gown and hadn't had any coffee; every time I'd made a move towards the coffee machine during our Deep and Meaningful, Tim had accused me of not Taking It Seriously, which I suppose I wasn't, but as it was evidently a Bad Thing, I felt obliged to pretend that I was.

Thank God, I thought, as Euthanasia dived head first into a mixing bowl full of cornflakes and milk, there wasn't really anybody else left to hassle me. I poured two mugs of wonderful, vibrant, wholesome, radiant coffee, and sank gratefully into a chair.

I had the cup halfway to my mouth, and was basking in the wonderful smell, when Moses jumped on the table, yelling about injustice. By the time I had him settled down with a plate of Snappy Tom, Gran was ready for a refill. I began to understand why women at home with several children have that harried look in their eyes, and dubious colour co-ordination.

It was obviously not a good time to explain to Gran that I'd changed my mind about killing my husband. It's always a mistake to get into any kind of difficult conversation when one's not dressed. This was probably why I hadn't been able to avoid the Deep and Meaningful, I mused. When you're in your dressing gown, with your hair tangled and a temperature probably coming on, and the other person is all freshly showered and suited and dripping with cologne, well you're just putty in their hands, aren't you?

***

It was just as well I hadn't said anything, I reflected as we coaxed Euthanasia onto the number 67 tram.

When Gran got it into her mind to Go Shopping, it was best not to complicate things any further.

'Um, Gran?'

'Yes, dear?'

'What are we going shopping for, exactly?'

'A chip fryer.'

I was silent for a moment, digesting this. I had often stayed at Gran's house in the country, and I didn't think I'd ever eaten chips there. Come to think of it, I'd never had them at home, either. In my family, potatoes are either boiled or roasted. Chips were something you had at take-away places; I doubted if my mother had ever seen one. What was a chip fryer, anyway? Surely Gran wasn't going to buy one of those great tank things they have in fish shops.

'What are you going to do with it?'

Gran shot me a look of utter loathing and contempt.

'Stupid girl! What does one do with them?'

To which there seemed to be no adequate answer. I looked out of the window all the way to the city, while Euthanasia growled warningly at the tram driver.

***

I was expecting to go through the city to some northern industrial type suburb where one bought fish shop equipment, but we got off at Bourke Street as usual. Gran headed confidently down the mall, with Euthanasia bustling importantly ahead of her, clearing a way through the crowd.

Now one place I do know my way around is the Bourke Street Mall. You can buy most things there, including jeans, jewellery, scent, cosmetics and all kinds of household things from David Jones. You can get books in Myers, although it's better to go around the corner to Bookworld or across the street to Collins or Angus & Robertson. You can't really get pet shop things, but you can get just about anything else you might want.

But I was absolutely sure you couldn't get one of those big oil tank things they have in fish shops.

So I couldn't really see why we were going into David Jones.

'Um, Gran?'

'For Heaven's sake, Fiona, must you say "um" before every sentence? You don't have a cleft palate as far as I know.'

'What are we going into David Jones for? You can't get a chip thing here.'

'In the first place, Fiona, *we* are not going into David Jones. *I* am going into David Jones, and you and Euthanasia will wait for me outside. In the second place, I am quite confident that I will be able to buy a chip fryer here, and if I can't, then we'll go over the road to Billy Guyatt's.'

'But what d'you want it for?' I wailed despairingly. I was eaten up with curiosity. Was she going to convert it into a Japanese bath? Store old shoes in it? God knew she was capable of anything.

She looked at me as though I were mad.

'It's for you, Fiona. So that you can cook chips for your husband.'

'But I don't have any chips – I mean any husband – I mean –'

Gran fixed me with a steely glare.

'Tonight, Fiona, you will cook chips for your husband. And you will continue to cook chips for your husband, on a regular basis, for as long as it takes.'

'But why? As long as what takes?'

'I'll explain later, it's too public here. You look after Euthanasia, buy him an ice cream if he gets restless.'

She disappeared into David Jones without a backward glance.

'Chips!' I muttered disgustedly to Euthanasia. 'Why on earth chips?'

There's no explaining the behaviour of old people.

***

Euthanasia and I were both getting pretty bored by the time Gran emerged from David Jones. She was carrying a large square box in a David Jones bag, which she handed to me.

'Here, Fiona, this is for you.'

For a wild moment I thought she'd bought me a present to cheer me up. Could it be the new perfume, that I'd been lusting after some of for months? If it was it must be the huge bottle. The box was about the size of four shoe boxes put together, perhaps a bit larger. I ripped it open.

Disappointment struck me like a blow. The box contained some kind of foreign electrical appliance.

Fortunately, I have been Carefully Brought Up, and therefore knew exactly what to say.

'Gosh, thanks, Gran. Just what I wanted! Um... what is it?'

❧CHAPTER TWENTY-FOUR☙

*At which day of Marriage, if any man do
alledge and declare any impediment,
why they may not be coupled together in
Matrimony, by God's Law, or the Laws
of this Realm; and will be bound, and
sufficient sureties with him, to the
parties; or else put in a Caution (to the
full value of such charges as the persons
to be married do thereby sustain) to
prove his allegation: then the
solemnization must be deferred, until
such time as the truth be tried.*

Book of Common Prayer

'Now you are just going to sit down here,
Fiona, and listen. Don't say anything, just
listen. Alright?'

'Can I have some raisin toast?'

Gran compressed her lips at me. I hate it when

people do that, as if you were some kind of annoying moron and they had to be patient with you. It was so unfair, too, after all I hadn't had any breakfast, what with feeding the multitudes and being dragged out shopping at the crack of dawn. Who, I asked myself, had had to stand around for nearly an hour in the Bourke Street mall, buying ice creams for a dog the size of a house and trying to find somewhere inoffensive to put the sticks? I had been attacked by some Greenie woman for keeping one of Nature's dumb beasts on a chain, and pointing out that I was just minding him for someone else only brought on a flood of recriminations for feeding him ecologically unsound snacks. I couldn't see, myself, what was so harmful about a packet of corn chips. I had also broken two of my fingernails when Euthanasia took exception to a blind man playing a didgeridoo. God knew what he'd get up to while we were in here having coffee, Gran had left him tied up to a post. I wondered why she couldn't have done that before.

There was a sort of uncomfortable silence until the waitress brought our coffee and my raisin toast, broken once or twice by Gran nagging at me not to fiddle with the little bags of sugar.

'Right, now listen, Fiona. And pay attention, are you paying attention?'

I couldn't say anything as I had my mouth full

of toast. I nodded frantically.

'Well, I just hope you are for once. Now, we already established that fishing line, black cotton and marbles are all out of the running, didn't we?'

Had we? I wasn't sure. Actually I thought the marbles were still quite a viable idea. I was about to say so when I remembered that I no longer wanted to murder my husband. I shut my mouth again quickly.

'What is the matter with you, Fiona, gaping like a fish? Drink your coffee and shut up.'

It was a bit much telling me to shut up, I thought. She never let me get a word in to say anything.

'Right. So, having eliminated fishing line, black cotton and marbles, what are we left with?'

Well, I thought, nearly everything, really. But Gran was obviously wanting a specific answer. I took a stab in the dark.

'Um, an axe?'

'An axe? For God's sake, Fiona, have you been listening to a word I've said? If you eliminate black cotton, marbles and fishing line, what's left?'

'Well, I don't see what's wrong with an axe.'

Gran glared at me, breathing heavily.

'And can you explain, Fiona, from the depths of your undoubtedly towering intelligence, just how we are going to use an axe to make someone fall down a flight of stairs?'

'Well, you could hit him in the head with it.'

'Ah, of course! Don't know why I didn't think of that myself, I must be getting senile. You hit him in the head with the axe, shove him down the stairs, and then at the inquest no doubt they'll conclude that he fell down the stairs from having a dizzy spell, and landed head-first on top of the axe which just happened to be lying about at the bottom of the stairs. Wonderful, Fiona. I can see you're an accomplished criminal. Nobody would suspect a thing.'

'Well, I only meant there are lots of ways to kill a person, not just black fishing line and stuff. There's poison, and fatal cultures of deadly diseases and things.' I still rather liked that idea, although not catching bubonic plague or whatever yourself after you'd infected them was a problem I hadn't yet managed to solve. Perhaps you could get vaccinated first.

'Fiona, you are without doubt the most exasperating person I have ever known. We were talking about having him fall down the stairs, weren't we? Remember, we'd already agreed that that was the most effective and least suspicious way to do the job. So, what other things are there that make a person fall down stairs?'

Being pushed, I wanted to say, but didn't dare. Still, I had to say something.

'Um, an epileptic fit?'

Gran glared at me disbelievingly.

'Fiona, tell me this. Do you want to kill your husband or not?'

Ah, at last, the perfect moment to tell her. I didn't let the moment pass me by, either. I was ready to seize the opportunity.

'Well, as a matter of fact, Gran, since you mention it, there's something I've been –'

'Right. And you're damned lucky to have me helping you to do it. Now, since you're obviously too busy devouring toast to think clearly, I will tell you the fourth, and ideal, solution to the problem. It is grease!'

'Grease?'

'Think, Fiona! How many times have you been

warned in your life to watch your step on slippery surfaces? There's nothing more dangerous than spilling grease on a concrete staircase.'

'Oh.'

'Now this is where the chip fryer comes in.'

'Oh, yes, you were saying this morning you wanted to buy one. Hadn't we better go and do that, before the shops shut?'

For a nasty moment I thought Gran was going to have a seizure. Whatever that is. When she spoke, it was through clenched teeth.

'Fiona. I have just spent one hundred and ninety-nine dollars and ninety-five cents buying you a chip fryer. Have the goodness to remember this fact for at least a few minutes.'

So that was what it was. I seemed to remember asking her that when I opened it, but she'd been so cross, and marched me off into this dim little cafe, and never actually said.

'Sorry, Gran.' That's the thing about old people, you always end up having to apologise whenever they've done something stupid.

The other thing about old people is that they have extremely short tempers.

***

Presently I got Gran calmed down. While she was sniffing at her smelling salts, I managed to order some more raisin toast. What was it, I wondered, about my family? Nobody seemed to recognise the importance of a good breakfast, and they were always rushing about getting into a fury and pretending to have heart attacks. I wondered if I'd suddenly get the urge to rush out and buy smelling salts when I turned forty.

'Now, Fiona, try to concentrate. I have bought you this chip thing so that you can make chips every night for your disgusting husband. I'm sure he likes greasy food, you can see by the whites of his eyes that he's got a malfunctioning liver, and by the pompous way he went on at your reception, it's obviously not from drink. No, don't interrupt. You will cook chips every night in the chip machine, for, oh let's say a week or two. Now, I'm sure you know not to pour grease down the sink, don't you?'

'Yes of course, everybody knows that.' Although why on earth not I'd never been able to imagine. After all, if it's a liquid, how could the drains tell the difference from water? It didn't seem like the time to say so, though, while we were in the middle of discussing a murder plot. Why were we, I wondered? I'd already tried to tell her I didn't want to go on with it. Well, I might as well at least listen to the new plan. She'd evidently gone to some trouble figuring it out. Perhaps we could take the chip thing back afterwards, when I'd explained my reasons for not wanting to do murder, and get a refund. What were my reasons, anyway? I couldn't seem to remember.

'...hits his head, kills himself, and there you are without a worry in the world.'

'Um, sorry, could you explain that bit again?'

'Which bit?'

'The bit after it being dangerous to put grease down the sink.'

'For God's sake, Fiona. Can't you listen for five minutes?'

'Sorry, Gran. I was thinking about drains.'

Gran breathed heavily out through her nose, flaring her nostrils. It looked exactly like what Moses does when he's about to bite someone.

'Gran, I was listening, honestly. I just didn't understand, not quite.'

'Look. Everyone knows that you shouldn't pour grease down drains. Never mind why for the moment.'

'But –'

'Never mind why, it's a fact. Now, you also can't keep grease that you've fried things in and use it again. That's a filthy habit and will give you ptomaine poisoning.'

'I'd never –'

'So, Fiona, in order to dispose of the used grease, you will carry it downstairs and pour it away somewhere.'

'Where?'

'Well, in the gutter, let's say.'

I certainly wasn't going to go running around the streets in the middle of the night pouring questionable substances down gutters. I started to say so.

On the other hand, sometimes discretion is the better part of valour.

Whatever that means.

'Now,' continued my sweet white-haired old grandmother, grinning with indecent relish, I thought, considering the subject, 'This is the really cunning part of the plan. Everybody who knows you at all, Fiona, knows your unshakeable dedication to covering up your mistakes.'

Well, that was true, I reflected complacently. I'd always been something of a perfectionist. I inclined my head graciously, to indicate modest agreement.

'Don't start falling asleep, Fiona. Really, you can be so aggravating. I sometimes wonder that Mary didn't put a pillow over your face when you were small. Yes, you've always had a furtive streak a mile wide, Heaven knows where you got it from, certainly not from my side of the family.'

Furtive! How dared she? Only filial piety and the hope that she might pay for our coffee stopped me from ramming her walking stick down her throat sideways.

'Yes,' Gran mused, obviously quite oblivious to the fact she'd already said more than enough, 'you've always had this remarkably strong tendency to cover unpleasant things up and pretend they don't exist. Rather like a cat going to the lavatory, I always think.'

This was too much, even for filial piety. I drew myself up to my full, regal height and stared at her down the bridge of my aristocratic nose.

'May I enquire,' I said in tones of icy politeness,

'what relevance any of this has to the matter at hand?'

I wish.

What actually happened was that I swallowed some coffee backwards.

It's amazing how a fluid can suddenly take on different characteristics. Take coffee, for instance. Warm, soft, soothing, the very breath of life. But get some up your nose and it's goodnight, Irene.

Of course my grandmother was kind and sympathetic.

'Really, Fiona, your table manners are an absolute disgrace. Here, wipe your nose for heaven's sake.'

I wiped my nose. I wiped my eyes. I coughed. I got out the little glass from my bag and looked at myself. My eyes had gone all red and puffy.

Gran snatched the glass out of my hand.

'Don't start primping now. We've got serious business to discuss. Now, as I was saying, knowing your absolute inability to admit that you've screwed anything up, and further knowing your extreme clumsiness, it will be totally in character when you spill the potful of grease on the stairs and say nothing about it. So you come back inside as if nothing had happened, wash the pot, and put it away. Then you go to bed and sleep the sleep of the just and righteous, and in the morning your despicable husband slips on the grease and falls to his death. We can leave it to chance who discovers the body, it won't matter, although it's probably best if it isn't you, you might not be able to act convincingly enough.'

'I can so, I was in the Dramatic Society at Uni.'

'Fiddlesticks!'

Another thing about old people is that they are graceless philistines with no appreciation of the Arts.

***

We bought some ready-made chips from the supermarket on the way home. Gran was outraged, she wanted to get potatoes, but since she had stayed outside with Euthanasia while I went in, she couldn't do anything. She also objected to the poly-unsaturated (whatever that means) cooking oil, and made me go back and buy three pounds of dripping.

The first lot of chips was not a great success. Tim, who was again home for dinner, a fact which had occasioned some extremely coarse biological speculations by Patrick, refused to eat them at all.

Gran said the oil had not been hot enough. I couldn't face them either, they swam around on the plate exuding grease like disgusting great crinkly worms.

Actually, no-one would eat them. I thought perhaps Euthanasia might, but Gran wouldn't let me give him any, claiming that she was watching his cholesterol levels. As if a dog had cholesterol. They don't become executives or play squash. I tried to point this out to Gran, but she got stubborn and mulish, and accused me of wanting to poison her dog, which given the reason I had made the chips at all struck me as the last word in hypocrisy.

***

As I was carefully pouring the disgusting melted dripping down the gutter, it suddenly struck me that I had still not succeeded in explaining to Gran that I no longer wanted to murder Tim, and that now we'd used the chip machine she wouldn't be able to get a refund for it.

Still, it was hardly the time to bring it up now, with Tim hanging around all over the place. I could talk to her about it tomorrow, calmly over a cup of coffee, without Tim or indeed Patrick hanging about getting in the way. I'd just calmly explain to her how murder was a vile sin and I wasn't willing to have it on my conscience. She'd certainly see it my way once I explained.

All I had to do now was think of an excuse not to have sex with Tim. Although the results from the Aids test wouldn't be ready till next Wednesday, I felt certain that he couldn't possibly have infected me with anything during the short time we'd been married so far, and as long as I managed to refrain from cohabiting with him any further I should be safe. Perhaps I could pretend I had my period, I thought with a sudden flash of inspiration. After all, he'd be dead within a couple of weeks, so I wouldn't have to keep it up for long.

Then I remembered that, if we didn't kill him, there was no reason to expect him to die any time soon. And I still didn't have a solution for anything. Really his death was the only decent way out of a terrible situation. Perhaps I ought to reconsider... but then I thought about hell, and prison, and being separated from Moses. No, I definitely couldn't risk it. I cried a little bit, thinking about being parted from Moses for years. No doubt my parents would take him back, but he'd always be looking for me. Every time footsteps went past outside the house he'd prick up his ears and go running to the door, making his little chirping noises. Year after year.

It was too terrible. I broke down and howled.

***

CRASH! The chip machine went flying as I was

knocked face-first into the gutter. I must be getting mugged, I thought dimly as an incredibly heavy weight dropped on my back, pressing my face uncomfortably into the nasty trickle of grease I'd just poured away. How lucky I wasn't carrying any money. Then my blood froze. What if it was a pervert evil rapist murderer? I tried to scream but couldn't draw enough breath with the weight pressing into my ribcage.

The weight shifted off me and I tried weakly to scrabble away. Something large wedged itself under my shoulder and rolled me over onto my back. It didn't feel like a hand. Dear God, I thought despairingly, it's a monster from the lake. Deep down I'd always known those stories were true. I kept my eyes tightly shut.

'Mary, help of Christians, pray for us,' I managed to gasp out. I hoped God realised I'd given up my evil plans to murder my husband.

Then I shut my mouth tightly. Something warm and wet was all over my face.

ಶCHAPTER TWENTY-FIVEಣ

Secondly, it was ordained for a remedy against sin, and to avoid fornication; that such persons as have not the gift of continence might marry, and keep themselves undefiled members of Christ's body.

Book of Common Prayer

I squeezed my eyes even more tightly shut, and mentally recited the Lord's prayer. Surely God wouldn't let me suffer long in the claws of the monster if I was actually praying? Please look after Moses, I thought despairingly. The very thing I'd been crying from imagining a few moments before was now coming true. I heard snuffling sounds.

'Euthanasia! What have you got there? Leave it!'

Gran?

'Drop it at once, bad dog! Yuk, dirty! Leave it!'

The monster rose up off me and leapt around, prancing and slavering. I could hear its toenails clicking on the pavement. I opened my eyes a little way. Euthanasia certainly looked pleased with himself. He jumped back to me and licked my face some more. Then he started jumping manically back and forth across me. Look, I've rescued you two nights running, he seemed to be saying.

'Good God, Fiona, what in Heaven's name are you doing rolling around in the gutter? Have a little self-respect, for goodness' sake. Look at you, you're covered in filth from head to foot!'

'He slimed me,' I gasped weakly.

'Oh, nonsense, he had a bath only last week. Get up, for goodness' sake, and what on earth have you done with the chip fryer? Really, Fiona, you are hopeless!'

***

I staggered into the flat hoping everyone might have gone to bed; so much time seemed to have passed since I'd gone out to empty the grease. But it was only eight-thirty, and Tim and Patrick were right in the middle of a tense silence. I really wish people wouldn't do things like that; the correct place for tense silences, I always think, is either just before dawn on a battlefield, or else during the last few minutes of Wimbledon. Not in my sitting room, anyway, I thought crossly as I washed the chip machine, surreptitiously checking it for dents and scratches. It would just about pass muster, I decided, if I put it with the handle to the left; the enamel was a bit nicked on the other side. I toyed briefly with the idea of taking it back and saying it was a factory defect and getting a nice new one, but then I remembered that I hadn't paid for it anyway.

Nobody came in to help me with the washing up. They were all too busy having tense silences, I supposed. I put on a pot of coffee and sat at the kitchen table to sulk. Even Moses was nowhere in sight. What I really needed was a nice hot bath. After all, I had been pushed face first into a gutter, and I felt sure I had done something to my nose, and probably skinned my knees as well. I was covered with sore bits, anyway, and my clothes were filthy. I tried in vain to plot a route to the bathroom that wouldn't involve going through the sitting room. If I climbed out of the kitchen window onto the balcony, I could go along to the other end and, by balancing on the balcony wall and leaning over only a little bit, I should be able to get in the bedroom window; from there I could get to the bathroom. Moses often did it. On the other hand, Moses, although large for a cat, was quite a bit smaller than me, and the bedroom window was one of those cheating ones that can only be opened about six inches. So, now I came to think of it, was the kitchen window. Damn. I thought how nice it must be to be a vampire. I could turn into a bat and go flying off to see the city lights. If Tim gave me any trouble, I'd just bite him in the neck. Could a vampire get Aids from biting someone who had it, I wondered? Well, I could ask Doctor Sanders when I went back for my test results.

Just then I remembered that there was quite a big mirror in the lavatory, which was right next to the front door so that I wouldn't have to go through the sitting room to get to it. I went in and locked the door carefully. Moses was in there, scratching around in his Booda Box. It really did work, you couldn't smell a thing. Not that it stopped him scattering the kittyflakes around as advertised, he just tossed them out through the little tunnel. Still, I felt, the smell was the important thing.

I had a look at myself in the glass and nearly fainted. My beautiful straight nose, of which I'd always been so proud, had vanished, and in its place was a huge red swollen monstrosity with a nasty weeping graze across the middle. There was grease all over the front of my sweater and one elbow was torn out. My jeans, although also filthy, seemed pretty well undamaged, but when I pulled the legs up

I found the skin was grazed off both knees. Dear God, no wonder I hurt.

I picked Moses up and sat down on the lavatory seat. It seemed like a pretty good place to be, under the circumstances. There was a lock on the door, so nobody could get at me, and presently when I felt a little better I could at least have a wash, as the lavatory had its own basin. Perhaps I'd stay here all night.

***

THUMP! THUMP! CRASH!

'Fiona, what the bloody hell are you doing in there, I have to GO!'

***

'Why not, for Christ's sake? It's been nearly three weeks, I have needs, you know.'

'I don't care. Shut up and let me go to sleep.'

***

'You have to be firm with him, Fiona. It's no use crying.'

***

'Tim! What are you doing? Stop it!'

'What does it bloody look like I'm doing, I'm having a wank, since my wife won't sleep with me.' He didn't even pause.

'Stop it!' I screamed. 'You're disgusting!'

I knew about masturbating, of course. You can't work in an office without hearing a million jokes about it. I'd never actually seen it, though. Although I was utterly disgusted and felt sick, it was weirdly fascinating. Tim had a strange glazed look on his face, as if he were in the grip of some kind of psychotic event. In fact, it was a bit like Moses when he gets into one of his paw-kneading, blanket-sucking trances. But Tim had none of Moses' graceful furry charm.

'Stop it, stop it, stop it! You pervert! I hate you!'

Tim paid no attention. Perhaps his mind had snapped under the stress of leading a double life. I was fairly sure I knew how to stop him, though. I hurried out to the kitchen, noticing on the way that Gran and Patrick, presumably awakened by all the shouting, were milling around in the sitting room. Ignoring their questions, I filled the largest pot I could find with cold water and marched back to the bedroom, trailing relatives.

'My goodness! What on earth is he –'

Snigger.

SPLASH!

'Ow, fuck, what the fuck are you doing, you stupid bitch!' Tim had leapt out of bed and was jumping around, literally dancing with rage, with no clothes on. I noticed with satisfaction that his penis had shrunk to the size of a walnut, he wouldn't be doing any more of his disgusting perverted acts in front of my cat, not that night, anyway.

Patrick was racked by uncontrollable giggling. Gran was hunting around in her dressing gown pocket, and presently produced her spectacles, through which she studied my husband with mild amazement. Moses, who had got splashed, was furiously washing himself on top of the dressing table, pausing every few licks to glare angrily at me.

Tim was struggling into some jeans, cursing wildly.

'...can't even have any fucking privacy in my own bedroom.'

'Young man, may I remind you that this is also your wife's bedroom, and your behaviour has exceeded the bounds of good taste.'

Tim didn't have anything to say to this. He shoved rudely past us and slammed out of the house.

Running out to the landing, where there was a window to the carpark, I saw him throw himself into his car and drive off with a squeal of brakes. I went back inside. Gran and Patrick had put on all the lights and the heater, and were discussing whether to have hot chocolate or sherry. They had that air of flushed, excited happiness that you see in the supporters of a winning football team, after a really big game.

'He won't come back tonight,' Gran was saying triumphantly. 'Mark my words, he'll be far too embarrassed, and besides, he knows the bed's wet.'

'Not as wet as it'd have been if he'd spoofed all over it.' Patrick was still having little fits of the giggles.

'Don't be silly, Patrick. Come and help me get the mattress off, we'll prop it up in here to dry in front of the heater. Really, Fiona, you were a bit excessive. I'm sure a cup full would have worked just as well.'

I started the hot chocolate while they were pulling my bed to pieces. I had no idea where I was going to sleep if my mattress was standing up in front of the heater, but it didn't seem worthwhile arguing about it. I didn't feel really tired anyway, perhaps I'd just stay up all night. It was so lovely not to be having the nightly wrangle about sex, and whether Moses should be allowed to sleep on the bed, and Our Relationship, perhaps I'd just be carried on till morning on a tide of celebration.

***

Tim didn't, in fact, come home that night, or all weekend. It was just as well, really, because it was Sunday afternoon before Gran finally pronounced the mattress dry enough to go back on the bed. It was lovely without him. I hadn't realised how tense I'd got, always watching out so I didn't set off one of his temper fits, and constantly having to monitor everything I said in case I let out that I knew about his mistress.

After having to share the sofa with Patrick for three nights, it was wonderful being able to put my bed back together again. Moses was even more pleased than I was and kept leaping onto the bed while I was making it, throwing himself down and purring contentedly. Eventually I got sick of moving him and just made him into the bed, there was a lump in the middle but so what? Tim wasn't around to criticise my housekeeping.

Because it was Sunday, and I hadn't been shopping, and Tim showed no signs of coming home, and Gloria had dropped in, I decided to send out for pizza instead of cooking. After all, I deserved a break from constantly ministering to all my house guests. I ordered one super-hot Mexican and one Supreme. There didn't seem to be any point ordering a Ham and Pineapple, as Tim probably wouldn't come home tonight either. If he did, he could either have what we were having or starve. Perhaps his mistress would give him dinner. I didn't care.

It was a nice relaxed dinner. Gran was still in a mellow frame of mind from witnessing Tim's disorderly exit, and Patrick was in a good mood because it was Sunday and I hadn't forced him to go to church. Moses was happy because he'd got his bed back, and also because he loves pizza. Euthanasia had been in an extra good mood ever since Tim had left, and was lying around looking dreamily affectionate and occasionally trying to give Moses a kiss, and getting his nose smacked.

The conversation at dinner was on a high intellectual plane.

'Um, Fiona?'

'Yeah, what?'

'I've been wanting to ask you ever since, you know...'

'You know, what?'

'You know, the other night. When Cedric... you know.'

'Patrick Aloysius MacDougall, I have told you a thousand times not to keep saying "you know" in between everything. If the person to whom you are speaking "knows", it is not necessary to say anything. It is an extremely vulgar habit.'

'Sorry, Gran. Look, Fiona, what I want to know is, what's wrong with his...' he hesitated, but didn't dare say it again. 'His, um, his willy.'

'What d'you mean, what's wrong with it?'

'Well, you kn– I mean, it was all sort of deformed and yucky looking.'

Gran took a deep breath and looked over the tops of her glasses. This made her look like an academic bullfrog.

'For your information, Patrick, that is what will happen to a male organ after years of self-abuse. I trust you will remember this dreadful warning.'

'Jesus, Mary and Joseph! The pig! Wouldn't it make the angels weep, at all? Well, the sooner we murder the bastard, the better, by all the holy saints.'

It was then that I heard the knock at the door.

Not just an ordinary knock, as it might be Tim sheepishly coming home without his keys, or a neighbour calling in to borrow some sugar.

A slow, measured, awful knock.

A knock of power.

A police knock.

❧CHAPTER TWENTY-SIX☙

With this ring I thee wed, with my body I thee worship, and with all my worldly goods I thee endow: In the Name of the Father, and of the Son, and of the Holy Ghost. Amen.

Book of Common Prayer

It's not true that your life flashes before your eyes in moments of crisis. At least, mine didn't. What actually flashed before my eyes was the sick realisation that the flat had no back way out.

'Jesus, Mary and Joseph,' screeched Gloria.

'Christ, I wish you wouldn't keep saying that all the fucking time!'

'Patrick Aloysius MacDougall, I cannot believe I am hearing those words from your lips! You will wash your mouth out with soap, young man.'

'For God's sake, Gran, what's it matter, we're all going to jail –'

The knock again, a little louder.

'WOOWOOWOOWOOWOOWOOWOOF'

'Shut up, Euthanasia. Quick, Fiona, hide the evidence.'

'Right. Um, what evidence?'

'WOOWOOWOOWOOWOOWOOWOOWO OF! AH-WOOOOOOOOH WOOF!'

'What? The evidence, girl, get it out of sight! We'll just have to brazen it out.'

'WOOWOOWOO! WOOF! WOOF! WOOF! ARGLEARGLEARGLE! ROWRFF!'

It was hard to think with Euthanasia baying like the Hounds of Doom. I looked around frantically, and finally caught sight of a little corner of Tim's insurance policy sticking out from under one of the sofa cushions. I shoved it out of sight and piled all the cushions up at that end. Was there anything else? I couldn't think of anything unless it was the chip thing. But after all, it's not a crime to own one of those.

'WOOWOOWOOWOOWOOWOOWOOOOOOOO

OOOOOOO! ROWFF! GRORFF! GARRRFF!'

'Euthanasia! Shut up or I'll kick you. Right, now Fiona, you go and open the door. Everybody just look natural.'

Gran's idea of looking natural was evidently to sit bolt upright with her feet firmly planted and her glasses on the end of her nose, clutching the arms of her chair. Patrick threw himself on the sofa with his shoes on, putting yet another black mark on the white upholstery. Gloria was crouched in a corner, muttering.

'...Pater noster, qui es in caelis...'

Euthanasia was dancing up and down in front of the door, slavering and hammering at it with his nose. I looked around but couldn't see Moses. I thought they'd probably take us straight away, in chains. Would they let me say goodbye to him?

I couldn't help it. I do cry easily.

KNOCK KNOCK KNOCK!

I opened the door. That is, I started to open the door. As it opened, Euthanasia rushed at it and got his shoulders jammed in the opening; since the door opened inwards, and he was pushing out, we were at an impasse.

'WOOWOOWOOWOOWOOWOO!
WAROOFF! GRUFF!'

'Dammit, Euthanasia, get back!'

'WAROOF!
GROWROWROWROWROWRORFFFF!' (Let me
deal with these alien scumbags for you, Auntie
Fiona. They'll be Dead Meat, I guarantee.)

For a second, I thought how lovely it would be
to let him break through and just kill whoever was on
the other side. We'd have no more trouble from
them, ever, whether it was the police or somebody
else. The history lessons I'd suffered through in high
school flashed through my mind. Just for an instant, I
felt the whole of human history was laid open to
view, comprehensible in the light of the moment; I
could really see the point of Fort Mayne.

I was still struggling with the door, and my
conscience, when a whistle blast split the air. The
silence that followed it was deafening. Euthanasia
put all his fur down and slunk backwards out of the
doorway; his legs had gone all sort of bendy. He
threw himself down in front of Gran's chair and let
out a great whiffly sigh. Aw, shucks, you're no fun,
he seemed to be saying. Couldn't you let me rough
them up just a little bit?

I opened the door. As I expected, there were two

policemen on the other side of it. My courage sank into the soles of my feet, where it kept on going, out through the floor and perhaps all the way to Japan. I wanted to run away, but was too paralysed with fright.

The younger policeman cleared his throat nervously.

'Um. Mrs Pinkpank?'

They had both removed their hats. Perhaps it was police etiquette to take one's hat off when arresting a lady.

'Mrs Timothy Pinkpank?'

I couldn't say anything. I was hunting frantically for my handkerchief. If I was going to be taken away in chains, I didn't want the neighbours seeing me with runny mascara.

'Mrs Pinkpank, I'm afraid we have some bad news for you. May we come in?'

'In?'

'Yes, may we come inside? I'm afraid we have some bad news.'

That was one way of looking at it, I supposed. Life imprisonment, hard labour. On the other hand, I hadn't actually done anything. Perhaps the sentence for conspiring to commit a felony wasn't as bad. Or was that in America? I couldn't think straight at all, it was all I could do to control my bladder and keep my nose from running.

'Fiona? Is anything wrong?'

Gran had sneaked up behind me and was looking like a sweet little old lady with her glasses on the end of her nose. If you didn't look carefully you'd have sworn she was wearing an apron.

'I am Fiona's grandmother. Please come inside, I gather there is some problem?'

The policemen shuffled inside sort of sideways, looking nervously about. They were clutching their hats and didn't seem to know what to do with them. Really, I thought, they didn't look as fierce as I expected. Not like the other time I'd got arrested, when I accidentally set off the burglar alarm at Marsh and Spacknall. The younger policeman jumped noticeably when he saw Euthanasia. Euthanasia didn't jump when he saw the policemen, but he did wrinkle his nose up and show all his teeth, which was quite an impressive sight.

God knew what the hell Gran thought she was up to. She fluttered around getting the policemen arranged into chairs and offering them sherry, which they declined.

The older policeman sat right on the edge of his chair, wriggling around and trying not to look at Euthanasia. He looked terribly uncomfortable.

'Mrs Pinkpank, I'm afraid we have some bad news for you.' He took out a handkerchief and mopped his face, which was red and sweaty. Gran had put him right next to the heater. He went on, sounding a bit desperate. 'I'm afraid it's your husband, Mrs Pinkpank.'

God, I wished he'd stop calling me by that ridiculous name. I had never had any intention of changing my name, even before I found out about Tim's mistress. I hoped they wouldn't call me Pinkpank all the time I was in jail.

'...on the South Eastern freeway.'

Damn, now I'd missed what he was saying. Would it be incriminating to ask him to repeat it? I noticed that Gloria had stopped praying and was crouched next to the sofa, staring at the policeman with enormous intensity, as though he was telling a really interesting story.

Before I could make up my mind to admit I hadn't been listening, Gran dived in.

'Ah, dear, dear. I can't say I'm very surprised,

Officer. I'm afraid he was a very wild young man. In fact, he hadn't even been home for three nights, that's why she's so upset. They'd not been married long. Fiona, dear, I think you'd better go and lie down for a while, this is a great shock. Come along, dear.'

There was a faint shriek from the policeman as he disappeared under Euthanasia, who had decided after all that he was a nice person and should be given a kiss.

'But...'

'Go on, dear, Gloria will go with you, won't you, Gloria.' It was not a request. Gloria got up like a zombie and shuffled towards the bedroom.

'But...'

'Patrick will make you a hot drink. Patrick –' she jerked her head towards the kitchen. Patrick scurried out.

'But...'

I decided not to argue. Gran seemed to be so much in control of everything, perhaps she could somehow convince them not to arrest me. Or to let me have bail so I could leave the country, or something.

The second we got into the bedroom, Gloria stopped her zombie impersonation and started jumping up and down on the bed, laughing silently. I grabbed her arm and pulled her off the bed.

'Gloria, what is it, what's going on?'

She looked at me in amazement.

'Holy saints and martyrs, weren't you listening?'

'Yes, of course I was, only I sort of didn't hear, that's all.'

'Dear heavenly Christ. He's dead, Fiona, he has ceased to be, gone to meet his Maker, he is an ex-husband!'

'Who?'

'Christ, I don't believe you! Tim, your philandering husband, the adulterer, that's who! Ex-adulterer, I mean, may God have mercy on him.' She stopped bouncing for a moment and crossed herself solemnly. 'You're free of the prick for good!'

'Oh, God. What, you mean he's really dead? Properly?'

'Yes, that's what the police are here for, to tell you about it. He was in an accident on the freeway, he was killed instantly.'

'What freeway?'

'Jesus, Fiona, the South-Eastern, what does it matter?'

'What was he doing on the South-Eastern freeway?'

'God, Fiona, I don't know, who cares? He was in the right place at the right time to get killed, that's what matters.'

I supposed it was. How lucky, I thought, that I'd already resolved not to murder him. Now I'd never have to worry about the state of my conscience.

Knock knock.

'Fiona, are you okay?' Patrick put his head around the door. 'Here, I brought you a belt of that sherry, she said cocoa but I thought you'd want to celebrate.'

I still felt woozy. I grabbed the mug and had a stiff belt. It brought tears to my eyes and I sat down rather suddenly on the bed. Sherry should be sipped, never gulped, I seemed to hear my mother saying from far away.

'The cops are leaving, Gran's seeing them out.

Cedric was drunk, they said the car was full of booze and he had a bimbo with him, that must have been Kathy-Wathy. Serve her right, the slut.'

Through a red haze I heard the front door close and presently Gran came into the room.

'Ah, good, I see young Patrick's got you a drink. Fiona, did you take that in? I thought you seemed a bit vague. You do realise Tim's been killed?'

They kept telling me he was dead, as I sat on the bed sipping sherry out of a coffee mug. Moses came in and curled up on my lap. Euthanasia came in and settled down huffily on the floor, blowing out great sighs of contentment, and occasionally rolling over to have his tummy rubbed. I had a great feeling of peace and comfort, like coming home after a long trip and seeing the lights shining out of the house windows.

It was Gloria who remembered first.

'Holy Mother of God, the insurance policy! Fiona, you're rich!'

***

The wake was even better than the reception. Black is better than white for red hair, and I had great success with the new pale makeup just coming into fashion. We didn't have Tim there in his coffin, though. I thought that would be a bit off-putting, and anyway the undertakers said there wasn't that much of him left, and it would be better to have the coffin closed up right away.

I didn't get a black ribbon for Moses, since he's black anyway it seemed a bit boring, so he had a beautiful primrose-yellow one that toned with his eyes. Euthanasia had a matching one, and I bought some amber beads just so we'd all go nicely together.

And I got to keep all the wedding presents.

THE END

Fiona's story concludes in Where The Heart Is.

ஐPROLOGUE௸

I knew all about life in the country. After all, hadn't I visited the Botanic gardens at least three times a year since I was a little girl? And hadn't I watched every single episode of Downton Abbey, and the first four seasons of Worzel Gummidge? And hadn't I even been down to the riverbank to see the bats go off from their colony? I knew I was prepared for anything the country could dish out.

Flies? I had a bottle of insect repellent that smelled like tropical flowers. Extreme weather? I had SPF30 – face it, when you're a redhead you don't leave home without it anyway. And as for the housekeeping, I still had my facsimile copy of Mrs Beeton's *Book of Household Management*. That covered things like straining hairs out of the milk and general observations on sheep, and after all, the country is all about sheep.

Isn't it?

&CHAPTER ONE&

The last proof of affection which we can give to those left behind, is to leave their worldly affairs in such a state as to excite neither jealousy, nor anger, nor heartrendings of any kind, at least for the immediate future.
Isabella Beeton, The Book of Household Management

'But I don't understand. Why can't I have the money now?'

I shifted in my chair. I'd been sitting here for at least twenty minutes listening to Mr Pilchard of Pilchard, Pilchard, Pilchard, Pilchard, Jones and Rowbottom spout gibberish. I didn't even know which Pilchard he was.

'Well, as I have been saying, the, ah, letters of administration have not yet been granted.'

'Well, can't you just write your own letters?'

Pilchard looked at me over the top of his glasses in that way he had. I didn't like it, but it was marginally better than when he pushed them up his nose and they reflected the light from the window, making his eyes disappear into blankness. That was creepy, and made him look like a huge praying mantis.

'Ahem. Letters of Administration are granted to the administrator of an estate where that estate is intestate. You see, Mrs Pinkpank, probate cannot be granted, for in the absence of any testamentary document, there is nothing to be proved.'

'Um, I don't use that name.' I'd told him at least five times that I still went by my own name. Perhaps those weird glasses interfered with his hearing. 'Anyway, if it's just letters, why can't you write them? These administration thingies.'

'They aren't something one writes, Mrs Pink– ah, Mrs MacDougall. Letters of Administration are granted by the Supreme Court, in cases where the deceased is intestate.'

'But he wasn't! Quite the reverse, actually.'

Pilchard looked startled, well, as startled as a lawyer can look, which isn't very. Anyway, he took off his glasses and started polishing them.

'Ah, you've found a will, then? But why didn't you say so, Mrs Pink-MacDougall? It changes everything.'

What was the man blathering about?

'No, I mean he wasn't intestate. He definitely had all his bits. Goodness, I should know, I was his wife. And he was always wandering about the house with nothing on.'

Pilchard had turned bright pink and appeared to be squirming in his chair. Why didn't he get on with it? I didn't have all day to be sitting around lawyers' offices.

'When I say intestate, Mrs Pink-MacDougall, I mean that the deceased, ah, um, that is to say your late husband,' he smirked and bowed, making me want to slap him, 'left no testamentary disposition, that is to say, will. No will.' He sat back, looking pleased with himself, as if he'd said something clever, put his glasses back on and stared blankly at me like a giant insect in a pinstriped suit.

'I could have another look, it might be there somewhere. I mean, you should see his desk, it's crammed with papers from the year dot.' I didn't like to tell Pilchard I hadn't actually got round to looking for the will. I'd meant to, but somehow there was always something more urgent I needed to do, and Tim's desk drawers were so stuffed full of rubbish... actually, I hadn't opened any of the drawers since we'd found the insurance policy. That had been the important thing at the time, and since he'd been killed, well there'd been celebrating, and then the funeral, and what with one thing and another the days had drifted by.

'So you see, I might have missed it in among all the papers. I'll go through them again.'

'Well, I shouldn't bother going too far back, Mrs Pink-MacDougall. There wouldn't be any point finding a will made before your marriage.'

'Why not? They don't go off, do they?'

'In point of fact, they do go off.' Pilchard smirked again. I wished he wouldn't. It made him look even more like a praying mantis. 'You see, Mrs Pink-MacDougall, a will is automatically revoked upon the testator's marriage. Except for certain special circumstances, for instance when the will has been made in contemplation–'

'Why?'

'Well, er... it is to lessen the possibility of injustice to the spouse. And of course, any... er...

issue. Let us say, for example, that an unmarried man makes a will giving all of his property to his brother, and then marries. If that earlier will were to take effect, his wife would be left destitute.'

I could feel my patience running out. Money was what I needed, not a lecture about the law of wills.

'Mr Pilchard, I've got the rent due. Well, overdue, and they wrote me a nasty letter. I need money now, to pay the rent.'

'I am sorry, Mrs Pink-MacDougall, but I cannot disburse any funds from the estate until administration has been granted, other than for funerary expenses, which we have, of course, already paid from your husband's funds.'

I knew that only too well. Tim's ashes were in a cardboard box, sitting on the mantelpiece. I hadn't known what else to do with them.

'Well, what about his life insurance?'

'The policy has not yet been paid. In any case, Mrs Pink-MacDougall, as your late husband did not name you as beneficiary on the policy, it is an asset of the estate, and as such must be paid into the estate.'

I wished he wouldn't keep calling me that.

Still, it was better than when he wrote to me, which he did at least once a week, addressing me as 'Dear Madam'. His letters were always at least three pages long and completely incomprehensible, which was why I'd come to see him. I'd hoped he might make more sense in person.

'Well, how long is all this going to take?'

'It is impossible to say with any certainty. But in general, it tends to be at least twelve months before disbursements are made. A grant of probate or administration must first be obtained, and then all the assets of the estate must be...'

He rabbited on for another twenty minutes before I could get away. I didn't understand a word of it, but one thing came through loud and clear.

I was not going to see a cent any time soon.

Also by Tabitha Ormiston-Smith

Dance of Chaos (Fiona MacDougall Book 1):
Lazy, frivolous, conceited and totally self centred,
Fiona MacDougall is not an asset to the workforce.
When she applies for a transfer to the Infotech
department of her company, she does so only in
order to get an afternoon off work.

Can she succeed in her challenging new job?

Can she save her little brother from the
consequences of his evil deeds?

Will Moses do something embarrassing to the
vicar's leg again?

**Gift of Continence (Fiona MacDougall Book
2):** With the perfect wedding dress, what can go
wrong? A great deal, as Fiona MacDougall rapidly
discovers. From the wedding from hell onwards,
Fiona successively discovers that her new husband
is stingy, bad-tempered and an adulterer.

**Where The Heart Is (Fiona MacDougall
Book 3):** Widowed, broke and unemployed, Fiona
moves to the country to save money. But she is not
prepared for the realities of country life... or for
whom she will meet.

King's Ransom: What really went on back in
1193? Was Richard Lionheart really the hero we
think? Was John really that bad? And who was
Robin Hood, no really, who was he?

Bloodsucking Bogans: Dingo Flats hasn't been the same since the Murphy family moved back to town. The boys are delinquents, the daughter's a disgrace, and old Granny Murphy is constantly causing trouble. Even the dogs are delinquents. The crime rate's doubled since they arrived.

And what's with all the dead rats that have started appearing on the doorsteps of local businesses? The tabloid thinks it's a plague, but Sam's dad is convinced it's warnings from the Mafia.

Meanwhile, Sam's friends are determined to make her over and marry her off, and she's staring down the barrel of having to give up her police dog pup. What's a cop to do?

The Secret Summer of Peter Fotheringay: Left at boarding school over the Christmas holidays, Peter expects to have a boring time. But when he goes exploring in the school's disused attic, he finds something that will change his world forever.

Reality Ever After: Rosalie can't remember much about her life before she was ill. Her life in the Gorgon Hotel is the same every day. But lately, Rosalie has started to dream, and the things she sees in her dreams are starting to make her think there is something very wrong at the Gorgon Hotel.

COLLECTIONS

Once Upon A Dragon: Collected short fiction. A non-themed, cross-genre collection of short fiction, including fantasy, science fiction and horror as well as general fiction.

With Coffee Spoons: Collected short fiction. A woman with a toxic mother-in-law, a man who crosses a social barrier and finds there is no way back, a man who loves his wife and reaps terrible trouble because of it, a homeless man, a dance teacher who just wants a few more students for his introductory Salsa class, an old woman confined in a nursing home, a big blue parrot, a young married couple, a dog who loves his man beyond the boundaries of death, a Christmas kitten, a scientist with a device of unimaginable power, a young graduate who goes looking for a thrill and finds more than he bargained for.

You'll laugh, you'll cry, and perhaps you'll even think about your life.

NOVELLAS

No Such Thing: Twelve-year-old Callie has taken on the responsibility of running the house and looking after her father, following her parents' divorce. When the bank threatens to foreclose on their home, Callie is forced to admit that this is a problem even she can't solve, until help comes from an unexpected quarter. But Callie learns that all actions have consequences, and sometimes the price for getting what you want can be too high...

Melanie's Diary: Melanie's life is out of control. Her status-hungry parents have forced her grandmother into a home, and she's under siege from the school bully. But things are going to get a lot worse before they get better...

Dancing Feet: Ashley is devastated when her widowed father returns from his business trip with a new wife and her two daughters in tow. Pushed to one side by the interlopers, can she make a new life for herself?

A modern-day Cinderella interpretation.

Operation Tomcat (Operation Tomcat Book 1): Left almost penniless after divorcing her cheating husband, Tammy moves to the country to reinvent her life. But life in a country town isn't as simple as it looks...

Operation Camilla (Operation Tomcat Book 2): A sleazy solicitor hacks into a dating website in order to boost his failing family law practice. But he doesn't count on Tom...

Operation Badger (Operation Tomcat Book 3): Detective Senior Constable Ben Jackson is handsome, kind, diligent, dedicated and a total mensch. He's also as thick as two planks.

His girlfriend, Tammy, is clever as anything, but sillier than a wet hen.

And then there is Tom. Tom is a cat.

NON-FICTION

Grammar Without Tears: Historical and fictional characters explain common grammatical errors in a funny-as-hell book that will forever change the way you see grammar.

Fifty Shades of Grammar: Everyone, it's said, has one book inside him, but getting it out can be problematical. Perhaps you can't English very well, or you work long hours and just don't have time, or you started writing and then got stuck? Fear not, for help is at hand.

Packed with friendly, no-nonsense advice, Fifty Shades of Grammar will answer all those questions you were too afraid to ask. From sentence structure to punctuation, from setting up your workspace to support your efforts to overcoming the dreaded 'writer's block', from traps and pitfalls to avoid to editing, the problems faced by the novice writer are clearly addressed – and with LOLCATS!

www.ingramcontent.com/pod-product-compliance
Lightning Source LLC
Chambersburg PA
CBHW020651110726
47901CB00001B/136